W9-AAG-105

DATE DUE

NOV 1 2 2001			

TIME
PROBE

SF

TIME PROBE:

The Sciences
in Science Fiction

COLLECTED AND WITH AN INTRODUCTION BY

ARTHUR C. CLARKE

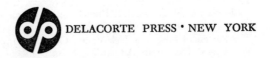 DELACORTE PRESS · NEW YORK

"Not Final!" by Isaac Asimov. Copyright 1941 by Street & Smith Publications, Inc. From *Astounding Science Fiction*. Reprinted by permission of the author.

"Take a Deep Breath," by Arthur C. Clarke. Copyright 1957 by Royal Publications, Inc. From *Infinity*. Reprinted by permission of the author and the author's agents, Scott Meredith Literary Agency, Inc.

"—And He Built a Crooked House," by Robert A. Heinlein. Copyright 1940 by Street & Smith Publications, Inc. From *Astounding Science Fiction*. Reprinted by permission of the author.

"The Tissue-Culture King," by Julian Huxley. Copyright 1927 by E. P. Company, Inc. From *Amazing Stories*. Reprinted by permission of the author.

"The Little Black Bag," by Cyril M. Kornbluth. Copyright 1950 by Street & Smith Publications, Inc. From *Astounding Science Fiction*. Reprinted by permission of Mrs. Mary Kornbluth.

"The Blindness," by Philip Latham. Copyright 1946 by Street & Smith Publications, Inc. From *Astounding Science Fiction*. Reprinted by permission of the author and the author's agents, Scott Meredith Literary Agency, Inc.

"The Wabbler," by Murray Leinster. Copyright 1942 by Street & Smith Publications, Inc. From *Astounding Science Fiction*. Reprinted by permission of the author.

"Grandpa," by James H. Schmitz. Copyright 1955 by Street & Smith Publications, Inc. From *Astounding Science Fiction*. Reprinted by permission of the author and the author's agents, Scott Meredith Literary Agency, Inc.

"The Artifact Business," by Robert Silverberg. Copyright 1957 by King-Size Publications, Inc. From *Fantastic Universe*. Reprinted by permission of the author and the author's agents, Scott Meredith Literary Agency, Inc.

"The Weather Man," by Theodore L. Thomas. Copyright 1962 by The Condé Nast Publications, Inc. From *Analog Science Fact-Science Fiction*. Reprinted by permission of the author.

"The Potters of Firsk," by Jack Vance. Copyright 1950 by Street & Smith Publications, Inc. From *Astounding Science Fiction*. Reprinted by permission of the author and the author's agents, Scott Meredith Literary Agency, Inc.

CONTENTS

INTRODUCTION:
Science and Science Fiction

Science fiction must be the most heavily anthologized of all fields of literature—which is, of course, a tribute to its vitality and its popularity. But this very popularity is embarrassing to the would-be anthologist; most of the best stories have been used over and over again, and it is difficult to think of a novel way of approaching the subject. Robots, Invaders from Space, Time Travel, Mutants—all these classic themes have already been employed to give coherence to collections (most of them edited by Groff Conklin).

Yet any anthology, unless it is compiled by sticking pins into a card index, must have some pattern or overall design. In this volume, the pattern is a very simple one, though to the best of my knowledge it has not been used before. These stories have all been selected because they illustrate some particular aspect of science or technology—preferably a striking or unfamiliar one.

Having said that, let me add a hasty reassurance. The prime function of a story is to *entertain*—not to instruct or to preach. No writer should ever forget Sam Goldwyn's immortal words: "If you've gotta message, use Western Union." Though these stories were first picked because of their scientific contents, the *final* selection was on the basis of entertainment. Thus numerous tales full of technical ingenuity were rejected, simply because they did not stand up as stories.

The acid test of any story comes when you reread it, preferably after a lapse of some years. If it's good, the second reading is as enjoyable as the first. If it's great, the second reading is more enjoyable. And if it's a masterpiece, it will improve on every rereading. Needless to say, there are very few masterpieces, in or out of science fiction, and I do not guarantee that there are any in this volume. But I am reasonably sure that all these tales are worth reading at least twice, and that most of them will leave a permanent mark on your memory. The test of a really mediocre story is that you can't remember if you've even read it once.

Fortunately, in this day and age there is no further need to defend science fiction against the illiterates who, until quite recently, were prone to attack it. However, most longtime enthusiasts such as myself still have automatic defense mechanisms; it is hard to ignore the instincts of a lifetime, and I can still remember the days when I used to hide the covers of my 1930 *Wonder* and *Amazing Stories*. (Now, *there* was Pop Art for you.) These instincts sometimes make one fly to the other extreme, as I did recently at a meeting of the PEN Club in New York, when I claimed that science fiction is a bridge between the celebrated "Two Cultures."

I now repudiate, or at least modify, that claim, as on further thought I don't believe there are two cultures; there is only culture and nonculture. A person who knows all about the plays of Aristophanes and nothing about the Second Law of Thermodynamics is as uncultured as one who has mastered quantum theory, but thinks von Gogh painted the roof of the Sistine Chapel. (Needless to say, these extreme types do not exist; but there are some good approximations to them.) So I would now claim not that science fiction is a bridge between the two cultures, but that it is one of the many bridges to culture, period. At the moment, it carries relatively little traffic; but it will carry more.

It is my hope that these stories—few of which have ever been anthologized before and some of which I am happy to have rescued from near oblivion—will appeal equally strongly to science-fiction fans and to those who think they couldn't care less about science. But above all, I hope they will ignite in many young readers that sense of wonder which, to the enquiring and imaginative mind, makes this type of literature more rewarding than any other.

I would like to thank my indefatigable agent, Scott Meredith, for suggesting the plan of this anthology; Bob Silverberg, for much research and the run of his nostalgia-provoking files of *Astoundings*, *Amazings*, *Wonders*, etc; Barbara Silverberg, for long hours of toil at the photocopy machine; and Don Fine, for deadline-stretching.

ARTHUR C. CLARKE
New York, June, 1965

TIME
PROBE

ROBERT A. HEINLEIN

Bob Heinlein is one of the founders of modern science fiction and the first exploiter of many of the themes that have become commonplace in the last thirty years. It is little exaggeration to say that his influence has been comparable to that of Wells, who also planted seeds that many later writers were happy to harvest.

And like Wells, Heinlein's chief interest has been the interaction of science upon society—*every* aspect of society, from politics to warfare, from religion to sport. An Annapolis graduate with a thorough understanding of engineering and technology, he made a notable attempt to alert the indifferent American public to the importance of space flight by writing the excellent movie *Destination Moon* (1950). Millions of popcorn-chewing skeptics then saw a U.S. astronaut propelling himself through vacuum by squirts from a cylinder of oxygen. (Where do science-fiction writers get these crazy ideas?)

The hilarious story that follows, though a quarter of a century old, is still one of my favorites, possibly for two reasons. It is about the fourth dimension, and I have always had a soft spot for that interesting place. The very first TV talk I ever gave was a thirty-minute lecture on the fourth dimension, delivered straight into the camera without a break; since *that*, all other TV exposures have been child's play.

The second reason involves *chez* Heinlein. A decade after writing this story, Bob and his charming wife Ginny did build a remarkable house—far from crooked—in the bracing environment of Colorado Springs. It was full of labor-saving features which, like other Heinlein ideas, have since become common property, and I had the privilege of inhabiting it for a week in 1952. I hope that one day I will have a chance to return Bob and Ginny's hospitality in the admittedly somewhat clammier climate of Colombo.

–And He Built a Crooked House

Americans are considered crazy anywhere in the world.

They will usually concede a basis for the accusation but point to California as the focus of the infection. Californians stoutly maintain that their bad reputation is derived solely from the acts of the inhabitants of Los Angeles County. Angelenos will, when pressed, admit the charge but explain hastily, "It's Hollywood. It's not our fault—we didn't ask for it; Hollywood just grew."

The people in Hollywood don't care; they glory in it. If you are interested, they will drive you up Laurel Canyon "—where we keep the violent cases." The Canyonites—the brown-legged women, the trunks-clad men constantly busy building and rebuilding their slaphappy unfinished houses—regard with faint contempt the dull creatures who live down in the flats, and treasure in their hearts the secret knowledge that they, and only they, know how to live.

Lookout Mountain Avenue is the name of a side canyon which twists up from Laurel Canyon. The other Canyonites don't like to have it mentioned; after all, one must draw the line somewhere!

High up on Lookout Mountain at number 8775, across the street from the Hermit—the original Hermit of Hollywood— lived Quintus Teal, graduate architect.

Even the architecture of southern California is different. Hot dogs are sold from a structure built like and designated "The Pup." Ice-cream cones come from a giant stucco ice-cream cone, and neon proclaims "Get the Chili Bowl Habit!" from the roofs of buildings which are indisputably chili bowls. Gasoline, oil, and free road maps are dispensed beneath the wings of tri-motored transport planes, while the certified rest rooms, inspected hourly for your comfort, are located in the cabin of the plane itself. These things may surprise, or amuse, the tourist, but the local residents, who walk bareheaded in the famous California noonday sun, take them as a matter of course.

Quintus Teal regarded the efforts of his colleagues in architecture as fainthearted, fumbling, and timid.

"What is a house?" Teal demanded of his friend, Homer Bailey.

"Well—" Bailey admitted cautiously— "speaking in broad terms, I've always regarded a house as a gadget to keep off the rain."

"Nuts! You're as bad as the rest of them."

"I didn't say the definition was complete—"

"Complete! It isn't even in the right direction. From that point of view we might just as well be squatting in caves. But I don't blame you," Teal went on magnanimously, "you're no worse than the lugs you find practicing architecture. Even the Moderns—all they've done is to abandon the Wedding Cake School in favor of the Service Station School, chucked away the gingerbread and slapped on some chromium, but at heart they are as conservative and traditional as a county courthouse. Neutra! Schindler! What have those bums got? What's Frank Lloyd Wright got that I haven't got?"

"Commissions," his friend answered succinctly.

"Huh? Wha' d'ju say?" Teal stumbled slightly in his flow of words, did a slight double take, and recovered himself. "Commissions. Correct. And why? Because I don't think of a house as an upholstered cave; I think of it as a machine for living, a vital process, a live dynamic thing, changing with the mood of the dweller—not a dead, static, oversized coffin. Why should we be held down by the frozen concepts of our ancestors? Any fool with a little smattering of descriptive geometry can design a house in the ordinary way. Is the static geometry of Euclid the only mathematics? Are we to completely disregard the Picard-Vessiot theory? How about modular systems? To say nothing of the rich suggestions of stereochemistry. Isn't there a place in architecture for transformation, for homomorphology, for actional structures?"

"Blessed if I know," answered Bailey. "You might just as well be talking about the fourth dimension for all it means to me."

"And why not? Why should we limit ourselves to the— Say!" He interrupted himself and stared into distances. "Homer, I think you've really got something. After all, why not? Think of the infinite richness of articulation and relationship in four dimensions. What a house, what a house—" He stood quite still, his pale bulging eyes blinking thoughtfully.

Bailey reached up and shook his arm. "Snap out of it. What the hell are you talking about, four dimensions? Time is the fourth dimension; you can't drive nails into *that*."

Teal shrugged him off. "Sure. Sure. Time is a fourth dimension, but I'm thinking about a fourth spatial dimension, like length, breadth and thickness. For economy of materials and convenience of arrangement you couldn't beat it. To say nothing of the saving of ground space—you could put an eight-room house on the land now occupied by a one-room house. Like a tesseract—"

"What's a tesseract?"

"Didn't you go to school? A tesseract is a hypercube, a square figure with four dimensions to it, like a cube has three, and a square has two. Here, I'll show you." Teal dashed out into the kitchen of his apartment and returned with a box of toothpicks, which he spilled on the table between them, brushing glasses and a nearly empty Holland gin bottle carelessly aside. "I'll need some plasticine. I had some around here last week." He burrowed into a drawer of the littered desk which crowded one corner of his dining room and emerged with a lump of oily sculptor's clay. "Here's some."

"What are you going to do?"

"I'll show you." Teal rapidly pinched off small masses of the clay and rolled them into pea-sized balls. He stuck toothpicks into four of these and hooked them together into a square. "There! That's a square."

"Obviously."

"Another one like it, four more toothpicks, and we make a cube." The toothpicks were now arranged in the framework of a square box, a cube, with the pellets of clay holding the corners together. "Now we make another cube just like the first one, and the two of them will be two sides of the tesseract."

Bailey started to help him roll the little balls of clay for the second cube, but became diverted by the sensuous feel of the docile clay and started working and shaping it with his fingers.

"Look," he said, holding up his effort, a tiny figurine, "Gypsy Rose Lee."

"Looks more like Gargantua; she ought to sue you. Now pay attention. You open up one corner of the first cube, interlock the second cube at one corner, and then close the corner. Then take eight more toothpicks and join the bottom of the first cube to the bottom of the second, on a slant, and the top of the first to the top of the second, the same way." This he did rapidly, while he talked.

"What's that supposed to be?" Bailey demanded suspiciously.

"That's a tesseract, eight cubes forming the sides of a hypercube in four dimensions."

"It looks more like a cat's cradle to me. You've only got two cubes there anyhow. Where are the other six?"

"Use your imagination, man. Consider the top of the first cube in relation to the top of the second; that's cube number three. Then the two bottom squares, then the front faces of each cube, the back faces, the right hand, the left hand—eight cubes." He pointed them out.

"Yeah, I see 'em. But they still aren't cubes; they're whatchamacallems—prisms. They are not square, they slant."

"That's just the way you look at it, in perspective. If you drew a picture of a cube on a piece of paper, the side squares would be slaunchwise, wouldn't they? That's perspective. When you look at a four-dimensional figure in three dimensions, naturally it looks crooked. But those are all cubes just the same."

"Maybe they are to you, brother, but they still look crooked to me."

Teal ignored the objections and went on. "Now consider this as the framework of an eight-room house; there's one room on the ground floor—that's for service, utilities, and garage. There are six rooms opening off it on the next floor, living room, dining room, bath, bedrooms, and so forth. And up at the top, completely enclosed and with windows on four sides, is your study. There! How do you like it?"

"Seems to me you have the bathtub hanging out of the living-room ceiling. Those rooms are interlaced like an octopus."

"Only in perspective, only in perspective. Here, I'll do it another way so you can see it." This time Teal made a cube of toothpicks, then made a second of halves of toothpicks, and set it exactly in the center of the first by attaching the corners of the small cube to the large cube by short lengths of toothpick. "Now—the big cube is your ground floor, the little cube inside is your study on the top floor. The six cubes joining them are the living rooms. See?"

Bailey studied the figure, then shook his head. "I still don't see but two cubes, a big one and a little one. Those other six things, they look like pyramids this time instead of prisms, but they still aren't cubes."

"Certainly, certainly, you are seeing them in different perspective. Can't you see that?"

"Well, maybe. But that room on the inside, there. It's completely surrounded by the thingamajigs. I thought you said it had windows on four sides."

"It has—it just looks like it was surrounded. That's the grand feature about a tesseract house, complete outside exposure for every room, yet every wall serves two rooms and an eight-room house requires only a one-room foundation. It's revolutionary."

"That's putting it mildly. You're crazy, Bud; you can't build a house like that. That inside room is on the inside, and there she stays."

Teal looked at his friend in controlled exasperation. "It's guys like you that keep architecture in its infancy. How many square sides has a cube?"

"Six."

"How many of them are inside?"

"Why, none of 'em. They're all on the outside."

"All right. Now listen—a tesseract has eight cubical sides, *all on the outside*. Now watch me. I'm going to open up this tesseract like you can open up a cubical pasteboard box, until it's flat. That way you'll be able to see all eight of the cubes." Working very rapidly he constructed four cubes, piling one on top of the other in an unsteady tower. He then built out four more cubes from the four exposed faces of the second cube in the pile. The structure swayed a little under the loose coupling of the clay pellets, but it stood, eight cubes in an inverted cross, a double cross, as the four additional cubes stuck out in four directions. "Do you see it now? It rests on the ground-floor room, the next six cubes are the living rooms, and there is your study, up at the top."

Bailey regarded it with more approval than he had the other figures. "At least I can understand it. You say that is a tesseract, too?"

"That is a tesseract unfolded in three dimensions. To put it back together you tuck the top cube onto the bottom cube, fold those side cubes in till they meet the top cube and there you are. You do all this folding through a fourth dimension of course; you don't distort any of the cubes, or fold them into each other."

Bailey studied the wobbly framework further. "Look here," he said at last, "why don't you forget about folding this thing up through a fourth dimension—you can't anyway—and build a house like this?"

"What do you mean, I can't? It's a simple mathematical problem—"

"Take it easy, son. It may be simple in mathematics, but you could never get your plans approved for construction. There isn't any fourth dimension; forget it. But this kind of a house—it might have some advantages."

Checked, Teal studied the model. "Hm-m-m—maybe you got something. We could have the same number of rooms, and we'd save the same amount of ground space. Yes, and we would set that middle cross-shaped floor northeast, southwest, and so forth, so that every room would get sunlight all day long. That central axis lends itself nicely to central heating. We'll put the dining room on the northeast and the kitchen on the south-east, with big view windows in every room. OK, Homer, I'll do it! Where do you want it built?"

"Wait a minute! Wait a minute! I didn't say you were going to build it for me—"

"Of course I am. Who else? Your wife wants a new house; this is it."

"But Mrs. Bailey wants a Georgian house—"

"Just an idea she had. Women don't know what they want—"

"Mrs. Bailey does."

"Just some idea an out-of-date architect has put in her head. She drives a 1941 car, doesn't she? She wears the very latest styles—why should she live in an eighteenth-century house? This house will be even later than a 1941 model; it's years in the future. She'll be the talk of the town."

"Well—I'll have to talk to her."

"Nothing of the sort. We'll surprise her with it. Have another drink."

"Anyhow, we can't do anything about it now. Mrs. Bailey and I are driving up to Bakersfield tomorrow. The company's bringing in a couple of wells tomorrow."

"Nonsense. That's just the opportunity we want. It will be a surprise for her when you get back. You can just write me a check right now, and your worries are over."

"I oughtn't to do anything like this without consulting her. She won't like it."

"Say, who wears the pants in your family anyhow?"

The check was signed about halfway down the second bottle.

Things are done fast in southern California. Ordinary houses there are usually built in a month's time. Under Teal's impassioned heckling the tesseract house climbed dizzily skyward in days rather than weeks, and its cross-shaped second story came jutting out at the four corners of the world. He had some trouble at first with the inspectors over these four projecting rooms but by using strong girders and folding money he had been able to convince them of the soundness of his engineering.

By arrangement, Teal drove up in front of the Bailey residence the morning after their return to town. He improvised on his two-tone horn. Bailey stuck his head out the front door. "Why don't you use the bell?"

"Too slow," answered Teal cheerfully. "I'm a man of action. Is Mrs. Bailey ready? Ah, there you are, Mrs. Bailey! Welcome home, welcome home. Jump in, we've got a surprise for you!"

"You know Teal, my dear," Bailey put in uncomfortably.

Mrs. Bailey sniffed. "I know him. We'll go in our own car, Homer."

"Certainly, my dear."

"Good idea," Teal agreed; " 'sgot more power than mine; we'll get there faster. I'll drive, I know the way." He took the keys from Bailey, slid into the driver's seat, and had the engine started before Mrs. Bailey could rally her forces.

"Never have to worry about my driving," he assured Mrs. Bailey, turning his head as he did so, while he shot the powerful car down the avenue and swung onto Sunset Boulevard; "it's a matter of power and control, a dynamic process, just my meat —I've never had a serious accident."

"You won't have but one," she said bitingly. "Will you *please* keep your eyes on the traffic?"

He attempted to explain to her that a traffic situation was a matter, not of eyesight, but intuitive integration of courses, speeds, and probabilities, but Bailey cut him short. "Where is the house, Quintus?"

"House?" asked Mrs. Bailey suspiciously. "What's this about a house, Homer? Have you been up to something without telling me?"

Teal cut in with his best diplomatic manner. "It certainly is a house, Mrs. Bailey. And what a house! It's a surprise for you from a devoted husband. Just wait till you see it—"

"I shall," she agreed grimly. "What style is it?"

"This house sets a new style. It's later than television, newer than next week. It must be seen to be appreciated. By the way," he went on rapidly, heading off any retort, "did you folks feel the earthquake last night?"

"Earthquake? What earthquake? Homer, was there an earthquake?"

"Just a little one," Teal continued, "about two A.M. If I hadn't been awake, I wouldn't have noticed it."

Mrs. Bailey shuddered. "Oh, this awful country! Do you hear that, Homer? We might have been killed in our beds and never have known it. Why did I ever let you persuade me to leave Iowa?"

"But, my dear," he protested hopelessly, "you wanted to come out to California; you didn't like Des Moines."

"We needn't go into that," she said firmly. "You are a man; you should anticipate such things. Earthquakes!"

"That's one thing you needn't fear in your new home, Mrs. Bailey," Teal told her. "It's absolutely earthquake-proof; every part is in perfect dynamic balance with every other part."

"Well, I hope so. Where is this house?"

"Just around this bend. There's the sign now." A large arrow sign, of the sort favored by real-estate promoters, proclaimed in letters that were large and bright even for southern California:

THE HOUSE OF THE FUTURE!!!

Colossal—Amazing—Revolutionary

SEE HOW YOUR GRANDCHILDREN WILL LIVE!

Q. Teal, Architect

"Of course that will be taken down," he added hastily, noting her expression, "as soon as you take possession." He slued around the corner and brought the car to a squealing halt in front of the House of the Future. "Voilà!" He watched their faces for response.

Bailey stared unbelievingly, Mrs. Bailey in open dislike. They saw a simple cubical mass, possessing doors and windows, but no other architectural features, save that it was decorated in intricate mathematical designs. "Teal," Bailey asked slowly, "what have you been up to?"

Teal turned from their faces to the house. Gone was the crazy tower with its jutting second-story rooms. No trace remained of the seven rooms above ground floor level. Nothing remained but the single room that rested on the foundations. "Great jumping cats!" he yelled. "I've been robbed!"

He broke into a run.

But it did him no good. Front or back, the story was the same: the other seven rooms had disappeared, vanished completely. Bailey caught up with him and took his arm.

"Explain yourself. What is this about being robbed? How come you built anything like this—it's not according to agreement."

"But I didn't. I built just what we had planned to build, an eight-room house in the form of a developed tesseract. I've been sabotaged; that's what it is! Jealousy! The other architects in town didn't dare let me finish this job; they knew they'd be washed up if I did."

"When were you last here?"

"Yesterday afternoon."

"Everything all right then?"

"Yes. The gardeners were just finishing up."

Bailey glanced around at the faultlessly manicured landscaping. "I don't see how seven rooms could have been dismantled and carted away from here in a single night without wrecking this garden."

Teal looked around, too. "It doesn't look it. I don't understand it."

Mrs. Bailey joined them. "Well? Well? Am I to be left to amuse myself? We might as well look it over as long as we are here, though I'm warning you, Homer, I'm not going to like it."

"We might as well," agreed Teal, and drew a key from his pocket with which he let them in the front door. "We may pick up some clues."

The entrance hall was in perfect order, the sliding screens that separated it from the garage space were back, permitting them to see the entire compartment. "This looks all right," observed Bailey. "Let's go up on the roof and try to figure out what happened. Where's the staircase? Have they stolen that, too?"

"Oh, no," Teal denied, "look—" He pressed a button below the light switch; a panel in the ceiling fell away and a light, graceful flight of stairs swung noiselessly down. Its strength members were the frosty silver of duralumin, its treads and risers transparent plastic. Teal wriggled like a boy who has successfully performed a card trick, while Mrs. Bailey thawed perceptibly.

It was beautiful.

"Pretty slick," Bailey admitted. "Howsomever it doesn't seem to go any place—"

"Oh, that—" Teal followed his gaze. "The cover lifts up as you approach the top. Open stair wells are anachronisms. Come on." As predicted, the lid of the staircase got out of their way as they climbed the flight and permitted them to debouch at the top, but not, as they had expected, on the roof of the single room. They found themselves standing in the middle one of the five room which constituted the second floor of the original structure.

For the first time on record Teal had nothing to say. Bailey echoed him, chewing on his cigar. Everything was in perfect order. Before them, through open doorway and translucent partition, lay the kitchen, a chef's dream of up-to-the-minute domestic engineering, Monel metal, continuous counter space, concealed lighting, functional arrangement. On the left the formal, yet gracious and hospitable, dining room awaited guests, its furniture in parade-ground alignment.

Teal knew before he turned his head that the drawing room and lounge would be found in equally substantial and impossible existence.

"Well, I must admit this *is* charming," Mrs. Bailey approved, "and the kitchen is just *too* quaint for words—though I would never have guessed from the exterior that this house had so much room upstairs. Of course *some* changes will have to be made. That secretary now—if we moved it over *here* and put the settle over *there*—"

"Stow it, Matilda," Bailey cut in brusquely. "What d'yuh make of it, Teal?"

"Why, Homer Bailey! The very id——"

"Stow it, I said. Well, Teal?"

The architect shuffled his rambling body. "I'm afraid to say. Let's go on up."

"How?"

"Like this." He touched another button; a mate, in deeper colors, to the fairy bridge that had let them up from below offered them access to the next floor. They climbed it, Mrs. Bailey expostulating in the rear, and found themselves in the master bedroom. Its shades were drawn, as had been those on the level below, but the mellow lighting came on automatically. Teal at once activated the switch which controlled still another flight of stairs, and they hurried up into the top-floor study.

"Look, Teal," suggested Bailey when he had caught his breath, "can we get to the roof above this room? Then we could look around."

"Sure, it's an observatory platform." They climbed a fourth flight of stairs, but when the cover at the top lifted to let them reach the level above, they found themselves, not on the roof, but *standing in the ground-floor room where they had entered the house.*

Mr. Bailey turned a sickly gray. "Angels in heaven," he cried, "this place is haunted. We're getting out of here." Grabbing his wife he threw open the front door and plunged out.

Teal was too much preoccupied to bother with their departure. There was an answer to all this, an answer that he did not believe. But he was forced to break off considering it because of hoarse shouts from somewhere above him. He lowered the staircase and rushed upstairs. Bailey was in the central room leaning over Mrs. Bailey, who had fainted. Teal took in the situation, went to the bar built into the lounge, and poured three fingers of brandy, which he returned with and handed to Bailey. "Here—this'll fix her up."

Bailey drank it.

"That was for Mrs. Bailey," said Teal.

"Don't quibble," snapped Bailey. "Get her another." Teal took the precaution of taking one himself before returning with a dose earmarked for his client's wife. He found her just opening her eyes.

"Here, Mrs. Bailey," he soothed, "this will make you feel better."

"I never touch spirits," she protested, and gulped it.

"Now tell me what happened," suggested Teal. "I thought you two had left."

"But we did—we walked out the front door and found ourselves up here, in the lounge."

"The hell you say! Hm-m-m—wait a minute." Teal went into the lounge. There he found that the big view window at the end of the room was open. He peered cautiously through it. He stared, not out at the California countryside, but into the ground-floor room—or a reasonable facsimile thereof. He said nothing, but went back to the stairwell, which he had left open, and looked down it. The ground-floor room was still in place. Somehow, it managed to be in two different places at once, on different levels.

He came back into the central room and seated himself opposite Bailey in a deep, low chair, and sighted him past his upthrust bony knees. "Homer," he said impressively, "do you know what has happened?"

"No, I don't—but if I don't find out pretty soon, something is going to happen and pretty drastic, too!"

"Homer, this is a vindication of my theories. This house is a real tesseract."

"What's he talking about, Homer?"

"Wait, Matilda—now Teal, that's ridiculous. You've pulled some hanky-panky here and I won't have it—scaring Mrs. Bailey half to death, and making me nervous. All I want is to get out of here, with no more of your trapdoors and silly practical jokes."

"Speak for yourself, Homer," Mrs. Bailey interrupted, "I was *not* frightened; I was just took all over queer for a moment. It's my heart; all of my people are delicate and highstrung. Now about this tessy thing—explain yourself, Mr. Teal. Speak up."

He told her as well as he could in the face of numerous interruptions the theory back of the house. "Now as I see it, Mrs. Bailey," he concluded, "this house, while perfectly stable in three dimensions, was not stable in four dimensions. I had built a house in the shape of an unfolded tesseract; something happened to it, some jar or side thrust, and it collapsed into its normal shape—it folded up." He snapped his fingers suddenly. "I've got it! The earthquake!"

"Earthquake?"

"Yes, yes, the little shake we had last night. From a four-dimensional standpoint this house was like a plane balanced on edge. One little push and it fell over, collapsed along its natural joints into a stable four-dimensional figure."

"I thought you boasted about how safe this house was."

"It is safe—three-dimensionally."

"I don't call a house safe," commented Bailey edgily, "that collapses at the first little temblor."

"But look around you, man!" Teal protested. "Nothing has been disturbed, not a piece of glassware cracked. Rotation through a fourth dimension can't affect a three-dimensional figure any more than you can shake letters off a printed page. If you had been sleeping in here last night, you would never have awakened."

"That's just what I'm afraid of. Incidentally, has your great genius figured out any way for us to get out of this booby trap?"

"Huh? Oh, yes, you and Mrs. Bailey started to leave and landed back up here, didn't you? But I'm sure there is no real difficulty—we came in, we can go out. I'll try it." He was up and hurrying downstairs before he had finished talking. He flung open the front door, stepped through, and found himself staring at his companions, down the length of the second-floor lounge. "Well, there does seem to be some slight problem," he admitted blandly. "A mere technicality, though—we can always go out a window." He jerked aside the long drapes that covered the deep French windows set in one side wall of the lounge. He stopped suddenly.

"Hm-m-m," he said, "this is interesting—very."

"What is?" asked Bailey, joining him.

"This." The window stared directly into the dining room, instead of looking outdoors. Bailey stepped back to the corner where the lounge and the dining room joined the central room at ninety degrees.

"But that can't be," he protested, "that window is maybe fifteen, twenty feet from the dining room."

"Not in a tesseract," corrected Teal. "Watch." He opened the window and stepped through, talking back over his shoulder as he did so.

From the point of view of the Baileys he simply disappeared.

But not from his own viewpoint. It took him some seconds

to catch his breath. Then he cautiously disentangled himself from the rosebush to which he had become almost irrevocably wedded, making a mental note the while never again to order landscaping which involved plants with thorns, and looked around him.

He was outside the house. The massive bulk of the ground-floor room thrust up beside him. Apparently he had fallen off the roof.

He dashed around the corner of the house, flung open the front door and hurried up the stairs. "Homer!" he called out, "Mrs. Bailey! I've found a way out!"

Bailey looked annoyed rather than pleased to see him. "What happened to you?"

"I fell out. I've been outside the house. You can do it just as easily—just step through those French windows. Mind the rosebush, though—we may have to build another stairway."

"How did you get back in?"

"Through the front door."

"Then we shall leave the same way. Come, my dear." Bailey set his hat firmly on his head and marched down the stairs, his wife on his arm.

Teal met them in the lounge. "I could have told you that wouldn't work," he announced. "Now here's what we have to do: As I see it, in a four-dimensional figure a three-dimensional man has two choices every time he crosses a line of juncture, like a wall or a threshold. Ordinarily he will make a ninety-degree turn through the fourth dimension, only he doesn't feel it with his three dimensions. Look." He stepped through the very window that he had fallen out of a moment before. Stepped through and arrived in the dining room, where he stood, still talking.

"I watched where I was going and arrived where I intended to." He stepped back into the lounge. "The time before I didn't watch and I moved on through normal space and fell out of the house. It must be a matter of subconscious orientation."

"I'd hate to depend on subconscious orientation when I step out for the morning paper."

"You won't have to; it'll become automatic. Now to get out of the house this time—Mrs. Bailey, if you will stand here with your back to the window, and jump backward, I'm pretty sure you will land in the garden."

Mrs. Bailey's face expressed her opinion of Teal and his ideas. "Homer Bailey," she said shrilly, "are you going to stand there and let him suggest such—"

"But Mrs. Bailey," Teal attempted to explain, "we can tie a rope on you and lower you down eas——"

"Forget it, Teal," Bailey cut him off brusquely. "We'll have to find a better way than that. Neither Mrs. Bailey nor I are fitted for jumping."

Teal was temporarily nonplused; there ensued a short silence. Bailey broke it with, "Did you hear that, Teal?"

"Hear what?"

"Someone talking off in the distance. D'you s'pose there could be someone else in the house, playing tricks on us, maybe?"

"Oh, not a chance. I've got the only key."

"But I'm sure of it," Mrs. Bailey confirmed. "I've heard them ever since we came in. Voices. Homer, I can't stand much more of this. Do something."

"Now, now, Mrs. Bailey," Teal soothed, "don't get upset. There can't be anyone else in the house, but I'll explore and make sure. Homer, you stay here with Mrs. Bailey and keep an eye on the rooms on this floor." He passed from the lounge into the ground-floor room and from there to the kitchen and on into the bedroom. This led him back to the lounge by a straight-line route, that is to say, by going straight ahead on the entire trip he returned to the place from which he started.

"Nobody around," he reported. "I opened all of the doors and windows as I went—all except this one." He stepped to the window opposite the one through which he had recently fallen and thrust back the drapes.

He saw a man with back toward him, four rooms away. Teal snatched open the French window and dived through it, shouting, "There he goes now! Stop, thief!"

The figure evidently heard him; it fled precipitately. Teal pursued, his gangling limbs stirred to unanimous activity, through drawing room, kitchen, dining room, lounge—room after room, yet in spite of Teal's best efforts he could not seem to cut down the four-room lead that the interloper had started with.

He saw the pursued jump awkwardly but actively over the low sill of a French window and in so doing knock off his hat. When he came up to the point where his quarry had lost his headgear, he stooped and picked it up, glad of an excuse to stop and catch his breath. He was back in the lounge.

"I guess he got away from me," he admitted. "Anyhow, here's his hat. Maybe we can identify him."

Bailey took the hat, looked at it, then snorted and slapped it on Teal's head. It fitted perfectly. Teal looked puzzled, took the hat off, and examined it. On the sweat band were the initials "Q.T." It was his own.

Slowly comprehension filtered through Teal's features. He went back to the French window and gazed down the series of rooms through which he had pursued the mysterious stranger. They saw him wave his arms semaphore fashion. "What are you doing?" asked Bailey.

"Come see." The two joined him and followed his stare with their own. Four rooms away they saw the backs of three figures, two male and one female. The taller, thinner of the men was waving his arms in a silly fashion.

Mrs. Bailey screamed and fainted again.

Some minutes later, when Mrs. Bailey had been resuscitated and somewhat composed, Bailey and Teal took stock. "Teal," said Bailey, "I won't waste any time blaming you; recriminations are useless and I'm sure you didn't plan for this to happen, but I suppose you realize we are in a pretty serious predicament. How are we going to get out of here? It looks now as if we would stay until we starve; every room leads into another room."

"Oh, it's not that bad. I got out once, you know."

"Yes, but you can't repeat it—you tried."

"Anyhow we haven't tried all the rooms. There's still the study."

"Oh, yes, the study. We went through there when we first came in, and didn't stop. Is it your idea that we might get out through its windows?"

"Don't get your hopes up. Mathematically, it ought to look into the four side rooms on this floor. Still we never opened the blinds; maybe we ought to look."

" 'Twon't do any harm anyhow. Dear, I think you had best just stay here and rest—"

"Be left alone in this horrible place? I should say not!" Mrs. Bailey was up off the couch where she had been recuperating even as she spoke.

They went upstairs. "This is the inside room, isn't it, Teal?" Bailey inquired as they passed through the master bedroom and climbed on up toward the study. "I mean it was the little cube in your diagram that was in the middle of the big cube, and completely surrounded."

"That's right," agreed Teal. "Well, let's have a look. I figure this window ought to give into the kitchen." He grasped the cords of Venetian blinds and pulled them.

It did not. Waves of vertigo shook them. Involuntarily they fell to the floor and grasped helplessly at the pattern on the rug to keep from falling. "Close it! Close it!" moaned Bailey.

Mastering in part a primitive atavistic fear, Teal worked his way back to the window and managed to release the screen. The window had looked *down* instead of *out*, down from a terrifying height.

Mrs. Bailey had fainted again.

Teal went back after more brandy while Bailey chafed her wrists. When she had recovered, Teal went cautiously to the window and raised the screen a crack. Bracing his knees, he studied the scene. He turned to Bailey. "Come look at this, Homer. See if you recognize it."

"You stay away from there, Homer Bailey!"

"Now, Matilda, I'll be careful." Bailey joined him and peered out.

"See up there? That's the Chrysler Building, sure as shooting. And there's the East River, and Brooklyn." They gazed straight down the sheer face of an enormously tall building. More than a thousand feet away a toy city, very much alive, was spread out before them. "As near as I can figure it out, we are looking down the side of the Empire State Building from a point just above its tower."

"What is it? A mirage?"

"I don't think so—it's too perfect. I think space is folded over through the fourth dimension here and we are looking past the fold."

"You mean we aren't really seeing it?"

"No, we're seeing it all right. I don't know what would happen if we climbed out this window, but I for one don't want to try. But what a view! Oh, boy, what a view! Let's try the other windows."

They approached the next window more cautiously, and it was well that they did, for it was even more disconcerting, more reason-shaking, than the one looking down the gasping height of the skyscraper. It was a simple seascape, open ocean and blue sky—but the ocean was where the sky should have been, and contrariwise. This time they were somewhat braced for it, but they both felt seasickness about to overcome them at the sight of waves rolling overhead; they lowered the blind quickly without giving Mrs. Bailey a chance to be disturbed by it.

Teal looked at the third window. "Game to try it, Homer?"

"Hrrumph—well, we won't be satisfied if we don't. Take it easy." Teal lifted the blind a few inches. He saw nothing, and raised it a little more—still nothing. Slowly he raised it until the window was fully exposed. They gazed out at—nothing.

Nothing, nothing at all. What color is nothing? Don't be silly! What shape is it? Shape is an attribute of *something*. It had neither depth nor form. It had not even blackness. It was *nothing*.

Bailey chewed at his cigar. "Teal, what do you make of that?"

Teal's insouciance was shaken for the first time. "I don't know, Homer, I don't rightly know—but I think that window ought to be walled up." He stared at the lowered blind for a moment. "I think maybe we looked at a place where space *isn't*. We looked around a fourth-dimensional corner and there wasn't anything there." He rubbed his eyes. "I've got a headache."

They waited for a while before tackling the fourth window. Like an unopened letter, it might *not* contain bad news. The doubt left hope. Finally the suspense stretched too thin and Bailey pulled the cord himself, in the face of his wife's protests.

It was not so bad. A landscape stretched away from them,

right side up, and on such a level that the study appeared to be a ground-floor room. But it was distinctly unfriendly.

A hot, hot sun beat down from lemon-colored sky. The flat ground seemed burned a sterile, bleached brown and incapable of supporting life. Life there was, strange stunted trees that lifted knotted, twisted arms to the sky. Little clumps of spiky leaves grew on the outer extremities of these misshapen growths.

"Heavenly day," breathed Bailey, "where is that?"

Teal shook his head, his eyes troubled. "It beats me."

"It doesn't look like anything on Earth. It looks more like another planet—Mars, maybe."

"I wouldn't know. But, do you know, Homer, it might be worse than that, worse than another planet, I mean."

"Huh? What's that you say?"

"It might be clear out of our space entirely. I'm not sure that that is our sun at all. It seems too bright."

Mrs. Bailey had somewhat timidly joined them and now gazed out at the outré scene. "Homer," she said in a subdued voice, "those hideous trees—they frighten me."

He patted her hand.

Teal fumbled with the window catch.

"What are you doing?" Bailey demanded.

"I thought if I stuck my head out the window I might be able to look around and tell a bit more."

"Well—all right," Bailey grudged, "but be careful."

"I will." He opened the window a crack and sniffed. "The air is all right, at least." He threw it open wide.

His attention was diverted before he could carry out his plan. An uneasy tremor, like the first intimation of nausea, shivered the entire building for a long second, and was gone.

"Earthquake!" They all said it at once. Mrs. Bailey flung her arms around her husband's neck.

Teal gulped and recovered himself, saying, "It's all right, Mrs. Bailey. This house is perfectly safe. You know you can expect settling tremors after a shock like last night." He had just settled his features into an expression of reassurance when the second shock came. This one was no mild shimmy but the real seasick roll.

In every Californian, native-born or grafted, there is a deep-rooted primitive reflex. An earthquake fills him with soul-shaking claustrophobia which impels him blindly to *get outdoors!* Model Boy Scouts will push aged grandmothers aside to obey it. It is a matter of record that Teal and Bailey landed on top of Mrs. Bailey. Therefore, she must have jumped through the window first. The order of precedence cannot be attributed to chivalry; it must be assumed that she was in readier position to spring.

They pulled themselves together, collected their wits a little, and rubbed sand from their eyes. Their first sensations were relief at feeling the solid sand of the desert land under them. Then Bailey noticed something that brought them to their feet and checked Mrs. Bailey from bursting into the speech that she had ready.

"Where's the house?"

It was gone. There was no sign of it at all. They stood in the center of flat desolation, the landscape they had seen from the window. But aside from the tortured, twisted tree there was nothing to be seen but the yellow sky and the luminary overhead, whose furnacelike glare was already almost insufferable.

Bailey looked slowly around, then turned to the architect. "Well, Teal?" His voice was ominous.

Teal shrugged helplessly. "I wish I knew. I wish I could even be sure that we were on Earth."

"Well, we can't stand here. It's sure death if we do. Which direction?"

"Any, I guess. Let's keep a bearing on the sun."

They had trudged on for an undetermined distance when Mrs. Bailey demanded a rest. They stopped. Teal said in an aside to Bailey, "Any ideas?"

"No . . . no, none. Say, do you hear anything?"

Teal listened. "Maybe—unless it's my imagination."

"Sounds like an automobile. Say, it *is* an automobile!"

They came to the highway in less than another hundred yards. The automobile, when it arrived, proved to be an elderly, puffing light truck, driven by a rancher. He crunched to a stop at their hail. "We're stranded. Can you help us out?"

"Sure. Pile in."

"Where are you headed?"

"Los Angeles."

"Los Angeles? Say, where is this place?"

"Well, you're right in the middle of the Joshua-Tree National Forest."

The return was as dispiriting as the Retreat from Moscow. Mr. and Mrs. Bailey sat up in front with the driver while Teal bumped along in the body of the truck, and tried to protect his head from the sun. Bailey subsidized the friendly rancher to detour to the tesseract house, not because they wanted to see it again, but in order to pick up their car.

At last the rancher turned the corner that brought them back to where they had started. But the house was no longer there.

There was not even the ground-floor room. It had vanished. The Baileys, interested in spite of themselves, poked around the foundations with Teal.

"Got any answers for this one, Teal?" asked Bailey.

"It must be that on that last shock it simply fell through into another section of space. I can see now that I should have anchored it at the foundations."

"That's not all you should have done."

"Well, I don't see that there is anything to get downhearted about. The house was insured, and we've learned an amazing lot. There are possibilities, man, possibilities! Why, right now I've got a great new revolutionary idea for a house—"

Teal ducked in time. He was always a man of action.

MURRAY LEINSTER

Murray Leinster was writing science fiction before most of us were born; he is now in his very young seventies, and his total output since 1917 would fill at least a hundred volumes of small print. Yet that colossal production has seldom been at the expense of quality, and Will F. Jenkins—to give him his real name—has pioneered many of the basic themes of modern science fiction. Alternate time tracks ("Sideways In Time"), passage through solid matter ("The Mole Pirates"), and the concept of the giant, self-sustaining interstellar ship ("Proxima Centauri") are some of the ideas that he was among the first to use. And his story of man's encounter with aliens in the depths of space ("First Contact") is such a classic that a Soviet writer recently found it necessary to take a poor view of it. (The Russian's thesis: since all advanced races *must* be good communists, there is no possibility of conflict. Chinese papers, please copy.)

"The Wabbler" is a story of cybernetics, though it was written six years before Norbert Wiener put that word into circulation (1948). It is the best example I know of an author's getting into the "mind" of a machine, and making the reader identify himself with it. As such, it merits careful study by all computer-programmers, anxious to outthink their moronic charges.

On rereading this story after some twenty years, I suddenly realized that I was very familiar with the Wabbler's territory. Only two years after Murray Leinster wrote his story, the 30,000-ton British battleship *Valiant* was eased into the world's largest floating dock, on the east coast of Ceylon. The distressful events that then followed were almost identical in result, though not in cause, with the climax of this tale; I have described them in *The Reefs of Taprobane* (Chapter 16, "A Very Expensive Night"). "The Wabbler" vividly invokes my own dives through the gloomy wreckage, inhabited by ten-foot groupers, that still lies along the bottom of Trincomalee harbor.

The Wabbler

The Wabbler went westward, with a dozen of its fellows, by night and in the belly of a sleek, swift-flying thing. There were no lights anywhere save the stars overhead. There was a sustained, furious roaring noise, which was the sound the sleek thing made in-flying. The Wabbler lay in its place, with its ten-foot tail coiled neatly above its lower end, and waited with a sort of deadly patience for the accomplishment of its destiny. It and all its brothers were pear-shaped, with absurdly huge and blunt-ended horns, and with small round holes where eyes might have been, and shielded vents where they might have had mouths. They looked chinless, somehow. They also looked alive, and inhuman, and filled with a sort of passionless hate. They seemed like bodiless demons out of some metallic hell. It was not possible to feel any affection for them. Even the men who handled them felt only a sort of vengeful hope in their capacities.

The Wabblers squatted in their racks for long hours. It was very cold, but they gave no sign. The sleek, swift-flying thing roared on and roared on. The Wabblers waited. Men moved somewhere in the flying thing, but they did not come where the Wabblers were until the very end. But somehow, when a man came and inspected each one of them very carefully and

poked experimentally about the bottoms of the racks in which
the Wabblers lay, they knew that the time had come.

The man went away. The sleek thing tilted a little. It seemed
to climb. The air grew colder, but the Wabblers—all of them—
were indifferent. Air was not their element. Then, when it was
very, very cold indeed, the roaring noise of the flying thing
ceased abruptly. The cessation of the noise was startling. Presently little whistling, whispering noises took the place of the
roar, as hearing adjusted to a new level of sound. That whistling
and whining noise was wind, flowing past the wings of the flying
thing. Presently the air was a little warmer—but still very cold.
The flying thing was gliding, motors off, and descending at a
very gradual slant.

The Wabbler was the fourth in the row of its brothers on
the port side of the flying thing. It did not stir, of course, but
it felt an atmosphere of grim and savage anticipation. It seemed
that all the brothers coldly exchanged greetings and farewell.
The time had definitely come.

The flying thing leveled out. Levers and rods moved in the
darkness of its belly. The feeling of anticipation increased.
Then, suddenly, there were only eleven of the Wabblers. Wind
roared where the twelfth had been. There were ten. There were
nine, eight, seven, six—

The Wabbler hurtled downward through blackness. There
were clouds overhead now. In all the world there was no speck
of actual light. But below there was a faint luminosity. The
Wabbler's tail uncurled and writhed flexibly behind it. Wind
screamed past its ungainly form. It went plunging down and
down and down, its round holes—which looked so much like
eyes—seeming incurious and utterly impassive. The luminosity
underneath separated into streaks of bluish glow, which were
phosphorescences given off by the curling tips of waves. Off
to westward there was a brighter streak of such luminosity. It
was surf.

Splash! The Wabbler plunged into the water with a flare of
luminescence and a thirty-foot spout of spume and spray rising
where it struck. But then that spouting ceased, and the Wabbler was safely under water. It dived swiftly for twenty feet. Perhaps thirty. Then its falling checked. It swung about, and its

writhing tail settled down below it. For a little while it seemed almost to intend to swim back to the surface. But bubbles came from the shielded opening which seemed to be a mouth. It hung there in the darkness of the sea—but now and then there were little fiery streaks of light as natives of the ocean swam about it —and then slowly, slowly, slowly it settled downward. Its ten-foot tail seemed to waver a little, as if groping.

Presently it touched. Ooze. Black ooze. Sea bottom. Sixty feet overhead the waves marched to and fro in darkness. Some-how, through the stilly silence, there came a muffled vibration. That was the distant surf, beating upon a shore. The Wabbler hung for an instant with the very tip of its tail barely touching the bottom. Then it made small sounds inside itself. More bubbles came from the round place like a mouth. It settled one foot; two feet; three. Three feet of its tail rested on the soft ooze. It hung, pear-shaped, some seven feet above the ocean bottom, with the very tip of its horns no more than four feet higher yet. There was fifty feet of empty sea above it. This was not its destiny. It waited passionlessly for what was to happen.

There was silence save for the faint vibration from the distant surf. But there was an infinitesimal noise, also, within the Wabbler's bulk, a rhythmic, insistent, hurried *tick-tick-tick-tick* —It was the Wabbler's brain in action.

Time passed. Above the sea the sleek, swift-flying thing bel-lowed suddenly far away. It swerved and went roaring back in the direction from which it had come. Its belly was empty now, and somewhere in the heaving sea there were other Wabblers, each one now waiting as the fourth Wabbler did, for the thing that its brain expected. Minutes and minutes passed. The seas marched to and fro. The faraway surf rumbled and roared against the shore. And higher yet, above the clouds, a low-hang-ing and invisible moon dipped down toward a horizon which did not show anywhere. But the Wabbler waited.

The tide came. Here, so far from the pounding surf, the stir-ring of the lower levels of the sea was slight indeed. But the tide moved in toward the land. Slowly, the pressure of water against one of the Wabbler's sides became evident. The Wab-bler leaned infinitesimally toward the shore. Presently its flexible tail ceased to be curved where it lay upon the ooze. It straightened out. There were little bluish glows where it stirred the phosphorescent mud. Then the Wabbler moved. Shoreward. It trailed its tail behind it and left a little glowing track of ghostly light.

Fish swam about it. Once there was a furry purring sound, and propellers pushed an invisible, floating thing across the surface of the sea. But it was far away and the Wabbler was impassive. The tide flowed. The Wabbler moved in little jerks. Sometimes three feet or four, and sometimes eight or ten. Once, where the sea bottom slanted downward for a space, it moved steadily for almost a hundred yards. It came to rest then, swaying a little. Presently it jerked onward once more. Somewhere an indefinite distance away were its brothers, moving in in the same fashion. The Wabbler went on and on, purposefully, moved by the tide.

Before the tide turned, the Wabbler had moved two miles nearer to the land. But it did not move in a straight line. Its trailing, flexible tail kept it in the deepest water and the strongest current. It moved very deliberately and almost always in small jerks, and it followed the current. The current was strongest where it moved toward a harbor entrance. In moving two miles shoreward, the Wabbler also moved more than two miles nearer to a harbor.

There came a time, though, when the tide slackened. The Wabbler ceased to move. For half an hour it hung quite still, swaying a little and progressing not at all, while the *tick-tick-tick-tick* of its brain measured patience against intent. At the end of the half-hour there were small clanking noises within its body. Its shielded mouth emitted bubbles. It sank, and checked, and gave off more bubbles, and sank again. It eased itself very cautiously and very gently into the ooze. Then it gave off more bubbles and lay at rest.

It waited there, its brain ticking restlessly within it, but with its appearance of eyes impassive. It lay in the darkness like some creature from another world, awaiting a foreordained event.

For hours it lay still with no sign of any activity at all. Toward the end of those hours, a very faint graying of the upper sea became manifest. It was very dim indeed. It was not enough, in all likelihood, for even the Wabbler to detect the slight move-

ment of semi-floating objects along the sea floor, moved by the
ebb tide. But there came a time when even such movements
ceased. Again the sea was still. It was full ebb. And now the
Wabbler stirred.

It clanked gently and wavered where it lay in the ooze. There
was a cloud of stirred-up mud, as if it had emitted jets of water
from its under parts. It wabbled to one side and the other,
straining, and presently its body was free, and a foot or two and
then four or five feet of its tail—but it still writhed and wabbled
spasmodically—and then suddenly it left the sea floor and
floated free.

But only for a moment. Almost immediately its tail swung
free, the Wabbler spat out bubbles and descended gently to
the bottom again. It rested upon the tip of its tail. It spat more
bubbles. One—two—three feet of its tail rested on the mud. It
waited. Presently the flood tide moved it again.

It floated always with the current. Once it came to a curve in
the deeper channel to which it had found its way, and the tide
tended to sweep it up and out beyond the channel. But its tail
resisted the attempt. In the end, the Wabbler swam grandly
back to the deeper water. The current was stronger there. It
went on and on at a magnificent two knots.

But when the current slowed again as the time of the tide
change neared, the Wabbler stopped again. It swung above
the yard-length of its tail upon the mud. Its brain went *tick-tick-
tick-tick* and it made noises. It dribbled bubbles. It sank, and
checked, and dribbled more bubbles, and sank cautiously again
—It came cautiously to rest in the mud.

During this time of waiting, the Wabbler heard many
sounds. Many times during slack tide, and during ebb tide, too,
the water brought humming, purring noises of engines. Once
a boat came very near. There was a curious hissing sound in the
water. Something—a long line—passed very close overhead. A
minesweeper and a minesweep patrolled the sea, striving to detect and uproot submarine mines. But the Wabbler had no
anchor cable for the sweep to catch. It lay impassively upon the
bottom. But its eyes stared upward with a deadly calm until
the minesweeper passed on its way.

Once more during the light hours the Wabbler shook itself

free of the bottom ooze and swam on with the tide. And once more—with another wait on the mud while the tide flowed out —at night. But day and night meant little to the Wabbler. Its ticking brain went on tirelessly. It rested, and swam, and swam, and rested, with a machinelike and impassive pertinacity, and always it moved toward places where the tide moved faster and with channels more distinct.

At last it came to a place where the water was no more than forty feet deep, and a distinct greenish-blue light came down from the surface sunshine. In that light the Wabbler was plainly visible. It had acquired a coating of seaweed and slime which seemed to form a sort of aura of wavering greenish tentacles. Its seeming of eyes appeared now to be small and snakelike and very wise and venomous. It was still chinless, and its trailing tail made it seem more than ever like some bodiless demon out of a metallic hell. And now it came to a place where for a moment its tail caught in some minor obstruction, and as it tugged at the catch, one of its brothers floated by. It passed within twenty feet of the fourth Wabbler, and they could see each other clearly. But the fourth Wabbler was trapped. It wavered back and forth in the flood tide, trying to pull free, as its fellow swam silently and implacably onward.

Some twenty minutes after that passage there was a colossal explosion somewhere, and after that very many fuzzy, purring noises in the sea. The Wabbler may have known what had happened, or it may not. A submarine net across a harbor entrance is not a thing of which most creatures have knowledge, but it was a part of the Wabbler's environment. Its *tick-tick-ticking* brain may have interpreted the explosion quite correctly as the destiny of its brother encountering that barrier. It is more likely that the brain only noted with relief that the concussion had broken the grip of the obstruction in the mud. The Wabbler went onward in the wake of its fellow. It went sedately, and solemnly, and with a sort of unholy purposefulness, following the tidal current. Presently there was a great net that stretched across the channel, far beyond any distance that the Wabbler could be expected to see. But right where the Wabbler would pass, there was a monstrous gaping hole in that net. Off to one side there was the tail of another Wabbler, shattered away from that other Wabbler's bulk.

The fourth Wabbler went through the hole. It was very simple indeed. Its tail scraped for a moment, and then it was inside the harbor. And then the *tick-tick-ticking* of the Wabbler's brain was very crisp and incisive indeed, because this was its chance for the accomplishment of its destiny. It listened for sounds of engines, estimating their loudness with an uncanny precision, and within its rounded brainpan it measured things as abstract as variations in the vertical component of terrestrial magnetism. There were many sounds and many variations to note, too, because surface craft swarmed about the scene of a recent violent explosion. Their engines purred and rumbled, and their steel hulls made marked local changes in magnetic force. But none of them came quite close enough to the Wabbler to constitute its destiny.

It went on and on as the flood tide swept in. The harbor was a busy one, with many small craft moving about, and more than once in these daylight hours flying things alighted upon the water and took off again. But it happened that none came sufficiently near. An hour after its entrance into the harbor the Wabbler was in a sort of eddy, in a basin, and it made four slow, hitching circuits about the same spot—during one of which it came near to serried ranks of piling—before the time of slack water. But even here the Wabbler, after swaying a little without making progress for perhaps twenty minutes, made little clanking noises inside itself and dribbled out bubbles and eased itself down in the mud to wait.

It lay there, canted a little and staring up with its small, round, seeing eyes with a look of unimpassioned expectancy. Small boats roved overhead. Once engines rumbled, and a wooden-hulled craft swam on the surface of the water to the very dock whose pilings the Wabbler had seen. Then creaking sounds emanated from those pilings. The Wabbler may have known that unloading cranes were at work. But this was not its destiny either.

There came other sounds of greater import. Clankings of gears. A definite, burbling rush of water. It continued and con-

tinued. The Wabbler could not possibly be expected to understand, of course, that such burbling underwater sounds are typical of a drydock being filled—the filling beginning near low tide
when a great ship is to leave at high. Especially, perhaps, the
Wabbler could not be expected to know that a great warship
had occupied a vastly important drydock and that its return to
active service would restore much power to an enemy fleet.
Certainly it could not know that another great warship waited
impatiently to be repaired in the same basin. But the restless
tick-tick-tick-tick which was the Wabbler's brain was remark-
ably crisp and incisive.

When flood tide began once more, the Wabbler jetted water
and wabbled to and fro until it broke free of the bottom. It
hung with a seeming impatience—wreathed in seaweed and
coated with greenish slime—above the tail which dangled down
to the harbor mud. It looked alive, and inhuman, and chinless,
and it looked passionately demoniac, and it looked like something out of a submarine Gehenna. And, presently, when the
flood tide began to flow and the eddy about the docks and the
drydock gates began, the Wabbler inched as if purposefully
toward the place where water burbled through flooding valves.

Sounds in the air did not reach the Wabbler. Sounds under
water did. It heard the grinding rumble of steam winches, and
it heard the screeching sound as the drydock gates swung open.
They were huge gates, and they made a considerable eddy of
their own. The Wabbler swam to the very center of that eddy
and hung there, waiting. Now, for the first time, it seemed excited. It seemed to quiver a little. Once when it seemed that the
eddy might bring it to the surface, it bubbled patiently from
the vent which appeared to be a mouth. And its brain went
tick-tick-tick-tick within it, and inside its brainpan it measured
variations in the vertical component of terrestrial magnetism,
and among such measurements it noted the effect of small tugs
which came near but did not enter the drydock. They only sent
lines within, so they could haul the warship out. But the tugs
were not the Wabbler's destiny either.

It heard their propellers thrashing, and they made, to be sure,
a very fine noise. But the Wabbler quivered with eagerness as
somewhere within itself it noted a vast variation in the vertical

magnetic component, which increased and increased steadily. That was the warship moving very slowly out of its place in the drydock. It moved very slowly but very directly toward the Wabbler, and the Wabbler knew that its destiny was near.

Somewhere very far away there was the dull, racking sound of an explosion. The Wabbler may have realized that another of its brothers had achieved its destiny, but paid no heed. Its own destiny approached. The steel prow of the battleship drew nearer and nearer, and then the bow plates were overhead, and something made a tiny click inside the Wabbler. Destiny was certain now. It waited, quivering. The mass of steel within the range of its senses grew greater and greater. The strain of restraint grew more intense. The *tick-tick-ticking* of the Wabbler's brain seemed to accelerate to a frantic—to an intolerable—pace. And then—

The Wabbler achieved its destiny. It turned into a flaming ball of incandescent gases—three hundred pounds of detonated high explosive—squarely under the keel of a thirty-five-thousand-ton battleship which at the moment was only halfway out of a drydock. The watertight doors of the battleship were open, and its auxiliary power was off, so they could not be closed. There was much need for this drydock, and repairs were not completed in it. But it was the Wabbler's destiny to end all that. In three minutes the battleship was lying crazily on the harbor bottom, half in and half out of the drydock. She careened as she sank, and her masts and fighting tops demolished sheds by the drydock walls. Battleship and dock alike were out of action for the duration of the war.

And the Wabbler—

A long, long time afterward—years afterward—salvage divers finished cutting up the sunken warship for scrap. The last irregularly cut mass of metal went up on the salvage slings. The last diver down went stumbling about the muddy harbor water. His heavy, weighted shoes kicked up something. He fumbled to see if anything remained to be salvaged. He found a ten-foot, still-flexible tail of metal. The rest of the Wabbler had ceased to exist. Chronometer, tide-time gear, valves, compressed-air tanks, and all the balance of its intricate inwards had been blown to atoms when the Wabbler achieved its destiny. Only the flexible metal tail remained intact.

The salvage diver considered that it was not worth sending the sling down for again. He dropped it in the mud and jerked on the lifeline to be hauled up to the surface.

THEODORE L. THOMAS

This is a story with a deceptively innocuous, yet wholly accurate title. One day men will be able to *do* something about the weather—and when that time comes, the patterns of global power will have irrevocably changed. But there is much more besides meteorology and politics in "The Weather Man"; it concerns personal relations, the irrational impulses which sometimes motivate human beings—and ends with a close and terrifying glimpse of our nearest star, the sun. On all levels, it is a *tour-de-force* of science fiction.

Theodore Thomas, who lives in Lancaster, Pennsylvania, is a successful patent attorney whose hobbies include skin-diving; I once saw him cross the Delaware in a manner that would have astonished Washington. Under the name "Leonard Lockhard" he has written some hilarious, yet fundamentally serious, article-stories, poking fun at the tottering chaos of U.S. patent law. One in which I am morbidly interested concerned the impossibility of taking out a patent for a communications satellite until it was too late to be of any value.

The Weather Man

. . . And the name "Weather Bureau" continued to be used, although the organization itself was somewhat changed in form. Thus the Weather Congress consisted of three arms. First was the political arm, the Weather Council. Second was the scientific arm, the Weather Advisors. Third was the operating arm, the Weather Bureau. All three arms were relatively independent, and each . . .

                    The Columbia Encyclopedia, 32nd Edition
                              Columbia University Press

Jonathan H. Wilburn opened his eyes and immediately felt the tension in the day. He lay there, puzzled, seeking the source of it. It was the start of just another day in Palermo. The street noises were normal, his apartment was quiet, and he felt good. That was it. He felt good, very good, full of vigor and strong of mind, and with the feeling that he was ready for anything that might happen.

In one movement he threw back the cover and rolled to his feet alongside the bed. Not bad for a man who had turned fifty last week. He stepped into the shower and dissolved his pajamas into a rich foam of cleansing lather. He dried and stood motionless in the center of his dressing room. The tension and the excitement were still with him. He depilated and dressed, and as he slipped into his jacket it came to him.

Sometime during the night in his sleep he had made up his mind that the time had come for him to make a move. He was fifty years old, he had carefully built a good reputation, and he had come as far as he could in the normal course of events. It was now time to push, time to take a chance. To reach the top in politics you have to take a chance.

Wilburn finished slipping into his jacket. He bared his teeth at himself in the mirror. Now he knew why the day felt different. But knowing the reason did nothing to diminish the tension. He would live with it from now on; this he knew for a certainty. He would live and work on the tips of his toes, looking for a way to seize the god of luck and give him a good ringing out.

For a quarter of a century he had moved cautiously, planning each move, insuring its success before he committed himself to it. Slowly he had climbed through the tiers of politics, the

House, the Senate, the United Nations, an ambassadorship, several emergency chairmanships, and finally, the most elite of all bodies, the Weather Congress. His reputation was made, he was known as a brilliant, affable diplomat, one with high skill at bringing about agreement among other hostile Councilmen. He had built a strong following among the two hundred members in the Weather Council. But in politics as in everything else, the higher one climbs, the tougher the advancement. Wilburn suddenly came to a realization that he had not made any advancements in four years. Then came his fiftieth birthday.

Jonathan Wilburn ate breakfast with his wife that morning. Harriet was a slim woman, quietly wise in her role of the wife of a member of the Council of the Weather Congress. In one quick glance she saw that her husband was tight as a wire, and she touched the Diner and placed coffee in front of him. While he sipped it she touched out a set of onion-flavored eggs and carefully hand-basted them with the pork sauce he loved so much; she did not trust the Diner to do it right. While she worked she chatted about the news in the morning paper. Wilburn ate his breakfast, part listening, part smiling and grunting responses, and part staring into space. He kissed her goodbye then, and went out and stepped on a walk.

He rode the walk through the soft Sicilian air, and then became impatient with standing still. He stepped off the walk and strode alongside, and he felt pleased at the way his legs stretched. Off in the distance he could see the dome of the main Council building, and it brought his mind back to the problem at hand. But, even as he thought it, he knew it was nothing he could reason out in advance. This was something he would have to pick up on the spur of the moment. And he would have to stay alert to recognize it when it came.

Wilburn stepped back on the walk and rode it to the Council.

He entered the Great Hall by the north stairs and walked along the east wall toward the stairs to his office. A group of sightseers were being guided across the Great Hall by a uniformed guide, and the guide was describing the wonders of the Hall. When the guide saw Wilburn coming, he interrupted his lecture to say, "And coming toward us from our left is Council-

man Wilburn of an eastern United States District of whom you
have all heard and who will play such an important part in the
vote today to reduce the water available to northern Australia."

The sightseers stopped, stumbling into one another at the
unexpected appearance of such a celebrity. Wilburn smiled and
waved at them, and this confounded them even more, but he
did not stop to talk. He knew from the guide's remarks that
none of his constituents were in the group; the guide would
have contrived to warn him so that he could act accordingly.
Wilburn smiled to himself—an officeholder had many advantages over a mere candidate for office.

Wilburn turned to the stairs and rode up with Councilman
Georges DuBois, of Middle Europe. DuBois said, "I heard him.
Decided yet how you are to vote on this Australian situation,
Jonathan?"

"I lean toward an aye, but I don't know. Do you?"

DuBois shook his head. "I feel the same. It is a thing we
should do only with the greatest of caution. It is a terrible thing
to make men suffer, and even worse to do it to women and
children. I don't know."

They rode in silence to the top of the stairs, and just before
they parted Wilburn said, "My wife stands with me in everything I do, Georges."

DuBois looked at him thoughtfully for a moment, and then
said, "Yes, I understand you. The women there are as much
to blame as the men, and deserve punishment as much. Yes,
that will help me if I vote aye. I will see you in Council." They
nodded goodbye to each other in a wordless gesture of mutual
respect and understanding. DuBois was one of the thoughtful
Councilmen who knew better than most the fearful responsibility carried by the political arm of the Weather Congress.

Wilburn nodded to his staff as he passed through the outer
office. Once at his desk he swiftly settled down to take care
of the many chores. The small pile of papers stacked neatly in
the center of his desk melted away as he picked up one after
another, dictated the words that disposed of it, and dropped it
on another pile.

He was just finishing when a gentle masculine voice said through the speaker, "Have you time to see a friend?"

Wilburn smiled, and got up to open the door of his office for Councilman Gardner Tongareva. The two men smiled and shook hands, and Tongareva settled back deep into one of Wilburn's chairs. He was a yellow-skinned man, a Polynesian, wrinkled and old and wise. His trousers were full and short, reminiscent of the sarong worn by his ancestors. His hair was white and his face was warm and kindly. Tongareva was one of those rare men whose mere presence brought smiles to the faces of his companions and peace to their hearts. He was a man of enormous influence in the Council solely by virtue of his personality.

His District was 15–30 degrees north latitude 150–165 degrees east longitude, the same fifteen-degree-on-a-side landed area of the Earth as the District of each of the other Councilmen. But in Tongareva's case the land was vanishingly small. The only land in the entire region was Marcus Island, one square mile in area, and supporting exactly four people. This was quite a contrast with the 100 million people living in Wilburn's District of 30–45 degrees north latitude 75–90 degrees west longitude. Yet time after time when the population-weighted votes of the two hundred Councilmen were counted, it was apparent that Tongareva had swayed a large percentage of the entire globe.

Wilburn leaned back in his chair and said to Tongareva, "Have you reached a decision yet about the Australian drought?"

Tongareva nodded. "Yes, I have. I believe we have no choice but to subject them to a year's drought. Naughty children must be spanked, and for two years these people have persisted in maintaining an uneven balance of trade. What is really involved here, Jonathan, is a challenge to the supreme authority of the Weather Congress over the peoples of the world. These people in Queensland and the Northern Territory are a hardy lot. They don't really believe that we can or will chastise them by controlling their weather to their detriment. They must be punished immediately or other sections of the world will begin acting up, too. At this time a simple drought to take away their lush pros-

perity for a year ought to serve. Later it might become necessary
to make them suffer, and none of us wants that. Yes, Jonathan,
my vote will be cast in favor of the Australian drought."

Wilburn nodded soberly. He saw now that the vote almost
certainly would be in favor of punishment. Most of the Councilmen seemed to feel it was necessary, but were reluctant to cause
suffering. But when Tongareva stated his position as he just had,
the reluctance would be put aside. Wilburn said, "I agree with
you, Gardner. You have put into words the thoughts of most
of us in this matter. I will vote with you."

Tongareva said nothing, but he continued to stare sharply at
Wilburn. It was not a discomfiting stare; nothing Tongareva
did was ever discomfiting. Tongareva said, "You are a different
man this morning, my good friend. Just as you have been still
a different man for the last three weeks. You have resolved whatever it is that has been disturbing you, and I am pleased. No,"
he raised a hand as Wilburn was about to speak, "it is quite unnecessary to discuss it. When you want me, I will be there to
help you." He stood up. "And now I must go to discuss the Australian situation with some of the others." He smiled and left
before Wilburn could say anything.

Wilburn stared after him, awed at the enormous ability of
Tongareva to understand what he had been going through. He
shook his head and gathered himself and then went out into his
waiting room to talk to the dozen people who were waiting to
see him.

"I'm sorry to keep you waiting," he said to all of them, "but
things are hectic around the Council this morning, as I guess
you know. Please forgive me for not seeing each of you alone,
but we will be summoned for Council business in a few minutes.
I did not want to miss the chance to see all of you for a moment
or two at least. Perhaps we can get together this afternoon or
tomorrow morning."

And Wilburn moved around the room shaking hands and
fixing in his mind the name of each visitor. Two of them were
not constituents. They were lobbyists representing the northern
Australian Districts, and they launched into a tirade against the
taking of any punitive action against the Districts.

Wilburn held up his hand and said, "Gentlemen, this topic

may not be discussed under these circumstances. I will listen to
the arguments for and against on the Floor of the Council, nowhere else. That is all." He smiled and began to pass on. The
younger of the two seized his arm and turned him to face him,
saying, "But, Councilman, you must listen. These poor people
are being made to suffer for the acts of a few of their leaders.
You cannot—"

Wilburn shrugged away from the restraining arm, stepped
swiftly to the wall and pressed a button there. The lobbyist
turned pale and said, "Oh, now, Councilman, I meant no harm.
Please do not lodge a protest against me. Please—"

Two men in the uniform of the Weather Congress swept in
the outer door. Wilburn's voice was calm and his face impassive,
but his eyes glinted like ice crystals. He pointed and said to the
guards, "This man grabbed my arm to try to force me to listen
to his arguments on Council business. I lodge a protest against
him."

It all happened so fast the rest of the visitors had difficulty
recalling exactly what had happened. But the recording tapes
showed, and Wilburn knew that the lobbyist would never again
be allowed in the halls of the Weather Congress. The two
guards softly hustled him out of the room. The other lobbyist
said, "I am sorry, Councilman. I feel responsible for his con-
duct; he is new."

Wilburn nodded and started to speak, but a low musical
chime sounded repeatedly in the room. Wilburn said to the
visitors, "Please excuse me. I must go to the Council Floor now.
If you wish, you may watch the proceedings from the Visitor's
Auditorium. Thank you for coming up to see me, and I hope we
can talk more another time." He waved and smiled and went
back into his office.

Hurriedly he checked his staff to see that they were ready for
the day's business. All were in position, all knew their roles in
the coming debate. Wilburn then took the belt to the Floor,
walking the last hundred yards out in the public hall where he
could be seen. As he came to the main doors several newspaper-
men asked permission to approach, but he refused; he wanted to
get to his desk early and start work.

He went through the doors and down the short wide hall that

led to the Floor. He came out into the huge room and went
down the main aisle toward his desk. A few Councilmen were
already there, and as the Recorder called off Wilburn's name,
they looked up and waved at him. He waved back and continued
on his way to his high-seniority desk up front. He sat down and
began flipping the buttons and switches that put him in touch
with everything that was going on. Immediately a light glowed
indicating that one of the seated Councilmen wanted to talk
to him. Councilman Hardy of 165–180 west longitude 30–45
south latitude—containing most of New Zealand—said to him,
"Well, Jonathan, have you talked with Tongareva yet?"

"Yes, George, I have."

"Going to vote the way he wants?"

"Yes, although I want to wait and hear what is said in opposition before I finally make up my mind. Where do you stand?"

There was a perceptible pause, then, "I will probably vote
against it, unless someone expresses the extreme reluctance of
the Council to vote for drought."

"Why don't you do it, George?"

"Maybe I will. Thank you, Jonathan." And he cut the circuit.

Wilburn looked around the huge chamber, and as always, he
became a little awed at what he saw. It was more than the impressive array of the two hundred huge desks, the raised President's chair, the great board that showed the weather at the
moment on every part of the Earth's surface, and the communications rooms set off from the main room. There was an aura
about this great chamber that was felt by all the men and
women who entered it, whether to work in it or simply to visit.
The fate of the Earth was centered here, and had been for fifty
years. From this chamber flowed the decisions that controlled
the world.

The Weather Congress was the supreme body of Earth, able
to bend states, nations, continents, and hemispheres to its will.
What dictator, what country, could survive when no drop of
rain fell for a year? Or what dictator, what country could survive when blanketed under fifty feet of snow and ice? The
Weather Congress could freeze the Congo River or dry up the
Amazon. It could flood the Sahara or Tierra del Fuego. It could

thaw the tundra, and raise and lower the levels of the oceans at will. And here, in this chamber, all the political decisions had been made, and the chamber seemed to acquire some of the feeling that had been expressed over the last half century, from the stormy early days, to the more settled and reflective present. It was a powerful chamber, and it made its power felt by those who sat in it.

A great many Councilmen had seated themselves. Another chime sounded, and the weather requests began to be relayed to the Councilmen. The Recorder read off the requests, and his voice reached each desk through a tiny speaker. At the same time the written request flashed on the big board. In this manner the Councilmen could busy themselves with other duties while keeping an eye on the requests.

The first request, as usual, came from the Lovers of the Lowly Cactus Plant, and they wanted less rainfall and more desolation in Death Valley to keep the barrel cactus from becoming extinct.

Wilburn rang Tongareva's desk and said, "How many have you talked to, Gardner?"

"About forty, Jonathan. I caught a large group having a cup of coffee."

"Have you talked to Maitland?"

There was a perceptible pause. Maitland seemed always to be against anything Wilburn stood for. His District was 60–75 west longitude 30–45 north latitude, adjoining Wilburn's and including New York City and Boston. Maitland always made it plain that he considered Wilburn unfit for the position of influence he held in the Council. "No," said Tongareva, and Wilburn could see him shake his great head, "no, I did not talk to Maitland."

Wilburn signed off, and listened and watched. The president of Bolivia complained that the region around Cochabamba was running a little too cool to suit his taste. The mayor of Avigait in Greenland stated that the corn crop was ten per cent lower this year due to an extra two inches of rainfall and too much cloud cover. Wilburn nodded; there was one that should be treated seriously, and he pushed a button on his desk marked "favorable" to ensure that it would be considered by the entire Council.

His phone rang. It was a constituent asking him to address the Combined Rotary Club at their annual meeting October 27th next. The clear light flashed as Wilburn's staff, monitoring and checking everything, indicated that he was free on that day. "Why, thank you, yes," said Wilburn, accepting the invitation. "I shall be grateful for the chance to talk to your group." He knew he had made no address in that region for a year, and it was high time. Probably his staff had subtly set it up in the first place.

A farmer outside of Gatrun, Libya, wanted his neighbor's water cut back so that all their crops would be the same height.

Then a conference was called among half a dozen Councilmen to discuss the order of speeches on the Australian situation. While they worked this out, Wilburn noted a request from Ceylon to be allowed to go over from rice in the inland sections to wheat, with the attendant reduction in rainfall and average temperature. He pushed the "favorable" button.

It was decided that Georges DuBois, of Middle Europe, should introduce the drought resolution, with appropriately reluctant language.

One George Andrews of Holtville, California, wanted to see snow fall again before he died, which would be in a few weeks now, no matter that it was July. He could not leave the semitropical environment of Holtville.

Tongareva would second the resolution, and then they would hear the Councilmen from the Australian Districts present their reasons why the punishment should not be instituted. After that they would play it by ear.

The seaport city of Stockholm requested an additional fifteen centimeters of elevation for the Baltic Sea. Kobdo, Mongolia, complained that there had been two disastrous avalanches due to the extra snow burden. And it was there that the hairs on the back of Wilburn's neck began to prickle.

He stiffened in his seat and looked around to see the source of the strange sensation. The floor bustled with activity, all of it normal. He stood up, but he could see nothing more. He saw

Tongareva looking over at him. He shrugged his shoulders and sat down and stared at the barrage of lights on his desk. His skin almost crawled and the adrenalin poured into his veins and he felt wildly exhilarated. What was it? He grabbed the edge of the desk and closed his eyes and forced himself to think. He blanked out all the activity around him and forced his mind to relax and find the source of the stimulation. Australian problem? No, not that. It was . . . it was something in the weather requests. He opened his eyes, and pushed the playback button and watched the requests again.

One by one, more quickly now, they flashed on the miniature screen on his desk. Avalanches, Baltic Sea level, snow in southern California, Ceylon's rice to wheat, the Libyan farmer, the— Wait. He had it now, so he turned back to it and read it very slowly.

George Andrews of Holtville, California, wanted to see snow fall again before he died soon, and he would be unable to leave the semitropical environment of southern California. The more Wilburn stared at it, the more it seemed to have everything he needed. It had universal appeal: a dying man with a final request. It would be difficult: snow in July in southern California was unheard of; he wasn't even certain that it could be carried out. It was almost completely irrational; the Council had never bothered with such requests in the past. The more Wilburn looked at it, the more he became convinced he had found the proper cause on which to risk his career. People the world over would be behind him if he could bring it off. He remembered how it had been in the tradition of American presidents to show an occasional high concern over some unimportant individual. If he failed, he would probably be finished in politics, but that was the chance to take. And there was something about that name George Andrews, something that set off a vague, disturbing memory in the back of his mind, something that had attracted him to the request in the first place. No matter. It was time for him to call up for action all the forces he could muster.

He cut his entire staff into his circuit, and cut all others out. He said, "I am considering supporting the George Andrews request." He paused to allow the statement to sink in, smiling to

himself at the shock to his staff; never had they heard of anything so wild from him. "Check out everything you can about
George Andrews. Make certain that his request is bona fide and
isn't some sort of trap for an innocent Councilman like me. In
particular, make certain that no connection exists between
George Andrews and Councilman Maitland. Check with Greenberg in the Advisors as to the chances of coming up with a solution to the problem of snow in July in southern California in
an extremely restricted region. Given that answer, check with
the Bureau, probably Hechmer—he's up on the sun right now
—and see what the chances are of carrying it out. This must be
completed in . . . just a moment." Wilburn looked around
him. The weather requests had ended, and Councilman Yardley
had left his desk and was walking toward the front of the Floor
to assume his role as President. "You have four hours to get all
the information. Go, and good luck. We will all need it this
time." And Wilburn sat back. There was no time to relax,
however.

Calls had piled up while he had set the investigation in motion. He began clearing them as President Yardley called the
Council to order, swiftly dispensed with the old business, and
then brought up the matter of the censure of Australia. Wilburn
kept an ear on the transactions on the Floor as he continued to
handle the incoming calls and other demands on his time. The
President stated the order of the speeches for and against the
drought resolution, and the Council sat back to listen. Councilman DuBois made his preliminary remarks, expressing the deep
and abiding regret that the Council found it necessary in this
manner to uphold the principles of the Weather Congress. It
was a good speech, thought Wilburn. There could be no doubt
of DuBois' sincerity, and when he solemnly stated the resolution
itself, there were tears in his eyes, and his voice shook. Then the
first of the Councilmen from Australia got up to argue against
the resolution.

Wilburn pocketed the portable receiver, punched the button
that showed he was listening via receiver, and left the Floor.
Many other Councilmen did the same, most of them heading
for the Councilmen's Closed Restaurant, where they could have

a cup of coffee without having to deal with constituents, the press, lobbyists, or any of a multitude of organizations. They sipped their coffee and nibbled sweet cakes and talked. The conversation was all on the coming vote, and it was easy to see that opinion was hardening in favor of the resolution. The Councilmen talked in low voices so they could follow the trend of the arguments being made back on the floor; each Councilman had his portable receiver with him and each listened through the bone microphone behind an ear. The talk grew louder as it became apparent that the Australian Councilman was advancing nothing more than the same old arguments, don't-cause-suffering and give-us-another-chance. The vote was now almost a certainty.

Wilburn wandered back to the floor and handled some more of the day's business at his desk. He went out for more coffee, and returned. He rose to make a brief speech in favor of the resolution, expressing regret for the necessity. Then, as the arguments pro and con began to draw toward the end, the information on George Andrews began to come in.

George Andrews was one hundred and twenty-six years old with a heart condition, and the doctors had given him six weeks to live. There was no discernible connection between Andrews and Councilman Maitland. Wilburn interrupted to ask, "Who checked on that?"

"Jack Parker," was the answer, and Wilburn heard a slight chuckle, which he forgave. Jack Parker was one of the keenest investigators in the business, and Wilburn noted to himself that the staff member who had thought of putting Parker on that particular investigation was due for a bonus. At least Wilburn could now make a decision without fear of walking into a political trap of some kind. But the report continued.

"As I guess you know, Andrews came very close to being one of the most famous men in the world a hundred years ago. For a while it looked like Andrews would get credit for inventing the sessile boats, but he was finally beaten by Hans Daggensnurf. There used to be a few people around who insisted that Andrews was the real inventor all along, and that dirty politics, shrewd lawyers, unethical corporations, and filthy money com-

bined to make a goat out of him. The name 'sessile boats' was
Andrews' name for the sun boats, and the name has stuck. But
then, you could never have called them Daggensnurf boats."

Wilburn remembered now, awed that his subconscious mind
should have somehow alerted him to need to check out the
name George Andrews. Andrews had been the George Seldon
of the automobile industry, the William Kelly of the so-called
Bessemer steel process. All were forgotten men; someone else
reaped the immortality. In Andrews' case, he had, according to
some, been the man who invented the sun boats, those marvelous devices that made the entire Weather Congress possible.
Sliding on a thin film of gaseous carbon, the sessile boats safely
traversed the hell of the sun's surface, moving from place to
place to stir up the activity needed to produce the desired
weather. Without the sessile boats there would be no Weather
Bureau staffed by lean, hard-eyed men, working the sun to produce the results called for by the Weather Council. Yes, Wilburn was lucky indeed to have dragged out his piece of ancient
history just when he needed it.

The report continued, "We checked with the Weather Advisors, particularly Bob Greenberg. He says there is a fair chance
they can find a way to pull snow in southern California this
time of year, but he's not guaranteeing anything. One of his
people has the beginnings of a new theory that might just work,
and our request might be the one to test it out. But he doesn't
want to be quoted on any of this. He's got a personnel problem
with the genius who would do the work if our request was official. I gathered he would like for us to push it through so he
could settle things one way or the other with this bright-eyed
genius."

Wilburn asked, "How about the Bureau?"

"Well, we talked to Hechmer as you suggested. It is his tour
on the sun right now, so he's in close touch. He says they've only
got one Boat Master in the entire Bureau with enough guts and
imagination, and he's having some kind of trouble at home. But
Hechmer says if we come up with something special, he'll find
a way to make his man produce."

Wilburn listened to many other details relating to the Andrews situation. His first assistant had added a feature of his own to the investigation, one which showed why he was such a highly paid member of Wilburn's staff. He had supervised a quiet opinion survey to find how Wilburn's constituents would react to his sponsoring a motion to grant Andrews' request. The result was predictable: If the request went through quickly and smoothly, and if the snow fell, Wilburn would be a wise, humane, and generous man. If acrimony developed in a debate and if snow did not fall, Wilburn would be a man who had blundered badly.

The report ended. Wilburn cleared his desk of all activity and took a quick look out at the Floor. The debate was winding up. The Councilmen were visibly restless to get on to the voting, and it was now clear that the vote was overwhelmingly in favor of the resolution calling for a drought. Wilburn sat back to think.

But even as he sat back he knew the answer; there was really no need to make a decision here. He was going to do it. The only question was: How? And as he turned his mind to the timing of presenting his motion, he saw that here and now was the time. When better than right at the time the Council was finishing an unpleasant piece of business? He might be able to slip his motion through to help take the unpleasant taste from the mouths of the Councilmen. That was it. Wilburn sat back to wait the vote. In another ten minutes it started.

And in twenty minutes it was over. The vote in favor of the drought resolution was 192 to 8. The President lifted his gavel to adjourn the session. Wilburn stood up.

"Mr. President," he said, "we have just had to carry out a necessary but unpleasant duty. I now wish to move that the Council carry out an unnecessary but pleasant duty. I respectfully direct the attention of the honorable members to Weather Request Number 18, today's date."

He paused while the members, looking puzzled, punched the button on their desks that would play back for them the Andrews request. Wilburn waited until he saw most of the faces turned toward him in disbelief. Then he said, "I just said that our duty in this matter was unnecessary, but in a larger sense we have never had a more necessary duty in conscience to see that justice . . ." And Wilburn stated his case for Andrews. He briefly traced the history of George Andrews' career, and the debt owed him by the human race, a debt that had never been paid. As he talked, Wilburn smiled to himself at the phone calls he knew were racing from desk to desk on the Floor. "What's got into Jonathan?" "Has Wilburn lost his mind?" "Watch yourself on this one; he's up to something."

Wilburn stated the difficulty of knowing for certain whether the request was even within the realm of technological possibility. Only the Weather Advisors could tell. And even if it were possible, the Bureau might not be able to carry it out. But such considerations should not stop the Council from trying. And he concluded with an impassioned plea for this act of grace to show the world that the Council was made up of men who never lost sight of the individual.

He sat down amidst silence. Then Tongareva rose, and with soft words and gentle manner he supported the resolution, emphasizing the warmth and humanity of the motion at a time when there would be many who thought the Council too harsh. He sat down, and Maitland rose to the Floor. To Wilburn's astonishment, Maitland, too, supported the resolution. But as Wilburn listened, he understood that Maitland supported the resolution only because he saw disaster in it for Wilburn. It took nerve for Maitland to do it. He could not know what Wilburn had in mind, but Maitland was willing to trust his judgment that a mistake had been made and to try to capitalize on it.

Wilburn answered all the incoming calls from his fellow Councilmen, all of whom wanted to know if Wilburn wanted them to rise in support of the motion. Some of these were his friends, others were those who owed him a favor. To all of them Wilburn urged support in the form of a brief supporting speech. For forty minutes Councilmen bobbed up, spoke for a moment, and then sat down. When the vote came, it was one of the few unanimous votes in the history of the Council. The Australian drought was forgotten, both on the floor and on the video screens of the world. All thoughts were turned to the little town of Holtville, California.

Wilburn heard the gavel adjourn the session, and he knew he was fully committed. His fate was in the hands of others; his work was done for now, possibly forever.

But after all, if one wants to reach the top in politics, one has to take a chance.

Anna Brackney wandered up the broad steps of the Weather Advisors Building half an hour early, as usual. At the top she stopped and looked out over the city of Stockholm. It was a pretty city, sturdy under its heavy roofs, sparkling under the early morning sun, and quiet and restful. Stockholm was a fine place for the Advisors. In fact it was such an excellent choice for the kind of work the Advisors did, Anna wondered all over again how it was possible for men to have chosen it. She turned and went in.

The Maintenance Supervisor, Hjalmar Froding, directed the Polishing Machine around the lobby. He saw Anna Brackney and immediately guided the Machine to lay down a tic-tac-toe pattern in wax on the floor, and then he bowed to her. She stopped, put her finger in her mouth, and then pointed to the upper right-hand square. The Machine put an "O" on it, and then placed an "X" in the center square for Froding. The game went on until Froding had three "Xs" in a row, and the Machine triumphantly ran a straight line through them. Hjalmar Froding bowed to Anna Brackney, and she bowed to him and went on her way. She ignored the escalator and walked up the stairs, feeling pleased that she again was able to have Froding win in an unobvious manner. Anna Brackney was fond of Froding; he seldom spoke or smiled, and treated her as if she were the queen of Sweden. It was too bad some of the other men around here couldn't be guided as simply.

She had to pass through the main Weather Room on her way to her office. A great globe of the world occupied the center of the room, and it showed the weather at the moment on every part of the Earth. The globe was similar in purpose to the map in the Weather Council, but it had a few additional features. Every jet stream, density variation, inversion, every front, isobar, isallobar, isotherm, precipitation area, clouded area, and air mass showed on the globe. The globe was a mass of shifting colors, undecipherable to the untrained eye, making sense only to the mathemeteorologists who made up the technical staff of the Advisors. The curved walls of the room were covered with the instruments that made up the Weather Net, the senses of the Advisors. The entire room looked like something out of a nightmare with its seething globe and dancing lights and shimmering dials. Anna walked through without noticing with the callousness of long proximity. She headed for the private wire from the Weather Council to see if that strange request had come in yet.

The guard in the Council Communications Room saluted and stepped aside for her. She went in and sat down and began to flip through the night's messages from the Council. She picked up the one that related to the imposition of a drought in northern Australia, and read it. She snorted when she finished, and said aloud to herself, "Nothing, no problem at all. A child could figure out how to bring that about." And on down the stack of messages she went.

She found it and read it carefully, and read it again. It was just as the news flashes had reported: snow in July on a one-square-mile area in southern California. The latitude and the longitude of the area were given, and that was all there was to it. But Anna Brackney felt the excitement grow within her. Here was the nastiest problem to confront the Advisors in decades, one that probably could not be solved by standard technics. She put her finger in her mouth. Here was what she had been waiting for, the chance to prove out her theory. Now all she had to do was convince Greenberg to give her the problem. She restacked the messages and went to her office.

It was a small office measuring about eight by eight feet, but Anna Brackney still thought it too big. Her desk was in one corner facing one wall to give her the illusion of being more cramped than she really was. Anna could not stand the feeling of open spaces when she worked. There was no window, no picture on any of the walls, nothing distracting against the plain dark-gray walls. Other Advisors had different ideas on the proper working environment. Some used bright splashes of color, others used woodland or ocean scenes, Greenberg had his walls covered with a black and white maze, and Hiromaka's walls were covered with nudes. Anna shuddered with disgust as she thought of it.

Instead of sitting at her desk, she stood in the middle of the small room, thinking how she could persuade Greenberg to assign the Andrews problem to her. This would be hard. She knew that Greenberg did not like her, and she knew it was only because he was a man and she was a woman. None of the men liked her, and as a result her work never received the credit it deserved. A woman in a man's world was never allowed to be judged on the basis of her work alone. But if she could get the Andrews problem, she would show them. She would show them all.

But time was short. The Andrews problem had to be solved immediately. Sometimes the Advisors' weather programs took weeks to put into operation, and if this turned out to be one like that it would be too late. It had to be worked on and solved now to see if there was enough time. She spun on her heels and ran out of the office and down the escalator to the wide steps at the front door of the building. She would waste no time. She would meet Greenberg as he came in.

She had a ten-minute wait, and Greenberg was early at that. Anna Brackney pounced on him as he reached the top step. She said, "Dr. Greenberg, I am ready to start work immediately on the Andrews problem. I feel—"

"You've been waiting for me?" he said.

"I feel I am best equipped to solve the Andrews problem since it will call for new procedures and . . ."

"What on Earth is the Andrews problem?"

She looked at him blankly and said, "Why, that's the problem that came in during the night, and I want to be the one who . . ."

"But you've nailed me out here on the steps before I've had a chance to go inside. How do I know what problems came in during the night? I haven't been upstairs yet."

"But you must know . . . you have heard of it, it's all on the news."

"There's a lot of junk on the news about our work, most of it untrue. Now why don't you wait until I get a look at it so I know what you're talking about."

They went up the escalator together in silence, he annoyed at being accosted in such a manner, and she annoyed at his obvious effort to put off doing what she wanted.

He started to go into his office first, but she said, "It's over in the Council Communications Room, not in your office."

He started to retort, but thought better of it, and went on in and read the message. She said, "Now may I have it?"

"Look, damn it. This request is going to be treated like any other until we understand its ramifications. I am going to give it to Upton as I do all the others for a preliminary opinion and a recommendation as to assignment. After I have that recommendation I will decide what to do. Now don't bother me until Upton's had a look at it." He saw her mouth curve down and her eyes begin to fill. He had been through these crying sessions before, and he did not like them. "See you later," he said, and he all but ran to his office and locked the door. One thing nice at the Advisors Building. A locked door was inviolate. It meant the person inside did not want to be disturbed, and the caliber of the work was such that the wish was honored.

Anna Brackney raged back to her office. There it was again. A woman did not stand a chance around here; they refused to treat her like a man. Then she went and waited at Upton's office to explain the whole thing to him.

Upton was a portly man with an easy disposition and a mind like a razor. What's more, he understood the operation of a single-tracked mind. Anna had got out no more than half her tale of woe when he recognized that the only way to get her off his back for the day was to review the Andrews request. He sent for it, looked at it, whistled and sat down at a twenty-six-fifty computer. For half an hour he fed in data and sat back while the computer chewed and then spat out the results. The job grew, so he called in some help and soon there were three men working on the computers. In another three hours Upton swung around to Anna, who had been standing behind him the entire time.

He said, "Do you have some ideas on this?"

She nodded.

"Care to tell me something about it?"

She hesitated, then said, "Well, I don't have it all yet. But I think it can be done by—" she paused and glanced at him shyly as if to see in advance whether or not he was laughing at her— "a vertical front."

Upton's jaw fell. "A ver—— . . . You mean a true front that is tipped perpendicular to the Earth's surface?"

She nodded, and put her finger in her mouth. Far from laughing, Upton stared at the floor for a moment, and then headed for Greenberg's office. He walked in without knocking and said to Greenberg, "There is a forty-six per cent chance of carrying out this Andrews mandate by conventional technics. And by the way, what's the matter with the Council? I've never known them to do such an idiotic thing before. What are they trying to do?"

Greenberg shook his head and said, "I don't know. I had a call asking about this from Wilburn. I've got the uncomfortable feeling that they're trying to see just what we *can* do here, sort of test us before they put some real big problem to us. They voted a drought for northern Australia yesterday, and maybe they are getting ready to put the real squeeze on some region and want to see what we can do first."

Upton said, "Drought in Australia? Well, they're getting a little tough, aren't they? That isn't like the good old easygoing Council that I know. Any difficulty with the Australian drought?"

"No. It was such a standard problem I didn't even bother to give it to you for screening. I turned it right over to Hiromaka. But there's something behind this Andrews thing, and I don't like it. We'd better find a way to carry it out."

Upton said, "Well, Brackney has an approach that's wild enough to work. Let's let her try to work out a solution, and then we can look it over and see if we feel it has a better chance to work than conventional technics."

Anna Brackney had been standing near the door. She came forward and said angrily, "What do you mean, 'wild'? There's nothing wrong with it at all. You just don't want me to be the one that solves it, that's all. You just—"

"No, no, Anna," said Greenberg, "that isn't it. You'll be the one to work it out, so don't—"

"Good, I'll start right now," said Anna, and she turned and left.

The two men looked at each other. Upton shrugged his shoulders, and Greenberg raised his eyes to the ceiling, shook his head, and sighed.

Anna Brackney sat herself down in her corner and stared at the wall. It was ten minutes before she put her finger into her mouth, and another twenty minutes before she pulled out a pad and pencil and began scribbling notations. It went fast then. With her first equation set up on a small sheet of paper, she left her office to find a resident mathemeteorologist; Anna refused to use the speaker at her desk to call one of them in.

The residents were all seated at desks in one large room, and when Anna entered they all bent over as if hard at work. Ignoring their behavior, Anna went up to the desk of Betty Jepson and placed the sheet of paper on it. Anna said without any preliminaries, "Run a regression analysis on this," and her finger traced out the equation in the form $y = a_1x_1 + a_2x_2 + \ldots + a_nx_n$, "noting that n equals 46 in this case. Take the observational data from the banks of Number Eighty-three computer. I want a fit better than ninety per cent." And she turned on her heels and returned to her office.

Half an hour later she was back with another equation for Charles Bankhead, then one for Joseph Pechio. With the pattern established, she asked for the aid of a full mathemeteorologist, and Greenberg assigned Albert Kropa to her. Kropa listened to her somewhat disjointed description of what she was trying to do, and then wandered around looking over the shoulders of the residents to see what they were doing. Gradually he understood, and finally he raced to his own office and began turning out the polynomial relationships on his own.

Each equation demanded the full use of a sixteen-fifty computer and its staff under the direction of a resident, plus six hours of time to arrive at even a preliminary fit. As Anna and Kropa turned out more of the needed basic equations, it was

apparent that too much time was being used in evolving each
one individually. Anna broke off and spent two hours working
out a method of programming a twenty-two-thirty to explore the
factors needed in each regression analysis. The computer began
producing the required equations at the rate of one every ten
minutes, so Anna and Kropa turned their attention to a method
of correlating the flood of data that would descend on them
when each analysis was complete. After half an hour it became
apparent that they could not finish that phase of it before the
data began coming in. They asked for and got two more full
mathemeteorologists.

The four of them moved out to the Weather Room so they
could be together as they worked. The correlating mathematics
began to unfold, and all the remaining residents were called in
to help with it. In another hour all the available sixteen-fifties
were tied up, and Greenberg called on the University of Stockholm for the use of theirs. This held for twenty minutes, and
then Greenberg called on half a dozen industrial computers in
the city. But that wasn't enough. The net of computers began
widening steadily out to the Continent, reaching in another two
hours to the cities on the eastern seaboard of the United States.
The overriding authority of the Advisors in the solving of a
weather problem was absolute.

It became necessary for Upton to join the group, and when
Greenberg himself took a chair at the large circle in the
Weather Room there was a brief break in the work for some
catcalls and some affectionately sarcastic remarks. Commitment
of the Advisors was total.

Anna Brackney seemed not to notice. Her eyes were glazed
and she spoke in crisp sharp sentences in contrast to her usual
vague and slurred sentences. She seemed to know just a little in
advance when a breakdown in the mounting flow of data was
impending, and she stepped in and supplied the necessary con-
tinuity. It was fifteen hundred before Hiromaka noticed that
none of them had eaten lunch. Greenberg sent for food, again
at twenty-three hundred, and again at zero nine hundred.

Everyone looked terrible, with sunken cheeks and rumpled
clothes and great hollows under the eyes. But there was fire in
the eyes of all of them, even down to the newest resident, a fire

born of participation in the most complex weather problem yet to confront the Advisors.

Upton took over the task of pulling together the mathematical models relating to the planet Earth. He kept under his control the regression analysis results relating to such variables as the various possible distances of Earth from the sun; the rotational positions of the Earth relating to the sun; the shape, position, density, variation, and charge of both Van Allen radiation belts; the velocity, temperature, direction, width, and mass of fourteen hundred jet streams; the heat flow of the major ocean currents; the effect on air drift of each major land mass; the heat content of the land masses; the Coriolis effect; and superimposed over all these factors and many more, the effect of the existing and programmed weather playing over the face of the entire Earth.

Greenberg took the sun and worked with the analysis results on the movement of each sunspot; the sun's rotations; fluctuating temperatures and pressures in the photosphere, reversing layer, chromosphere, and corona; spectrum variations; and the relative output from the carbon cycle and the proton-proton chain.

Anna wandered everywhere, now looking over Upton's shoulder, now on the phone to the computers in Washington, D. C., now guiding a resident on his next chore, now inventing a new notational system to simplify feeding newly derived mathematical models into the computers. She wandered as if in a dream, but when a question was asked or when something slowed down, her responses were far from dreamlike. Many a resident, several computer operators, and Upton himself felt the bite of one of her crisp sentences pointing out what could have been a rather obvious blunder. As time wore on and the work grew more frantic, the normally harsh lines on Anna's face softened, and she walked erect instead of with her usual slouch. Several of the mathemeteorologists, who formerly would not even have talked to her unless it was absolutely necessary, found themselves willingly turning to her for further guidance on their part of the problem.

The first partial solution was fully worked out for the first time at eleven hundred hours the next morning. It had only an eighty-one per cent fit, but that was good for the first time out; more would be coming soon. But Upton found a flaw. "No good," he said. "This solution would also increase that proposed drought in Australia by a factor of twelve. That would be nice. We pull something like that and we'll all be back reading electric meters."

The remark struck a responsive chord in the group, and the laughter spread and grew more intense. In moments every person in the Advisors Building was convulsed with violent laughter as the long strain finally took its hysterical toll. It was several minutes before the eyes were wiped and the people settled down to work again. Greenberg said, "Well, that's where our danger will be. Not necessarily in Australia, but anywhere. We've got to make sure we don't get a drastic reaction somewhere."

Anna Brackney heard him and said, "DePinza is working on a definite analysis to insure that there can be no undesirable reaction. He'll have it in an hour." She walked off, leaving Greenberg staring after her.

It was fifteen hundred when the final set of equations was completed. The fit was ninety-four per cent, and the checkout against DePinza's analysis was one hundred and two per cent. The residents and the mathemeteorologists gathered around the large table as Greenberg considered the results. They had finished none too soon. The procedure they had worked out called for sunside operations starting three hours after the beginning of the second shift, and that went on in four hours. Greenberg rubbed the heavy stubble on his face and said, "I don't know whether to let it go or not. We could report that our procedures are untried and ought not to be used all at once."

The eyes of the group turned to Anna Brackney, but she seemed supremely unconcerned. Upton voiced what was in everyone's mind. "There's a little bit of the heart of each one of us in there." He nodded to the equations. "Since they represent the very best that we can do, I don't see how we can report that they ought not to be used. Right now those equations represent the best Advisors output; in that sense they *are* the Advisors. Both we and the people who put us here have to stand or fall on our best efforts."

Greenberg nodded, and handed the two sheets of paper to a

resident and said, "Break it down to the sunside procedures and then send it up to the Weather Bureau. I hope they don't have to sweat it out the way we did." He rubbed his face. "Well, that's what we get paid for."

The resident took the sheets and went off. The others drifted away until only Greenberg and Upton were left. Upton said, "This will be quite a feather in Anna Brackney's cap. I don't know where she pulled her inspiration from."

"I don't either," said Greenberg. "But if she sticks her finger in her mouth again, I may quit the business."

Upton chuckled. "If she brings this one off, we'd better all learn to stick our fingers in our mouths."

James Eden rolled out of his bunk and stood poised on the balls of his feet. Yes, there was a faint, barely discernible chatter in the deck. Eden shook his head; the sun was rough, and it was going to be a bad day. If Base had a chatter, then the sessile boats would be hard to manage. Never knew it to fail. Try something tricky and you had to work in the worst possible conditions; try something routine, and conditions were perfect. But that was what you had to expect in the Bureau. Even the textbooks talked about it—an offshoot of an old Finagle Law.

Eden depilated and dressed, wondering what the job ahead of him would be like. They were always the last to hear anything, yet they were the ones who had to do all the dirty work. The whole Weather Congress depended on the Bureau. The Council was nothing more than a bunch of rich old fat politicians who scratched each other's backs and spent their days cooking up Big Deals. The Advisors were a bunch of nuts who sat on their duffs and read out loud all the stuff the computers figured out. But the Bureau was something else again, a fine body of dedicated men who did a job so that the planet Earth could flourish. It was good to be in the Weather Bureau—and there it was again.

Eden could not keep his thoughts away from the problem that had been nagging at him during this entire tour. He rubbed his forehead and wondered again at the perversity of women. Rebecca, black-haired and black-eyed, with warm white skin, waited for him when his tour was over, but only if he left the

Bureau. He could see her now, close to him, looking deep into his eyes, the soft palm of her hand pressed against his cheek, saying, "I will not share you with any person or any thing, even your beloved Bureau. I want a complete husband. You must decide." With other women he could have laughed and picked them up and swung them around and quickly jogged them out of the mood, but not Rebecca, not Rebecca of the long black hair, damn it!

He swung around and stepped out of his tiny cabin and headed for the mess hall. There were half a dozen men already there when he entered, and they were talking and laughing. But they stopped what they were doing and looked at him and hailed him as he came in through the door. "Hey, Jim." "About time you were rolling out." "Good to see you, boy."

Eden recognized the symptoms. They were tense, and they were talking and laughing too loud. They were relieved to have him join them. They needed somebody to lean on, and Eden pitied them a little for it. Now they would not have to make such an effort to appear normal. The others had felt the chatter in the deck, too.

Eden sat down and said, "Morning. Anything on the Board yet about the shift's work?"

The others shook their heads, and Pisca said, "Not a word. They always wait and tell us last. Everybody on the planet knows what's going on, but not us. All we get are rumors until it's time to go out and do it."

"Well," said Eden, "communication with the Bureau is not the easiest thing in the world, don't forget. We can't expect to hear everything as soon as it happens. But I sort of agree with you anyway; seems to me they could keep us posted better as things develop back on Earth."

They nodded, and then applied themselves to the breakfast. They chatted over coffee until a soft chime sounded throughout Base. They rose. It was time for the briefing, and they headed for the briefing room up at the top of the Base. Commander Hechmer was there when they walked in and took their seats. Eden watched carefully as he found a seat and sat down. In the past he had sometimes wondered if Hechmer had taken particular notice of him—an extra glance, closer attention when he asked a question, talking more to him than to the others at a briefing, little things, but important nevertheless.

Commander John H. Hechmer was a legend in the Weather Bureau at the age of forty-five years. It was he who had evolved and perfected the Pinpoint Stream technic, in which a thin stream of protons could be extracted from the 4,560-degree level in a sunspot and directed against any chosen sunside part of Earth. In the days when Hechmer was the Senior Boat Master in the Bureau, great strides had been made in weather control. A fineness and detail of weather patterns on Earth had become possible that had astonished all the experts. Hechmer had even guided the Advisors, showing them the broadened scope of the Bureau's abilities. His handling of a sun boat had never been matched, and it was one of the goals in Eden's career—if he chose to stay with it—to be thought of as the man who most nearly approximated Hechmer.

Eden watched, and finally when Hechmer looked up from the table it seemed to Eden that his eyes swept the group to rest for an instant on Eden, and then they moved on. It was as if Hechmer wanted to assure himself that Eden was there. Eden could not be sure of this, but the possibility of it made him sit straighter in his chair.

Hechmer said, "Here is Phase One of the next shift's operation as received from the Advisors." He flashed the requisite portion of the page on the upright panel behind him. It took Eden one quick glance to see that it represented a substantial departure from customary procedure. Immediately he began to slump down in his seat as he lost himself in the problem of studying out how to handle it. He did not notice that Hechmer saw his instant grasp of the problem. It was a moment or two before several low whistles announced that the others had grasped it, too.

Hechmer sat quietly while they studied over the page. All of them were now thinking out how the report had to be modified to place it in useful condition for the Bureau to use. The Advisors always prided themselves on stating their solutions in clear and explicit terminology. But as a practical matter their solutions were totally unusable as received for they did not mention many of the sun conditions that the Bureau had to cope with. These are accomplishments not explained by mathematics. It was one of the quiet jokes of the Bureau to listen to the talk of an Advisor about the thoroughness of his solution and about the lack of thinking required by the Bureau, and then to ask the Advisor what he knew about "reversing granulation." No one except a working member of the Bureau could experience that strange upwelling sometimes found in the lower regions of the reversing layer.

The silence grew long. Eden's forehead was wrinkled with concentration as he tried to find some way to break into the problem. He finally saw a possible entry, and he pulled over a pad and began trying for a method of breakdown. Hechmer began to polish his own figures while the rest stared at the page on the wall as if hypnotized. It was ten minutes before another of the men finally began to make notes.

Eden sat back and looked over what he had written. With growing excitement he realized that his possible answer had never been tried before. As he looked at it more closely, though, he realized that it might not ever be done; it was a radical approach, calling for Boat performance not mentioned in the Boat specifications.

Hechmer said, "Gentlemen, we must begin. To start things off, here is my proposed answer. Pick it apart if you can."

Eden looked up at it. It was different, too, but it differed in that it called for the use of every single Boat on the sun, a thing never before needed. Hechmer's answer was to carry out the mission by sheer weight of numbers, and by this means to dig from the various levels in the sun's atmosphere the total of the streams and sheets needed to bring about the desired weather on Earth. But as he looked at it Eden began to see flaws. The streams, being taken from different parts of the sun's surface, would strike the Earth and its environs at angles slightly different from those that were called for. Hechmer's answer might work, but it did not seem to have as good a chance as Eden's answer.

Hechmer said, "The main feature wrong with this plan is the wide scattering of the impinging streams. Can you think of any way to overcome that?"

Eden could not, but his mind was more occupied with his

own plan. If he could be certain that the Boats could stand submersion in the sun's surface for the required length of time, there would be few problems. Oh, communication might be more difficult, but with only one Boat down there would be a much reduced need for communication; the Boat would succeed or not, and no instructions from anywhere else could help.

One of the other men was beginning to suggest the unfeasible modification of having all the Boats work closer together, a grave mistake since the Boats could not control their toruses with sufficient nicety. Eden interrupted him without thinking. "Here is a possible answer." And he dropped his page on the desk.

Hechmer continued to look at the man who had been talking, waiting politely for him to finish. The man avoided an embarrassing situation by saying, "Let's see what Jim has to offer before we go on with this one."

Hechmer slipped Eden's page into the viewer, and they all studied it. It had the advantage at least of being readily understandable, and they all began talking at once, most of them saying that it couldn't be done. "You'll lose the Boat." "Yes, and the men in it, don't forget." "Won't work even if the Boat holds up." "You can't get a Boat that deep."

Eden carefully watched Hechmer's face while he studied the plan. He saw Hechmer's eyes widen, and then narrow again, and Hechmer realized that Eden was watching him closely. For a moment the room faded from Hechmer's mind, replaced by another similar room, many years ago, when a younger and rasher Hechmer sat and anxiously watched his superior eye a new kind of plan. Hechmer said, without taking his eyes from the projected page, "Assuming the Boat can get down there, why won't this plan work?"

"Well," said the man who had stated it wouldn't work, "the streams and sheets won't necessarily emerge in the direction . . . " But as he talked he noticed that the energy of the sunspot's field was channeled to serve as a focusing lens, and his words faded.

Hechmer nodded approval. "Glad you saw it. Anybody else? Any flaws in it once the Boat gets down and stays long enough?" The men worried at it, but could find nothing wrong, given the stated assumption. Hechmer continued, "All right, now why won't a Boat stand that kind of submersion?"

One answered, "The sessile effect is not as great on the top. Burn right through."

Eden popped out, "No. Double the carbon feed to the top torus. That'll do it."

They argued for half an hour, Eden and two others defending the concept, and in the end there was no more opposition. They all worked at polishing the plan to take out as much risk as possible. By the time they finished there really was no decision for Hechmer to make. The group of Boat captains had accepted the plan, and it went without saying that Eden's Boat would be the deep Boat. There was a bare half an hour to the start of the shirt, so they went to get ready.

Eden struggled into the lead suit, muttering the same curses every Boatman since the first had muttered. The Boats had ample shielding, and the suits were to provide protection only if a leak allowed in some stray radiation. But on the sun it seemed unlikely that a leak would allow in only a little radiation. It seemed much more likely that a leak would allow in so much of the sun's atmosphere that the men in the Boat would never know what hit them. A lead suit then would be like trying to dam a volcano with a feather. Nevertheless, lead suits were mandatory.

Entering the Boat from Base was always a tricky maneuver. The torus above the joining lock was not a permanent part of the lock, and if it moved, the full gravitational field of the sun could pull at the man, pulling his entire body down into his shoes. Eden slipped through and made the rounds of the Boat on the standard captain's inspection before he went to his chair and began the start-up procedure.

He noted the continuing roughness of the sun. First he checked the carbon supply, the material which vaporized and then in the form of a thin film protected the entire Boat from the searing heat of the sun's surface. The Boats rode the layer of vaporized carbon the way a drop of water rides a layer of vaporized water on a red-hot plate; this was the sessile effect. Next he checked the overhead torus. Here in a circular path there traveled a few ounces of protons at a velocity approaching that of light. At these velocities the few ounces of protons weighed incalculable tons and thus offset the enormous gravitational attraction of the sun itself. The same magnetic tape that supplied the field to maintain the protons in their heavy-mass state also served to maintain a polarity the same as that of the adjacent sun's surface. Hence the torus and the sun's surface repelled each other. Objects under the torus were subjected to two gravitational fields, the one from the torus almost, but not quite, canceling the sun's. As a result men worked in the Boats and in the Base in a 1-G field.

Eden ran down the entire list checking off one by one the various functioning parts of the Boat. His crew of four worked with him, each responsible for a section of the Boat. Five minutes before castoff the board was green, and at zero time on the shift they shoved off.

The Boat felt good under his hands. It leaped and surged as the sun's surface roiled and boiled, but he kept it steadily headed outward, sliding ever downhill on its thin film of carbon vapor.

"How do you ride?" he said into the intercom.

A chorus of "fines" came back, so Eden tipped the Boat a little more to increase her speed. They were on a tight schedule and they had distance to make. As always Eden felt exhilarated as their speed increased, and he did the thing he always did when he felt that way.

Carefully, he drew back one after another of the sound-deadening panels on the bulkhead next to the pilot's seat. As the eighth panel drew back he could hear it faintly, and so he drew back the ninth panel slowly, and on the tenth the roar filled the pilot's cubicle. Eden sat bathed in a thunderous roar that washed over him, shaking his body with its fury, and taking everything from his mind except the need to fight and strain and hit back. This was the direct naked roar of the sun itself that came in upon him, the thunderous concatenation of a million fission bombs detonating every infinitesimal portion of a second. Its sound and fury were mind-staggering, and a man could only let a little of it in and keep his sanity. But that little was an awesome sound, cleansing, humbling, focusing a man's attention on the powers he controlled, warning him to mind his business.

This was a thing that Eden had never told to anyone, and no one had ever told him. It was his own secret, his own way of refreshing and replenishing whatever it was that made him the man he was. He supposed that he was the only one of the pilots that did this thing, and since on this one point he did not think clearly, it never occurred to him to wonder how it came about that the only movable sound-deadening panels in the entire Boat happened to be located right alongside the pilot's seat.

For half an hour Eden guided the Boat toward its first action point, easily coping with the usual roughness of the sun's surface. He checked the operation of the inertial guidance system exactly twice as often as was required by standard operating procedure to make sure that the extra bouncing did not affect its precise operation. As they approached the action point, Eden closed the sound-deadening panels and checked in with his crew. "Four minutes to operation. What color have you?"

Back came the answer from all four points. "All green, Master." Formalities aboard the sessile boat had started. Each man watched his own program, his fingers on the keys and his feet on the pedals, waiting for the position light. It winked on.

Out went the torpedolike capsules, down into the bowels of the sun where the carbon-nitrogen cycle raged. At a temperature of three point five million degrees the ablation head disintegrated and released into the inferno a charge of heavy nitrogen. The heavy nitrogen, appearing as it did at the end of the carbon-nitrogen cycle, disrupted the steady-state conditions and produced a floor of helium that served to dampen and cool the fusion reactions in the entire region. The resultant thermal shock to the interior caused an immediate collapse followed by an incredible increase in pressure with the attendant temperature rise. The vast explosion heaved its way to the surface and became a great prominence licking its way toward the Earth and channeling huge masses of protons toward the preselected site in the vicinity of the Earth. The initial phase of the operation appeared successful.

The next hour passed in moving from site to site and planting the proper charges, now to bring about a vast electron discharge at the correct angle, now to dampen a flare, now to shift the location of a spot. On two occasions the instruments showed that the detonations did not take place at a sufficiently precise location to meet the unusual requirements for accuracy, and so subsidiary detonations had to be made. They were in constant, if difficult, communication with the other three Boats and with Base. None of the Boats was specifically aware of it, but the beginnings of the Australian drought were set in motion during the second hour out.

There was no tension aboard Eden's Boat as the time for the deep operation approached; they were all too busy. When the time came Eden merely checked out over the communication net and reduced the polarity of the magnetic field on the overhead torus. The Boat went down fast, leaving the photosphere behind. Eden kept a careful check on the temperature drop across the walls of the Boat as they fell; when the sessile effect began to diminish, he wanted to know about it. The interior walls began to heat up sooner than he expected, and once they started, the heat-up proceeded ever more rapidly. A quick check showed that the rate of heating was faster than their rate of descent; they could not reach the required depth without becoming overheated. The Boat would not withstand the temperatures that Eden had thought it would. "Too hot, too hot," he said aloud. He checked the depth; they had another half a mile to go. There was no use in ever attempting to release the water where they were. It was half a mile deeper, or nothing. The plan was in jeopardy.

Eden did not really pause to make the decision. He simply drastically cut the power to the polarity-control generators to the torus, and the Boat fell like a stone toward the center of the sun. It dropped the half mile in forty seconds, the last few hundred yards in violent deceleration as Eden brought up the power level. The drop was so fast there was little additional heat-up. He hit the water releases and flung the Boat into the pattern that had been worked out, and in ten seconds the disruption was complete and a blast of oxygen 15 was started on its way to Earth. The plan, at least, was consummated.

Eden brought up the torus power to a high level and the Boat

began to rise to the relative safety of the surface. The time at
the deeper level had been sufficiently short that the interior
temperature of the Boat was at a tolerable 120 degrees F. The
control panel showed no signs of trouble until they rose to
within a thousand yards of the surface.

The steady rise slowed and drifted to a halt. The Boat sank
a little and then bobbed up and down and finally found a level,
and then it remained motionless. There was no way to
strengthen the polarity in the torus. The instruments showed
that full power flowed to the coils, and it was not enough. Eden
began a checkout. He had barely started when a voice spoke in
the intercom, "A portion of our right outboard coil is inoper-
ative, Master. Possibly burned away, but I am checking further."

Eden turned his attention to the coils and soon saw the telltale reduced output. He activated all the thermocouples and
other transducers in the vicinity of the coil, and in two minutes
he understood what had happened. The burn-out had occurred
at the point where the coil turned the corner. The sessile effect
there must have been slightly less effective than elsewhere. The
unexpectedly great heat had pushed past the film of carbon
vapor and destroyed a portion of the titanium-molybdenum
alloy wires. Full power to the coil was not enough now to increase the polarity sufficiently for the Boat to rise any farther.

Eden cut into the intercom and explained the situation to the
crew. A cheerful voice responded, "Glad to hear that there is
nothing seriously wrong then. It is just that we cannot move up.
Is that what you make of it, Master?"

"So far, yes. Anybody have any suggestions?"

"Yes, Master. I request a leave of absence."

"Granted," said Eden. "Now put in some time on this. We've
got to get up."

There was silence aboard the Boat, and the silence stretched
out to twenty minutes. Eden said, "I'll try to raise Base."

For ten minutes Eden tried to reach the Base or another Boat
with his long-long wavelength radio. He was about to give up
when he heard a faint and garbled reply. Through the noise he
could just recognize the call of the Boat mastered by Dobzhansky. He transmitted their situation, over and over, so that the
other Boat could fill in missing parts of any one message. Then

he listened and eventually learned that they understood and would notify Base. But as they listened to the faint retransmission all sound faded. A check of their position showed that they had drifted out of radio range, so Eden tipped the Boat and began a circle. Three quarters of the way around he picked up the signal again and listened. He heard nothing but routine communication.

One of his men said, "Fine thing. We can move in every direction with the greatest of ease except the one direction we want to go."

Base was now coming in through the other Boat, and Hechmer himself was speaking. All he had to say was, "Stand by while we see what we can do about this."

There was no levity aboard the Boat now. The Boat floated a thousand yards beneath the surface of the sun, and they began to realize that there was nothing anybody could do about it. A sharpened corner on a coil, and the Boat was helpless to return to the surface. Each man sat and stared at his instruments.

A dark-haired vision floated in front of Eden's panel, and in his mind's eye Eden could see the reproachful look on her face. This was what she meant, the black-haired Rebecca, when she said, "I will not share you with any thing." He understood, for now she would be sorry for him, trapped in a place where men had never been.

"Lost the Boat again, Master." The words jarred him. He tipped the Boat and began the circle again. The shadow of Rebecca was still on him, but suddenly he grew very annoyed. What was this? The worry of a woman to get in the way of his work? This was not for him; this was not for the Bureau. There could be no cloudiness of mind, no dichotomy of loyalty—and then he saw the way up.

As he completed the circle he checked the charts and found the nearest sunspot. It was an hour away. He came within radio range again and told Dobzhansky he was heading for the sunspot and that he would come up to the surface there. So saying he headed for it. By the most careful operation they cut their time to the spot to fifty minutes. The last ten minutes of time on the way they spent in building the speed of the Boat to the maximum obtainable. A thousand yards beneath the surface of the sun they entered the magnetic discontinuity that defined the sunspot.

They rode into it in a direction opposite to that of its rotation, and the great coils of the Boat cut across the lines of enormous magnetic force. The motion generated power, and the additional power flowed to the torus, and the Boat began to rise. It was a good spot, five thousand miles wide, and still in its prime. The Boat rode against the direction of its rotation and spiraled upward slowly as it went. It took great patience to note the fact that the Boat rose at all, but hour after hour they worked their way up and finally broke out on the indistinct surface. They rode the edges of the spot until Base came for them, and they docked the Boat and went aboard.

Eden reported to Hechmer, and they made arrangements to round off the relatively sharp corners on all coils. Most important of all, the deep technic appeared to be a success; it was added to the list of usable technics.

"Well," said Eden toward the end of the reporting session, stretching his tired muscles, "I see I'm due back on shift again in an hour. That doesn't give me much time to get rested up."

Then Hechmer said the thing that made Eden glad he had decided to stay in the Bureau. "Hm-m-m, that's right," said Hechmer, glancing up at the chronometer, "tell you what you do. You be an hour late getting back on duty."

George Andrews was very tired, and he had to work very hard to draw air into his lungs. He lay propped up on a soft bed out under the hot California sun, and his fingers plucked at the thin cover that lay over him. He was on a hilltop. Then he noticed an odd cylindrical-shaped cloud that seemed to rise from the level of the ground and reach way up through the scattered alto-cumulus clouds that dotted the blue sky. George Andrews smiled, for he could see it coming clearly now. The vertical cylinder of frothy clouds moved toward him, and he felt the chill as the leading edge touched him. He threw back the cover when the flakes began to fall so the snow could fall on him. He turned his face up to it, and it felt cold and it felt good. But more than that, he felt content.

Here was the snow he had loved so much when he was a boy. And the fact that it was here at all showed him that men had not changed much after all, for this was a foolish thing. He had no trouble with the air now; he needed none. He lay under the blanket of snow, and it was a good blanket.

ROBERT SILVERBERG

Archaeology is one of those subjects, like oceanography, which is not so much a single science as a compendium of sciences. Long the province of enthusiastic amateurs, it has recently been revolutionized by such techniques as carbon-14 dating, the results of which have caused consternation at many museums.

Robert Silverberg is one of the most prolific and far-ranging of the younger writers working in and around the science-fiction field. His slightly staggering output includes hundreds of stories and more than a dozen novels—all produced in a period of little more than ten years. Among his books are *Recalled to Life*, *Time of the Great Freeze*, and *Master of Life and Death*; in recent years he has concentrated on books of popular science, particularly on archaeological themes, such as the award-winning *Lost Cities and Vanished Civilizations*. A lifelong New Yorker, Bob and his wife Barbara inhabit a vast mansion which he is filling, floor by floor, with books— mostly his own.

The Artifact
Business

The Voltuscian was a small, withered humanoid whose crimson throat-appendages quivered nervously, as if the thought of doing archaeological fieldwork excited him unbearably. He gestured to me anxiously with one of his four crooked arms, urging me onward over the level silt.

"This way, friend. Over here is the Emperor's grave."

"I'm coming, Dolbak." I trudged forward, feeling the weight of the spade and the knapsack over my shoulder. I caught up with him a few moments later.

He was standing near a rounded hump in the ground, pointing downward. "This is it," he said happily. "I have saved it for you."

I fished in my pocket, pulled out a tinkling heap of arrow-shaped coins, and handed him one. The Voltuscian nodded his thanks effusively, and ran around behind me to help me unload.

Taking the spade from him, I thrust it into the ground and began to dig. The thrill of discovery started to tingle in me, as it does always when I begin a new excavation. I suppose that is the archaeologist's greatest joy, that moment of apprehension as the spade first bites into the ground. I dug rapidly and smoothly, following Dolbak's guidance.

"There it is," he said reverently. "And a beauty it is, too. Oh, Jarrell-sir, how happy I am for you!"

I leaned on my spade to recover my wind before bending to look. I mopped away beads of perspiration, and thought of the great Schliemann laboring in the stifling heat of Hissarlik to uncover the ruins of Troy. Schliemann has long been one of my heroes—along with the other archaeologists who did the pioneer work in the fertile soil of Mother Earth.

Wearily, I stooped to one knee and fumbled in the fine sand of the Voltuscian plain, groping for the bright object that lay revealed. I worried it loose from its covering of silt and studied it.

"Amulet," I said after a while. "Third Period; unspecified protective charm. Studded with emerald-cut gobrovirs of the finest water." The analysis complete, I turned to Dolbak and grasped his hand warmly. "How can I thank you, Dolbak?"

He shrugged. "Not necessary." Glancing at the amulet, he said, "It will fetch a high price. Some woman of Earth will wear it proudly."

"Ah—yes," I said, a trifle bitterly. Dolbak had touched on the source of my deep frustration and sorrow.

This perversion of archaeology into a source for trinkets and bits of frippery to adorn rich men's homes and wives has always rankled me. Although I have never seen Earth, I like to believe I work in the great tradition of Schliemann and Evans, whose greatest finds were to be seen in the galleries of the British Museum and the Ashmolean, not dangling on the painted bosom of some too rich wench who has succumbed to the current passion for antiquity.

When the Revival came, when everyone's interest suddenly turned on the ancient world and the treasures that lay in the ground, I felt deep satisfaction—my chosen profession, I thought, now was one that had value to society as well as private worth. How wrong I was! I took this job in the hope that it would provide me with the needed cash to bring me to Earth—but instead I became nothing more than the hired lackey of a dealer in women's fashions, and Earth's unreachable museums lie inch-deep in dust.

I sighed and returned my attention to the excavation. The amulet lay there, flawless in its perfection, a marvelous relic of the great race that once inhabited Voltus. Masking my sadness, I reached down with both hands and lovingly plucked the amulet from the grave in which it had rested so many thousands of years.

I felt a sudden impulse to tip Dolbak again. The withered alien accepted the coins gratefully, but with a certain reserve that made me feel that perhaps this whole business seemed as sordid to him as it did to me.

"It's been a good day's work," I told him. "Let's go back now. We'll get this assayed and I'll give you your commission, eh, old fellow?"

"That will be very good, sir," he said mildly, and assisted me in donning my gear once again.

We crossed the plain and entered the Terran outpost in silence. As we made our way through the winding streets to the assay office, hordes of the four-armed, purple-hued Voltuscian children approached us clamorously, offering us things for sale, things they had made themselves. Some of their work was quite lovely; the Voltuscians seem to have a remarkable aptitude for handicrafting. But I brushed them all away. I have made it a rule to ignore them, no matter how delightful a spun-glass fingerbowl they may have, how airy and delicate an ivory carving. Such things, being contemporary, have no market value on Earth, and a man of my limited means must avoid luxuries of this sort.

The assay office was still open, and I saw two or three men standing outside, each with his Voltuscian guide, as we approached.

"Hello, Jarrell," said a tall man raucously as I drew near.

I winced. He was David Sturges, one of the least scrupulous of the many Company archaeologists on Voltus—a man who thought nothing of breaking into the most sacred shrines of the planet and committing irreparable damage for the sake of ripping loose a single marketable item.

"Hello, Sturges," I said shortly.

"Have a good day, old man? Find anything worth poisoning you for?"

I grinned feebly and nodded. "Nice amulet of the Third

Period. I'm planning on handing it in immediately, but if you prefer I won't. I'll take it home and leave it on my table tonight. That way you won't wreck the place looking for it."

"Oh, that won't be necessary," Sturges said. "I came up with a neat cache of enameled skulls today—a dozen, of the Expansion Era, set with platinum scrollwork." He pointed to his alien guide, a dour-looking Voltuscian named Qabur. "My boy found them for me. Wonderful fellow, Qabur. He came home on a cache as if he's got radar in his nose."

I began to frame a reply in praise of my own guide when Zweig, the assayer, stepped to the front of his office and looked out. "Well, who's next? You, Jarrell?"

"Yes, sir." I picked up my spade and followed him inside. He slouched down behind his desk and looked up wearily.

"What do you have to report, Jarrell?"

I drew the amulet out of my knapsack and handed it across the desk. He examined it studiously, noticing the way the light glinted off the facets of the inset gobrovirs, and looked up. "Not bad," he said.

"It's a rather fine piece, isn't it?"

"Not bad," he repeated. "Seventy-five dollars, I'd say."

"What? I'd figured that piece for at least five hundred! Come on, Zweig, be reasonable. Look at the quality of those gobrovirs!"

"Very nice," he admitted. "But you have to understand that the gobrovir, while it's attractive, is intrinsically not a very valuable gem. And I must consider the intrinsic value as well as the historical, you know."

I frowned. Now would come the long speech about supply and demand, the scarcity of the gems, the cost of shipping the amulet back to Earth, marketing, on and on, on and on. I spoke before he had the chance. "I won't haggle, Zweig. Give me a hundred and fifty or I'll keep the thing myself."

He grinned slyly. "What would you do with it? Donate it to the British Museum?"

The remark stung. I looked at him sadly, and he said, "I'll give you a hundred."

"Hundred and fifty or I keep."

He reached down and scooped ten ten-dollar pieces from a drawer. He spread them out along his desk. "There's the offer," he said. "It's the best the Company can do."

I stared at him for an agonized moment, then scowled, took the ten tens, and handed over the amulet. "Here. You can give me thirty pieces of silver for the next one I bring in."

"Don't make it hard for me, Jarrell. This is only my job."

I threw one of the tens to the waiting Dolbak, nodded curtly, and walked out.

I returned to my meager dwelling on the outskirts of the Terran colony in a state of deep dejection. Each time I handed an artifact over to Zweig—and, in the course of the eighteen months since I had accepted this accursed job, I had handed over quite a few—I felt, indeed, a Judas. When I thought of the long row of glass cases my discoveries might have filled, in, say the Voltus Room of the British Museum, I ached. The crystal shields with double hand-grips; the tooth-wedges of finest obsidian; the sculptured ear-binders with their unbelievable filigree of sprockets—these were products of one of the most fertile creative civilizations of all, the old Voltuscians—and these treasures were being scattered to the corners of the galaxy as trinkets.

The amulet today—what had I done with it? Turned it over to—to a procurer, virtually, to ship back to Earth for sale to the highest bidder.

I glanced around my room. Small, uncluttered, with not an artifact of my own in it. I had passed every treasure across the desk to Zweig; I had no wish to retain any for myself. I sensed that the antiquarian urge was dying in me, choked to death by the wild commercialism that entangled me from the moment I signed the contract with the Company.

I picked up a book—Evans, *The Palace of Minos*—and looked at it balefully for a moment before replacing it on the shelf. My eyes throbbed from the day's anguish; I felt dried out and very tired.

Someone knocked at the door—timidly at first, then more boldly.

"Come in," I said.

The door opened slowly and a small Voltuscian stepped in.

I recognized him—he was an unemployed guide, too unreliable to be trusted. "What do you want, Kushkak?" I asked wearily.

"Sir? Jarrell-sir?"

"Yes?"

"Do you need a boy, sir? I can show you the best treasures, sir. Only the best—the kind you get good price for."

"I have a guide already," I told him. "Dolbak. I don't need another, thanks."

The alien seemed to wrinkle in on himself. He hugged his lower arms to his sides unhappily. "Then I am sorry I disturbed you, Jarrell-sir. Sorry. Very sorry."

I watched him back out despairingly. All of these Voltuscians seemed to me like withered old men, even the young ones. They were an utterly decadent race, with barely a shred of the grandeur they must have had in the days when the great artifacts were being produced. It was odd, I thought, that a race should shrivel so in the course of a few thousand years.

I sank into an uneasy repose in my big chair. About half past twenty-three another knock sounded.

"Come in," I said, a little startled.

The gaunt figure of George Darby stepped through the door. Darby was an archaeologist who shared my passionate desire to see Earth, shared my distaste for the bondage into which we had sold ourselves.

"What brings you here so late, George?" I asked, adding the conventional, "And how was your trip today?"

"My trip? Oh, my trip!" He seemed strangely excited. "Yes, my trip. You know my boy, Kushkak?"

I nodded. "He was just here looking for a job. I didn't know he'd been working with you."

"Just for a couple of days," Darby said. "He agreed to work for five percent, so I took him on."

I made no comment. I knew how things could pinch.

"He was here, eh?" Darby frowned. "You didn't hire him, did you?"

"Of course not!" I said.

"Well, I did. But yesterday he led me in circles for five hours before admitting he didn't really have any sites in mind, so I canned him and that's why I'm here."

"Why? Who'd you go out with today?"

"No one," Darby said bluntly. "I went out alone." For the first time, I noticed that his fingers were quivering, and in the dreary half-light of my room his face looked pale and drawn.

"You went out alone?" I repeated. "Without a guide?"

Darby nodded, running a finger nervously through his unruly white forelock. "It was half out of necessity—I couldn't find another boy in time—and half because I wanted to strike out on my own. The guides have a way of taking you to the same area of the Burial Ground all the time, you know. I headed in the other direction. Alone."

He fell silent for a moment. I wondered what it was that troubled him so.

After a pause he said, "Help me off with my knapsack."

I eased the straps from his shoulders and lowered the gray canvas bag to a chair. He undid the rusted clasps, reached in, and drew something out tenderly. "Here," he said. "What do you make of this, Jarrell?"

I took it from him with great care and examined it closely. It was a bowl, scooped by hand out of some muddy-looking black clay. Finger marks stood out raggedly, and the bowl was unevenly shaped and awkward-looking. It was an extremely uncouth job.

"What is it?" I asked. "Prehistoric, no doubt."

Darby smiled unhappily. " You think so, Jarrell?"

"It must be," I said. "Look at it—I'd say it was made by a child, if it weren't for the size of these fingerprints in the clay. It's very ancient or else the work of an idiot."

He nodded. "A logical attitude. Only—I found this in the stratum below the bowl." And he handed me a gilded tooth-wedge in Third Period style.

"This was below the bowl?" I asked, confused. "The bowl is more recent than the tooth-wedge, you're saying?"

"Yes," he said quietly. He knotted his hands together. "Jarrell, here's my conjecture, and you can take it for as much as you think it's worth. Let's discount the possibility that the bowl was made by an idiot, and let's not consider the chance that it might be a representative of a decadent period in Voltuscian pottery that we know nothing about.

"What I propose," he said, measuring his words carefully, "is that the bowl dates from classical antiquity—three thousand years back, or so. And that the tooth-wedge you're admiring so is perhaps a year old, maybe two at the outside."

I nearly dropped the tooth-wedge at that. "Are you saying that the Voltuscians are hoaxing us?"

"I'm saying just that," Darby replied. "I'm saying that in those huts of theirs—those huts that are taboo for us to enter—they're busy turning out antiquities by the drove, and planting them in proper places where we can find them and dig them up."

It was an appalling concept. "What are you going to do?" I asked. "What proof do you have?"

"None, yet. But I'll get it. I'm going to unmask the whole filthy thing," Darby said vigorously. "I intend to hunt down Kushkak and throttle the truth out of him, and let the universe know that the Voltuscian artifacts are frauds, that the *real* Old Voltuscian artifacts are muddy, ugly things of no aesthetic value and of no interest to—anyone—but—us—archaeologists," he finished bitterly.

"Bravo, George!" I applauded. "Unmask it, by all means. Let the Philistines who have overpaid for these pieces find out that they're not ancient, that they're as modern as the radiothermal stoves in their overfurnished kitchens. That'll sicken 'em—since they won't touch anything that's been in the ground less than a few millennia, ever since this Revival got under way."

"Exactly," Darby said. I sensed the note of triumph in his voice. "I'll go out and find Kushkak now. He's just desperate enough to speak up. Care to come along?"

"No—no," I said quickly. I shun violence of any sort. "I've got some letters to write. You take care of it."

He packed his two artifacts up again, rose, and left. I watched him from my window as he headed across the unpaved streets to the liquor-dispensary where Kushkak was usually to be found. He entered—and a few minutes later I heard the sound of voices shouting in the night.

The news broke the next morning, and by noon the village was in a turmoil.

Kushkak, taken unawares, had exposed all. The Voltuscians—brilliant handicrafters, as everyone knew—had attempted to sell their work to the wealthy of Earth for years, but there had been no market. "Contemporary? Pah!" What the customers wanted was antiquity.

Unable to market work that was labeled as their own, the Voltuscians had obligingly shifted to the manufacture of antiquities, since their ancestors had been thoughtless enough not to leave them anything more marketable than crude clay pots. Creating a self-consistent ancient history that would appeal to the imaginations of Earthmen was difficult, but they rose to the challenge and developed one to rank with that of Egypt and Babylonia and the other fabled cultures of Earth. After that, it was a simple matter of designing and executing the artifacts.

Then they were buried in the appropriate strata. This was a difficult feat, but the Voltuscians managed it with ease, restoring the disrupted strata afterward with the same skill for detail as they employed in creating the artifacts. The pasture thus readied, they led the herd to feast.

I looked at the scrawny Voltuscians with new respect in my eyes. Obviously they must have mastered the techniques of archaeology before inaugurating their hoax, else they would never have handled the strata relationships so well. They had carried the affair flawlessly—until the day when one of the Earthmen had unkindly disinterred a real Voltuscian artifact.

Conditions were still chaotic when I entered the square in front of the assay office later that afternoon. Earthmen and Voltuscians milled aimlessly around, not knowing what to do next or where to go.

I picked up a rumor that Zweig was dead by his own hand, but this was promptly squelched by the appearance of the assayer in person, looking rather dreadfully upset but still living. He came to the office and hung up a hastily scrawled card. It read:

NO BUSINESS
TRANSACTED TODAY

I smiled, then saw Dolbak go wandering by and called to him. "I'm ready to go out," I said innocently.

He looked at me, pity in his lidless eyes. "Sir, haven't you heard? There will be no more trips to the Burial Grounds."

"Oh? This thing is true, then?"

"Yes," he said sadly, "it's true."

Obviously he couldn't bear to talk further. He moved on, and I spotted Darby.

"You seem to have been right," I told him. "The whole thing's fallen apart."

"Of course. Once they were confronted with Kushkak's story, they saw the game was up. They're too fundamentally honest to try to maintain the pretense in the face of our accusation."

"It's too bad in a way." I said. "Those things they turned out were lovely, you know."

"Just a second, friend," said a deep voice from behind us. We turned to see David Sturges glaring bitterly.

"What do you want?" Darby asked.

"I want to know why you couldn't keep your mouth shut," said Sturges. "Why'd you have to ruin this nice setup for us? What difference did it make if the artifacts were the real thing or not? As long as people were willing to lay down cash for them, why rock the boat?"

Darby sputtered impotently at the bigger man, but said nothing.

"You've wrecked the whole works," Sturges went on. "What do you figure to do for a living now? Can you afford to go to another planet?"

"I did what was right," Darby said.

Sturges snorted derisively and walked away. I looked at Darby. "He's got a point, you know. We're going to have to go to another planet now. Voltus isn't worth a damn. You've succeeded in uprooting us and finishing the Voltuscian economy at the same time. Maybe you should have kept quiet."

He looked at me stonily for a moment. "Jarrell, I think I've overestimated you."

A ship came for Zweig the next day, and the assay office closed down permanently. The Company wouldn't touch Voltus again. The crew of the ship went rapidly through the Terran outpost distributing leaflets that informed us that the Company still required our services and could use us on other planets—provided we paid our own fares.

That was the catch. None of us had saved enough, out of the fees we had received from the Company, to get off Voltus. It had been the dream of all of us to see Earth someday, to explore the world from which our parent stock had sprung—but it had been a fool's dream. At Company rates, we could never save enough to leave.

I began to see that perhaps Darby had done wrong in exposing the hoax. It certainly didn't help us, and it was virtually the end of the world for the natives. In one swoop, a boundless source of income was cut off and their precarious economy totally wrecked. They moved silently through the quiet street, and any day I expected to see the vultures perch on the rooftops.

Three days after the bubble burst, a native boy brought me a note. It was from David Sturges, and it said, briefly, "There will be a meeting at my flat tonight."

When I arrived I saw that the entire little colony of Company archaeologists was there—even Darby.

"Good evening, Jarrell," Sturges said politely as I entered. "I think everyone's here now, and so we can begin." He cleared his throat.

"Gentlemen, some of you have accused me of being unethical," he said. "Even dishonest. You needn't deny it. I have been unethical. However," he said, frowning, "I find myself caught in the same disaster that has overtaken all of you, and just as unable to extricate myself. Therefore, I'd like to make a small suggestion."

"What's on your mind, Sturges?"

"This morning," he said, "one of the aliens came to me with an idea. It's a good one. Briefly, he suggested that, as expert archaeologists, we teach the Voltuscians how to manufacture Terran artifacts. There's no more market for anything from Voltus—but why not continue to take advantage of the skills of the Voltuscians as long as the market's open for things of Earth? We could smuggle the artifacts to Earth, plant them, have them dug up again and sold there—and we'd make the entire profit, not just the miserable fee the Company allows us!"

"It's shady, Sturges," Darby said hoarsely. "I don't like the idea."

"How do you like the idea of starving?" Sturges retorted. "We'll rot on Voltus unless we use our wits."

I stood up. "Perhaps I can make things clearer to Dr. Darby," I said. "George, we're caught in a cleft stick and all we can do is try to wriggle. We can't get off Voltus, and we can't stay here. If we accept Sturges' plan, we'll build up a cash reserve in a short time. We'll be free."

Darby remained unconvinced. He shook his head. "I can't condone counterfeiting Terran artifacts. No—if you try it, I'll expose you!"

A stunned silence fell over the room at the threat. Sturges glanced appealingly at me, and I moistened my lips. "You don't seem to understand, George. Once we have this new plan working, it'll spur genuine archaeology. Look—we dig up half a dozen phony scarabs in the Nile Valley. People buy them—and we keep on digging, with the profits we make. Earth experiences a sudden interest; there's a rebirth of archaeology. We dig up real scarabs."

His eyes brightened, but I could see he was still unpersuaded. I added my clincher.

"Besides, George, someone will have to go to Earth to supervise this project."

I paused, caught Sturges' silent approval. "I think," I said sonorously, "that it is the unanimous decision of this assembly that we nominate our greatest expert on Terran antiquity to handle the job on Earth—Dr. George Darby."

I didn't think he would be able to resist that. I was right.

Six months later, an archaeologist working near Gizeh turned up a scarab of lovely design, finely worked and inlaid with strange jewels.

In a paper published in an obscure journal to which most of us subscribe, he conjectured that this find represented an outcrop of a hitherto unknown area of Egyptology. He also sold the scarab to a jewelry syndicate for a staggering sum, and used the proceeds to finance an extensive exploration of the entire Nile Valley, something that hadn't been done since the decline of archaeology more than a century earlier.

Shortly afterward, a student working in Greece came up with a remarkable Homeric shield.

What had been a science as dead as alchemy suddenly blossomed into new life; the people of Earth discovered that their own world contained riches as desirable as those on Voltus and Dariak and the other planets the Companies had been mining for gewgaws, and that they were also much less costly.

The Voltuscian workshops are now going full blast, and the only limitation on our volume is the difficulty of smuggling the things to Earth and planting them. We're doing quite well financially, thank you. Darby, who's handling the job brilliantly on Earth, sends us a fat check every month, which we divide equally among ourselves after paying the Voltuscians.

Occasionally I feel regret that it was Darby and not myself who won the coveted job of going to Earth, but I reconcile myself with the awareness that there was no other way to gain Darby's sympathies. I've learned things about ends and means. Soon, we'll all be rich enough to travel to Earth, if we want to.

But I'm not so sure I do want to go. There was a genuine Voltuscian antiquity, you know, and I've become as interested in that as I am in that of Greece and Rome. I see an opportunity to do some pure archaeology in a virgin field of research.

So perhaps I'll stay here after all. I'm thinking of writing a book on Voltuscian artifacts—the real ones, I mean, all crude things of no commercial value whatever. And tomorrow I'm going to show Dolbak how to make Aztec pottery of the Chichimec period. It's attractive stuff. I think there ought to be a good market for it.

JAMES H. SCHMITZ

Exobiology—the study of life-forms beyond the Earth—has been defined as a science without a subject. Despite this, its nonexistent material has fascinated mankind for at least two thousand years.

It is said that William Randolph Hearst once sent a famous astronomer this message: "IS THERE LIFE ON MARS CABLE THOUSAND WORDS," and received the following, repeated five hundred times: "NOBODY KNOWS." We are lucky enough to live in the age when more informative replies will be soon forthcoming. What, I wonder, would the old-time students of the red planet have thought of the volume that now lies on my desk entitled *Biology and the Exploration of Mars*, written by the Space Science Board of the National Academy of Science? I quote a few relevant passages: "The essence of our conclusions is that the exploration of Mars . . . does indeed merit the highest scientific priority in the nation's space program over the next decades. . . . Favorable opportunities for exploration between 1969 and 1973 can and should be exploited as vigorously as possible. . . . In the long run we believe that manned expeditions . . . will be part of the exploration of the planet. . . . Some of our readers will be as surprised as we were to discover the manned Martian missions will probably be feasible in the 1980's."

Long before that, of course, we hope to have at least preliminary answers from our Mariner probes, and from successors which will orbit the planet and survey it as the Tiros weather satellites now survey Earth. However, we must not be too impatient or expect too much before an actual landing. It is worth mentioning that only one of the first quarter million excellent Tiros photographs showed any evidence that the planet Earth bore intelligent life.

In the absence of hard facts, the science-fiction writers have not been idle. Indeed, far from it: much (possibly too much) of their endeavor since Lucian of Samos, second century A.D., has been devoted to portraying fantastic and often horrific inhabitants of other worlds. The traditional Bug-Eyed Monster has become the symbol of the cheapest form of science fiction, which meets its nadir in the horror movies.

If there is one lesson that we have learned from the biology of Earth, however, it is that the obvious menaces may not be the most lethal ones. To a visiting Martian, a cow might seem a far more dangerous monster than a rattlesnake. (He might even be right; if a rattler bit a Martian, the snake might be the one to die.) The modern science-fiction writer therefore avoids B.E.M.'s in favor of much more subtle perils, and this story of James Schmitz's suggests that, when we get to other worlds, we had better keep our wits about us. The natives may not always be as friendly as we think.

Noted for his whimsical imagination, Schmitz published his first story in *Unknown Worlds* in 1943, when he was serving with the Army Air Corps in the Pacific. Today he is a full-time writer and, like many practitioners of science fiction, lives in California.

Grandpa

A green-winged, downy thing as big as a hen fluttered along the hillside to a point directly above Cord's head and hovered there, twenty feet above him. Cord, a fifteen-year-old human being, leaned back against a skipboat parked on the equator of a world that had known human beings for only the past four Earth years, and eyed the thing speculatively. The thing was, in the free and easy terminology of the Sutang Colonial Team, a swamp bug. Concealed in the downy fur back of the bug's head was a second, smaller, semiparasitical thing, classed as a bug rider.

The bug itself looked like a new species to Cord. Its parasite might or might not turn out to be another unknown. Cord was a natural research man; his first glimpse of the odd flying team had sent endless curiosities thrilling through him. How did that particular phenomenon tick, and why? What fascinating things, once you'd learned about it, could you get it to *do*?

Normally, he was hampered by circumstances in carrying out any such investigation. The Colonial Team was a practical, hardworking outfit—two thousand people who'd been given twenty years to size up and tame down the brand-new world of Sutang to the point where a hundred thousand colonists could be settled on it, in reasonable safety and comfort. Even junior colonial students like Cord were expected to confine their curiosity to the pattern of research set up by the station to which they were attached. Cord's inclination toward independent experiments had got him into disfavor with his immediate superiors before this.

He sent a casual glance in the direction of the Yoger Bay Colonial Station behind him. No signs of human activity about that low, fortresslike bulk in the hill. Its central lock was still closed. In fifteen minutes, it was scheduled to be opened to let out the Planetary Regent, who was inspecting the Yoger Bay Station and its principal activities today.

Fifteen minutes was time enough to find out something about the new bug, Cord decided.

But he'd have to collect it first.

He slid out one of the two handguns holstered at his side. This one was his own property: a Vanadian projectile weapon. Cord thumbed it to position for anesthetic small-game missiles and brought the hovering swamp bug down, drilled neatly and microscopically through the head.

As the bug hit the ground, the rider left its back. A tiny scarlet demon, round and bouncy as a rubber ball, it shot toward Cord in three long hops, mouth wide to sink home inch-long, venom-dripping fangs. Rather breathlessly, Cord triggered the gun again and knocked it out in mid-leap. A new species, all right! Most bug riders were harmless plant-eaters, mere suckers of vegetable juice—

"*Cord!*" A feminine voice.

Cord swore softly. He hadn't heard the central lock click open. She must have come around from the other side of the station.

"Hi, Grayan!" he shouted innocently without looking around. "Come see what I got! New species!"

Grayan Mahoney, a slender, black-haired girl two years older than himself, came trotting down the hillside toward him. She was Sutang's star colonial student, and the station manager, Nirmond, indicated from time to time that she was a fine example for Cord to pattern his own behavior on. In spite of that, she and Cord were good friends, but she bossed him around considerably.

"Cord, you dope!" she scowled as she came up. "Quit acting like a collector! If the Regent came out now, you'd be sunk. Nirmond's been telling her about you!"

"Telling her what?" Cord asked, startled.

"For one," Grayan reported, "that you don't keep up on your assigned work. Two, that you sneak off on one-man expeditions of your own at least once a month and have to be rescued—"

"Nobody," Cord interrupted hotly, "has had to rescue me yet!"

"How's Nirmond to know you're alive and healthy when you just drop out of sight for a week?" Grayan countered. "Three," she resumed checking the items off on slim fingertips, "he complained that you keep private zoological gardens of unidentified and possibly deadly vermin in the woods back of the station. And four . . . well, Nirmond simply doesn't want the responsibility for you any more!" She held up the four fingers significantly.

"Golly!" gulped Cord, dismayed. Summed up tersely like that, his record *didn't* look too good.

"Golly is right! I keep warning you! Now Nirmond wants

the Regent to send you back to Vanadia—and there's a starship coming in to New Venus forty-eight hours from now!" New Venus was the Colonial Team's main settlement on the opposite side of Sutang.

"What'll I do?"

"Start acting like you had good sense mainly." Grayan grinned suddenly. "I talked to the Regent, too—Nirmond isn't rid of you yet! But if you louse up on our tour of the Bay Farms today, you'll be off the Team for good!"

She turned to go. "You might as well put the skipboat back; we're not using it. Nirmond's driving us down to the edge of the Bay in a treadcar, and we'll take a raft from there. Don't let them know I warned you!"

Cord looked after her, slightly stunned. He hadn't realized his reputation had become as bad as all that! To Grayan, whose family had served on Colonial Teams for the past four generations, nothing worse was imaginable than to be dismissed and sent back ignominiously to one's own homeworld. Much to his surprise, Cord was discovering now that he felt exactly the same way about it!

Leaving his newly bagged specimens to revive by themselves and flutter off again, he hurriedly flew the skipboat around the station and rolled it back into its stall.

Three rafts lay moored just offshore in the marshy cove, at the edge of which Nirmond had stopped the treadcar. They looked somewhat like exceptionally broad-brimmed, well-worn sugarloaf hats floating out there, green and leathery. Or like lily pads twenty-five feet across, with the upper section of a big, gray-green pineapple growing from the center of each. Plant animals of some sort. Sutang was too new to have had its phyla sorted out into anything remotely like an orderly classification. The rafts were a local oddity which had been investigated and could be regarded as harmless and moderately useful. Their usefulness lay in the fact that they were employed as a rather slow means of transportation about the shallow, swampy waters of the Yoger Bay. That was as far as the Team's interest in them went at present.

The Regent had stood up from the back seat of the car, where she was sitting next to Cord. There were only four in the party; Grayan was up front with Nirmond.

"Are those our vehicles?" The Regent sounded amused.

Nirmond grinned, a little sourly. "Don't underestimate them, Dane! They could become an important economic factor in this region in time. But, as a matter of fact, these three are smaller than I like to use." He was peering about the reedy edges of the cove. "There's a regular monster parked here usually—"

Grayan turned to Cord. "Maybe Cord knows where Grandpa is hiding."

It was well-meant, but Cord had been hoping nobody would ask him about Grandpa. Now they all looked at him.

"Oh, you want Grandpa?" he said, somewhat flustered. "Well, I left him . . . I mean I saw him a couple of weeks ago about a mile south from here—"

Grayan sighed. Nirmond grunted and told the Regent, "The rafts tend to stay wherever they're left, providing it's shallow and muddy. They use a hair-root system to draw chemicals and microscopic nourishment directly from the bottom of the bay. Well—Grayan, would you like to drive us there?"

Cord settled back unhappily as the treadcar lurched into motion. Nirmond suspected he'd used Grandpa for one of his unauthorized tours of the area, and Nirmond was quite right.

"I understand you're an expert with these rafts, Cord," Dane said from beside him. "Grayan told me we couldn't find a better steersman, or pilot, or whatever you call it, for our trip today."

"I can handle them," Cord said, perspiring. "They don't give you any trouble!" He didn't feel he'd made a good impression on the Regent so far. Dane was a young, handsome-looking woman with an easy way of talking and laughing, but she wasn't the head of the Sutang Colonial Team for nothing. She looked quite capable of shipping out anybody whose record wasn't up to par.

"There's one big advantage our beasties have over a skipboat, too," Nirmond remarked from the front seat. "You don't have to worry about a snapper trying to climb on board with you!" He went on to describe the stinging ribbon-tentacles the rafts spread around them under water to discourage creatures that might make a meal off their tender underparts. The snappers and two or three other active and aggressive species of the Bay hadn't yet learned it was foolish to attack armed human beings in a boat, but they would skitter hurriedly out of the path of a leisurely perambulating raft.

Cord was happy to be ignored for the moment. The Regent, Nirmond and Grayan were all Earth people, which was true of most of the members of the Team; and Earth people made him uncomfortable, particularly in groups. Vanadia, his own homeworld, had barely graduated from the status of Earth colony itself, which might explain the difference. All the Earth people he'd met so far seemed dedicated to what Grayan Mahoney called the Big Picture, while Nirmond usually spoke of it as "Our Purpose Here." They acted strictly in accordance with their Team Regulations—sometimes, in Cord's opinion, quite insanely. Because now and then the Regulations didn't quite cover a new situation and then somebody was likely to get killed. In which case, the Regulations would be modified promptly, but Earth people didn't seem otherwise disturbed by such events.

Grayan had tried to explain it to Cord:

"We can't really ever *know* in advance what a new world is going to be like! And once we're there, there's too much to do, in the time we've got, to study it inch by inch. You get your job done, and you take a chance. But if you stick by the Regulations you've got the best chances of surviving anybody's been able to figure out for you—"

Cord felt he preferred to just use good sense and not let Regulations or the job get him into a situation he couldn't figure out for himself.

To which Grayan replied impatiently that he hadn't yet got the Big Picture—

The treadcar swung around and stopped, and Grayan stood up in the front seat, pointing. "That's Grandpa, over there!"

Dane also stood up and whistled softly, apparently impressed by Grandpa's fifty-foot spread. Cord looked around in surprise. He was pretty sure this was several hundred yards from the spot where he'd left the big raft two weeks ago; and as Nirmond said, they didn't usually move about by themselves.

Puzzled, he followed the others down a narrow path to the water, hemmed in by tree-sized reeds. Now and then he got a glimpse of Grandpa's swimming platform, the rim of which just touched the shore. Then the path opened out, and he saw the whole raft lying in sunlit, shallow water; and he stopped short, startled.

Nirmond was about to step up on the platform, ahead of Dane.

"Wait!" Cord shouted. His voice sounded squeaky with alarm. "Stop!"

He came running forward.

They had frozen where they stood, looked around swiftly. Then glanced back at Cord coming up. They were well trained.

"What's the matter, Cord?" Nirmond's voice was quiet and urgent.

"Don't get on that raft—it's changed!" Cord's voice sounded wobbly, even to himself. "Maybe it's not even Grandpa—"

He saw he was wrong on the last point before he'd finished the sentence. Scattered along the rim of the raft were discolored spots left by a variety of heat-guns, one of which had been his own. It was the way you goaded the sluggish and mindless things into motion. Cord pointed at the cone-shaped central projection. "There—his head! He's sprouting!"

"Sprouting?" the station manager repeated uncomprehendingly. Grandpa's head, as befitted his girth, was almost twelve feet high and equally wide. It was armor-plated like the back of a saurian to keep off plant-suckers, but two weeks ago it had been an otherwise featureless knob, like those on all other rafts. Now scores of long, kinky, leafless vines had grown out from all surfaces of the cone, like green wires. Some were drawn up like tightly coiled springs, others trailed limply to the platform and over it. The top of the cone was dotted with angry red buds, rather like pimples, which hadn't been there before either. Grandpa looked unhealthy.

"Well," Nirmond said, "so it is. Sprouting!" Grayan made a choked sound. Nirmond glanced at Cord as if puzzled. "Is that all that was bothering you, Cord?"

"Well, sure!" Cord began excitedly. He hadn't caught the

significance of the word "all"; his hackles were still up, and he was shaking. "None of them ever—"

Then he stopped. He could tell by their faces that they hadn't got it. Or rather, that they'd got it all right but simply weren't going to let it change their plans. The rafts were classified as harmless, according to the Regulations. Until proved otherwise, they would continue to be regarded as harmless. You didn't waste time quibbling with the Regulations—apparently even if you were the Planetary Regent. You didn't feel you had the time to waste.

He tried again. "Look—" he began. What he wanted to tell them was that Grandpa with one unknown factor added wasn't Grandpa any more. He was an unpredictable, oversized life-form, to be investigated with cautious thoroughness till you knew what the unknown factor meant.

But it was no use. They knew all that. He stared at them helplessly. "I—"

Dane turned to Nirmond. "Perhaps you'd better check," she said. She didn't add, "—to reassure the boy!" but that was what she meant.

Cord felt himself flushing terribly. They thought he was scared—which he was—and they were feeling sorry for him, which they had no right to do. But there was nothing he could say or do now except watch Nirmond walk steadily across the platform. Grandpa shivered slightly a few times, but the rafts always did that when someone first stepped on them. The station manager stopped before one of the kinky sprouts, touched it and then gave it a tug. He reached up and poked at the lowest of the budlike growths. "Odd-looking things!" he called back. He gave Cord another glance. "Well, everything seems harmless enough, Cord. Coming aboard, everyone?"

It was like dreaming a dream in which you yelled and yelled at people and couldn't make them hear you! Cord stepped up stiff-legged on the platform behind Dane and Grayan. He knew exactly what would have happened if he'd hesitated even a moment. One of them would have said in a friendly voice, careful not to let it sound too contemptuous: "You don't have to come along if you don't want to, Cord!"

Grayan had unholstered her heat-gun and was ready to start Grandpa moving out into the channels of the Yoger Bay.

Cord hauled out his own heat-gun and said roughly, "I was to do that!"

"All right, Cord." She gave him a brief, impersonal smile, as if he were someone she'd met for the first time that day, and stood aside.

They were so infuriatingly polite! He was, Cord decided, as good as on his way back to Vanadia right now.

For a while, Cord almost hoped that something awesome and catastrophic would happen promptly to teach the Team people a lesson. But nothing did. As always, Grandpa shook himself vaguely and experimentally when he felt the heat on one edge of the platform and then decided to withdraw from it, all of which was standard procedure. Under the water, out of sight, were the raft's working sections: short, thick leaf-structures shaped like paddles and designed to work as such, along with the slimy nettle-streamers which kept the vegetarians of the Yoger Bay away, and a jungle of hair roots through which Grandpa sucked nourishments from the mud and the sluggish waters of the Bay, and with which he also anchored himself.

The paddles started churning, the platform quivered, the hair roots were hauled out of the mud; and Grandpa was on his ponderous way.

Cord switched off the heat, reholstered his gun, and stood up. Once in motion, the rafts tended to keep traveling un-hurriedly for quite a while. To stop them, you gave them a touch of heat along their leading edge; and they could be turned in any direction by using the gun lightly on the opposite side of the platform.

It was simple enough. Cord didn't look at the others. He was still burning inside. He watched the reed beds move past and open out, giving him glimpses of the misty, yellow and green and blue expanse of the brackish Bay ahead. Behind the mist, to the west, were the Yoger Straits, tricky and ugly water when the tides were running; and beyond the Straits lay the open sea, the great Zlanti Deep, which was another world entirely and one of which he hadn't seen much as yet.

Suddenly he was sick with the full realization that he wasn't

likely to see any more of it now! Vanadia was a pleasant enough
planet; but the wildness and strangeness were long gone from
it. It wasn't Sutang.

Grayan called from beside Dane, "What's the best route
from here into the farms, Cord?"

"The big channel to the right," he answered. He added somewhat sullenly, "We're headed for it!"

Grayan came over to him. "The Regent doesn't want to see
all of it," she said, lowering her voice. "The algae and plankton
beds first. Then as much of the mutated grains as we can show
her in about three hours. Steer for the ones that have been doing
best, and you'll keep Nirmond happy!"

She gave him a conspiratorial wink. Cord looked after her un-
certainly. You couldn't tell from her behavior that anything
was wrong. Maybe—

He had a flare of hope. It was hard not to like the Team
people, even when they were being rock-headed about their
Regulations. Perhaps it was that purpose that gave them their
vitality and drive, even though it made them remorseless about
themselves and everyone else. Anyway, the day wasn't over yet.
He might still redeem himself in the Regent's opinion. Something might happen—

Cord had a sudden cheerful, if improbable, vision of some
Bay monster plunging up on the raft with snapping jaws, and
of himself alertly blowing out what passed for the monster's
brains before anyone else—Nirmond, in particular—was even
aware of the threat. The Bay monsters shunned Grandpa, of
course, but there might be ways of tempting one of them.

So far, Cord realized, he'd been letting his feelings control
him. It was time to start thinking!

Grandpa first. So he'd sprouted—green vines and red buds,
purpose unknown, but with no change observable in his be-
havior-patterns otherwise. He was the biggest raft in this end
of the Bay, though all of them had been growing steadily in
the two years since Cord had first seen one. Sutang's seasons
changed slowly; its year was somewhat more than five Earth
years long. The first Team members to land here hadn't yet seen
a full year pass.

Grandpa then was showing a seasonal change. The other

rafts, not quite so far developed, would be reacting similarly a little later. Plant animals—they might be blossoming, preparing to propagate.

"Grayan," he called, "how do the rafts get started? When they're small, I mean."

Grayan looked pleased; and Cord's hopes went up a little more. Grayan was on his side again anyway!

"Nobody knows yet," she said. "We were just talking about it. About half of the coastal marsh-fauna of the continent seems to go through a preliminary larval stage in the sea." She nodded at the red buds on the raft's cone. "It *looks* as if Grandpa is going to produce flowers and let the wind or tide take the seeds out through the Straits."

It made sense. It also knocked out Cord's still half-held hope that the change in Grandpa might turn out to be drastic enough, in some way, to justify his reluctance to get on board. Cord studied Grandpa's armored head carefully once more—unwilling to give up that hope entirely. There were a series of vertical gummy black slits between the armor plates, which hadn't been in evidence two weeks ago either. It looked as if Grandpa were beginning to come apart at the seams. Which might indicate that the rafts, big as they grew to be, didn't outlive a full seasonal cycle, but came to flower at about this time of Sutang's year and died. However, it was a safe bet that Grandpa wasn't going to collapse into senile decay before they completed their trip today.

Cord gave up on Grandpa. The other notion returned to him —Perhaps he *could* coax an obliging Bay monster into action that would show the Regent he was no sissy!

Because the monsters were there, all right.

Kneeling at the edge of the platform and peering down into the wine-colored, clear water of the deep channel they were moving through, Cord could see a fair selection of them at almost any moment.

Some five or six snappers, for one thing. Like big, flattened crayfish, chocolate-brown mostly, with green and red spots on their carapaced backs. In some areas they were so thick you'd wonder what they found to live on, except that they ate almost anything, down to chewing up the mud in which they squatted.

However, they preferred their food in large chunks and alive, which was one reason you didn't go swimming in the Bay. They would attack a boat on occasion; but the excited manner in which the ones he saw were scuttling off toward the edges of the channel showed they wanted to have nothing to do with a big moving raft.

Dotted across the bottom were two-foot round holes which looked vacant at the moment. Normally, Cord knew, there would be a head filling each of those holes. The heads consisted mainly of triple sets of jaws, held open patiently like so many traps to grab at anything that came within range of the long, wormlike bodies behind the heads. But Grandpa's passage, waving his stingers like transparent pennants through the water, had scared the worms out of sight, too.

Otherwise, mostly schools of small stuff—and then a flash of wicked scarlet, off to the left behind the raft, darting out from the reeds! Turning its needle-nose into their wake.

Cord watched it without moving. He knew that creature, though it was rare in the Bay and hadn't been classified. Swift, vicious—alert enough to snap swamp bugs out of the air as they fluttered across the surface. And he'd tantalized one with fishing tackle once into leaping up on a moored raft, where it had flung itself about furiously until he was able to shoot it.

No fishing tackle. A handkerchief might just do it, if he cared to risk an arm—

"What fantastic creatures!" Dane's voice just behind him.

"Yellowheads," said Nirmond. "They've got a high utility rating. Keep down the bugs."

Cord stood up casually. It was no time for tricks! The reed bed to their right was thick with yellowheads, a colony of them. Vaguely froggy things, man-sized and better. Of all the creatures he'd discovered in the Bay, Cord liked them least. The flabby, sacklike bodies clung with four thin limbs to the upper sections of the twenty-foot reeds that lined the channel. They hardly ever moved, but their huge, bulging eyes seemed to take in everything that went on about them. Every so often, a downy swamp bug came close enough; and a yellowhead would open its vertical, enormous, tooth-lined slash of a mouth, extend the whole front of its face like a bellows in a flashing strike; and the bug would be gone. They might be useful, but Cord hated them.

"Ten years from now we should know what the cycle of coastal life is like," Nirmond said. "When we set up the Yoger Bay Station there were no yellowheads here. They came the following year. Still with traces of the oceanic larval form; but the metamorphosis was almost complete. About twelve inches long—"

Dane remarked that the same pattern was duplicated endlessly elsewhere. The Regent was inspecting the yellowhead colony with field glasses; she put them down now, looked at Cord and smiled. "How far to the farms?"

"About twenty minutes."

"The key," Nirmond said, "seems to be the Zlanti Basin. It must be almost a soup of life in spring."

"It is," nodded Dane, who had been here in Sutang's spring, four Earth years ago. "It's beginning to look as if the Basin alone might justify colonization. The question is still—" she gestured towards the yellowheads—"how do creatures like that get there?"

They walked off toward the other side of the raft, arguing about ocean currents. Cord might have followed. But something splashed back of them, off to the left and not too far back. He stayed, watching.

After a moment, he saw the big yellowhead. It had slipped down from its reedy perch, which was what had caused the splash. Almost submerged at the water line, it stared after the raft with huge pale-green eyes. To Cord, it seemed to look directly at him. In that moment, he knew for the first time why he didn't like yellowheads. There was something very like intelligence in that look, an alien calculation. In creatures like that, intelligence seemed out of place. What use could they have for it?

A little shiver went over him when it sank completely under the water and he realized it intended to swim after the raft. But it was mostly excitement. He had never seen a yellowhead come down out of the reeds before. The obliging monster he'd been looking for might be presenting itself in an unexpected way.

Half a minute later, he watched it again, swimming awkwardly far down. It had no immediate intention of boarding, at any rate. Cord saw it come into the area of the raft's trailing stingers. It maneuvered its way between them with curiously human swimming motions, and went out of sight under the platform.

He stood up, wondering what it meant. The yellowhead had appeared to know about the stingers; there had been an air of purpose in every move of its approach. He was tempted to tell the others about it, but there was the moment of triumph he could have if it suddenly came slobbering up over the edge of the platform and he nailed it before their eyes.

It was almost time anyway to turn the raft in toward the farms. If nothing happened before then—

He watched. Almost five minutes, but no sign of the yellowhead. Still wondering, a little uneasy, he gave Grandpa a calculated needling of heat.

After a moment, he repeated it. Then he drew a deep breath and forgot all about the yellowhead.

"Nirmond!" he called sharply.

The three of them were standing near the center of the platform, next to the big armored cone, looking ahead at the farms. They glanced around.

"What's the matter now, Cord?"

Cord couldn't say it for a moment. He was suddenly, terribly scared again. Something *had* gone wrong!

"The raft won't turn!" he told them.

"Give it a real burn this time!" Nirmond said.

Cord glanced up at him. Nirmond, standing a few steps in front of Dane and Grayan as if he wanted to protect them, had begun to look a little strained, and no wonder. Cord already had pressed the gun to three different points on the platform; but Grandpa appeared to have developed a sudden anesthesia for heat. They kept moving out steadily toward the center of the Bay.

Now Cord held his breath, switched the heat on full and let Grandpa have it. A six-inch patch on the platform blistered up instantly, turned brown, then black—

Grandpa stopped dead. Just like that.

"That's right! Keep burn——" Nirmond didn't finish his order.

A giant shudder. Cord staggered back toward the water. Then the whole edge of the raft came curling up behind him and went down again, smacking the Bay with a sound like a cannon shot. He flew forward off his feet, hit the platform face down and flattened himself against it. It swelled up beneath him. Two more enormous slaps and joltings. Then quiet. He looked round for the others.

He lay within twelve feet of the central cone. Some twenty or thirty of the mysterious new vines the cone had sprouted were stretched out stiffly toward him now, like so many thin green fingers. They couldn't quite reach him. The nearest tip was still ten inches from his shoes.

But Grandpa had caught the others, all three of them. They were tumbled together at the foot of the cone, wrapped in a stiff network of green vegetable ropes, and they didn't move.

Cord drew his feet up cautiously, prepared for another earthquake reaction. But nothing happened. Then he discovered that Grandpa was back in motion on his previous course. The heat-gun had vanished. Gently, he took out the Vanadian gun.

"Cord? It didn't get you?" It was the Regent.

"No," he said, keeping his voice low. He realized suddenly he'd simply assumed they were all dead. Now he felt sick and shaky.

"What are you doing?"

Cord looked at Grandpa's big armor-plated head with a certain hunger. The cones were hollowed out inside; the station's lab had decided their chief function was to keep enough air trapped under the rafts to float them. But in that central section was also the organ that controlled Grandpa's overall reactions.

He said softly, "I got a gun and twelve heavy-duty explosive bullets. Two of them will blow that cone apart."

"No good, Cord!" the pain-racked voice told him. "If the thing sinks, we'll die anyway. You have anesthetic charges for that gun of yours?"

He stared at her back. "Yes."

"Give Nirmond and the girl a shot each, before you do

anything else. Directly into the spine, if you can. But don't come any closer—"

Somehow, Cord couldn't argue with that voice. He stood up carefully. The gun made two soft spitting sounds.

"All right," he said hoarsely. "What do I do now?"

Dane was silent a moment. "I'm sorry, Cord. I can't tell you that. I'll tell you what I can—"

She paused for some seconds again. "This thing didn't try to kill us, Cord. It could have easily. It's incredibly strong. I saw it break Nirmond's legs. But as soon as we stopped moving, it just held us. They were both unconscious then—"

"You've got that to go on. It was trying to pitch you within reach of its vines or tendrils, or whatever they are, too, wasn't it?"

"I think so," Cord said shakily. That was what had happened, of course; and at any moment Grandpa might try again.

"Now it's feeding us some sort of anesthetic of its own through those vines. Tiny thorns. A sort of numbness—" Dane's voice trailed off a moment. Then she said clearly, "Look, Cord —it seems we're food it's storing up! You get that?"

"Yes," he said.

"Seeding time for the rafts. There are analogues. Live food for its seed probably; not for the raft. One couldn't have counted on that. Cord?"

"Yes. I'm here."

"I want," said Dane, "to stay awake as long as I can. But there's really just one other thing—this raft's going somewhere. To some particularly favorable location. And that might be very near shore. You might make it in then; otherwise it's up to you. But keep your head and wait for a chance. No heroics, understand?"

"Sure, I understand," Cord told her. He realized then that he was talking reassuringly, as if it weren't the Planetary Regent but someone like Grayan.

"Nirmond's the worst," Dane said. "The girl was knocked unconscious at once. If it weren't for my arm—But, if we can get help in five hours or so, everything should be all right. Let me know if anything happens, Cord."

"I will," Cord said gently again. Then he sighted his gun carefully at a point between Dane's shoulder blades, and the anesthetic chamber made its soft, spitting sound once more. Dane's taut body relaxed slowly, and that was all.

There was no point Cord could see in letting her stay awake; because they weren't going anywhere near shore.

The reed beds and the channels were already behind them, and Grandpa hadn't changed direction by the fraction of a degree. He was moving out into the open Bay—and he was picking up company!

So far, Cord could count seven big rafts within two miles of them; and on the three that were closest he could make out a sprouting of new green vines. All of them were traveling in a straight direction; and the common point they were all headed for appeared to be the roaring center of the Yoger Straits, now some three miles away!

Behind the Straits, the cold Zlanti Deep—the rolling fogs, and the open sea! It might be seeding time for the rafts, but it looked as if they weren't going to distribute their seeds in the Bay—

For a human being, Cord was a fine swimmer. He had a gun and he had a knife, in spite of what Dane had said; he might have stood a chance among the killers of the Bay. But it would be a very small chance, at best. And it wasn't, he thought, as if there weren't still other possibilities. He was going to keep his head.

Except by accident, of course, nobody was going to come looking for them in time to do any good. If anyone did look, it would be around the Bay Farms. There were a number of rafts moored there; and it would be assumed they'd used one of them. Now and then something unexpected happened and somebody simply vanished—by the time it was figured out just what had happened on this occasion, it would be much too late.

Neither was anybody likely to notice within the next few hours that the rafts had started migrating out of the swamps through the Yoger Straits. There was a small weather station a little inland, on the north side of the Straits, which used a helicopter occasionally. It was about as improbable, Cord decided dismally, that they'd use it in the right spot just now as it would be for a jet transport to happen to come in low enough to spot them.

The fact that it was up to him, as the Regent had said, sank in a little more after that! Cord had never felt so lonely.

Simply because he was going to try it sooner or later, he carried out an experiment next that he knew couldn't work. He opened the gun's anesthetic chamber and counted out fifty pellets—rather hurriedly because he didn't particularly want to think of what he might be using them for eventually. There were around three hundred charges left in the chamber then; and in the next few minutes Cord carefully planted a third of them in Grandpa's head.

He stopped after that. A whale might have showed signs of somnolence under a lesser load. Grandpa paddled on undisturbed. Perhaps he had become a little numb in spots, but his cells weren't equipped to distribute the soporific effect of that type of drug.

There wasn't anything else Cord could think of doing before they reached the Straits. At the rate they were moving, he calculated that would happen in something less than an hour; and if they did pass through the Straits, he was going to risk a swim. He didn't think Dane would have disapproved, under the circumstances. If the raft simply carried them all out into the foggy vastness of the Zlanti Deep, there would be no practical chance of survival left at all.

Meanwhile, Grandpa was definitely picking up speed. And there were other changes going on—minor ones, but still a little awe-inspiring to Cord. The pimply-looking red buds that dotted the upper part of the cone were opening out gradually. From the center of most of them protruded now something like a thin, wet, scarlet worm: a worm that twisted weakly, extended itself by an inch or so, rested and twisted again, and stretched up a little farther, groping into the air. The vertical black slits between the armor plates looked somehow deeper and wider than they had been even some minutes ago; a dark, thick liquid dripped slowly from several of them.

Under other circumstances Cord knew he would have been fascinated by these developments in Grandpa. As it was, they drew his suspicious attention only because he didn't know what they meant.

Then something quite horrible happened suddenly. Grayan started moaning loudly and terribly and twisted almost completely around. Afterwards, Cord knew it hadn't been a second before he stopped her struggles and the sounds together with another anesthetic pellet; but the vines had tightened their grip on her first, not flexibly but like the digging, bony green talons of some monstrous bird of prey. If Dane hadn't warned him—

White and sweating, Cord put his gun down slowly while the vines relaxed again. Grayan didn't seem to have suffered any additional harm; and she would certainly have been the first to point out that his murderous rage might have been as intelligently directed against a machine. But for some moments Cord continued to luxuriate furiously in the thought that, at any instant he chose, he could still turn the raft very quickly into a ripped and exploded mess of sinking vegetation.

Instead, and more sensibly, he gave both Dane and Nirmond another shot, to prevent a similar occurrence with them. The contents of two such pellets, he knew, would keep any human being torpid for at least four hours. Five shots—

Cord withdrew his mind hastily from the direction it was turning into; but it wouldn't stay withdrawn. The thought kept coming up again, until at last he had to recognize it:

Five shots would leave the three of them completely unconscious, whatever else might happen to them, until they either died from other causes or were given a counteracting agent.

Shocked, he told himself he couldn't do it. It was exactly like killing them.

But then, quite steadily, he found himself raising the gun once more, to bring the total charge for each of the three Team people up to five. And if it was the first time in the last four years Cord had felt like crying, it also seemed to him that he had begun to understand what was meant by using your head —along with other things.

Barely thirty minutes later, he watched a raft as big as the one he rode go sliding into the foaming white waters of the

Straits a few hundred yards ahead, and dart off abruptly at an angle, caught by one of the swirling currents. It pitched and spun, made some headway, and was swept aside again. And then it righted itself once more. Not like some blindly animated vegetable, Cord thought, but like a creature that struggled with intelligent purpose to maintain its chosen direction.

At least, they seemed practically unsinkable—

Knife in hand, he flattened himself against the platform as the Straits roared just ahead. When the platform jolted and tilted up beneath him, he rammed the knife all the way into it and hung on. Cold water rushed suddenly over him, and Grandpa shuddered like a laboring engine. In the middle of it all, Cord had the horrified notion that the raft might release its unconscious human prisoners in its struggle with the Straits. But he underestimated Grandpa in that. Grandpa also hung on.

Abruptly, it was over. They were riding a long swell, and there were three other rafts not far away. The Straits had swept them together, but they seemed to have no interest in one another's company. As Cord stood up shakily and began to strip off his clothes, they were visibly drawing apart again. The platform of one of them was half-submerged; it must have lost too much of the air that held it afloat and, like a small ship, it was foundering.

From this point, it was only a two-mile swim to the shore north of the Straits, and another mile inland from there to the Straits Head Station. He didn't know about the current; but the distance didn't seem too much, and he couldn't bring himself to leave knife and gun behind. The Bay creatures loved warmth and mud, they didn't venture beyond the Straits. But Zlanti Deep bred its own killers, though they weren't often observed so close to shore.

Things were beginning to look rather hopeful.

Thin, crying voices drifted overhead, like the voices of curious cats, as Cord knotted his clothes into a tight bundle, shoes inside. He looked up. There were four of them circling there; magnified seagoing swamp bugs, each carrying an unseen rider. Probably harmless scavengers—but the ten-foot wingspread was impressive. Uneasily, Cord remembered the venomously carnivorous rider he'd left lying beside the station.

One of them dipped lazily and came sliding down toward him. It soared overhead and came back, to hover about the raft's cone.

The bug rider that directed the mindless flier hadn't been interested in him at all! Grandpa was baiting it!

Cord stared in fascination. The top of the cone was alive now with a softly wriggling mass of the scarlet, wormlike extrusions that had started sprouting before the raft left the Bay. Presumably, they looked enticingly edible to the bug rider.

The flier settled with an airy fluttering and touched the cone. Like a trap springing shut, the green vines flashed up and around it, crumpling the brittle wings, almost vanishing into the long soft body—

Barely a second later, Grandpa made another catch, this one from the sea itself. Cord had a fleeting glimpse of something like a small, rubbery seal that flung itself out of the water upon the edge of the raft, with a suggestion of desperate haste—and was flipped on instantly against the cone where the vines clamped it down beside the flier's body.

It wasn't the enormous ease with which the unexpected kill was accomplished that left Cord standing there, completely shocked. It was the shattering of his hopes to swim to shore from here. Fifty yards away, the creature from which the rubbery thing had been fleeing showed briefly on the surface, as it turned away from the raft; and the glance was all he needed. The ivory-white body and gaping jaws were similar enough to those of the sharks of Earth to indicate the pursuer's nature. The important difference was that, wherever the white hunters of the Zlanti Deep went, they went by the thousands.

Stunned by that incredible piece of bad luck, still clutching his bundled clothes, Cord stared toward shore. Knowing what to look for, he could spot the telltale roilings of the surface now—the long, ivory gleams that flashed through the swells and vanished again. Shoals of smaller things burst into the air in sprays of glittering desperation and fell back.

He would have been snapped up like a drowning fly before he'd covered a twentieth of that distance!

But almost another full minute passed before the realization of the finality of his defeat really sank in.

Grandpa was beginning to eat!

Each of the dark slits down the sides of the cone was a mouth. So far only one of them was in operating condition, and the raft wasn't able to open that one very wide as yet. The first morsel had been fed into it, however: the bug rider the vines had plucked out of the flier's downy neck fur. It took Grandpa several minutes to work it out of sight, small as it was. But it was a start.

Cord didn't feel quite sane any more. He sat there, clutching his bundle of clothes and only vaguely aware of the fact that he was shivering steadily under the cold spray that touched him now and then, while he followed Grandpa's activities attentively. He decided it would be at least some hours before one of that black set of mouths grew flexible and vigorous enough to dispose of a human being. Under the circumstances, it couldn't make much difference to the other human beings here; but the moment Grandpa reached for the first of them would also be the moment he finally blew the raft to pieces. The white hunters were cleaner eaters, at any rate; and that was about the extent to which he could still control what was going to happen.

Meanwhile, there was the very faint chance that the weather station's helicopter might spot them—

Meanwhile also, in a weary and horrified fascination, he kept debating the mystery of what could have produced such a nightmarish change in the rafts. He could guess where they were going by now; there were scattered strings of them stretching back to the Straits or roughly parallel to their own course, and the direction was that of the plankton-swarming pool of the Zlanti Basin, a thousand miles to the north. Given time, even mobile lily pads like the rafts had been could make that trip for the benefit of their seedlings. But nothing in their structure explained the sudden change into alert and capable carnivores.

He watched the rubbery little seal-thing being hauled up to a mouth next. The vines broke its neck; and the mouth took it in up to the shoulders and then went on working patiently at what was still a trifle too large a bite. Meanwhile, there were more thin cat cries overhead; and a few minutes later, two more sea bugs were trapped almost simultaneously and added to the larder. Grandpa dropped the dead seal-thing and fed himself another bug rider. The second rider left its mount with a sudden hop, sank its teeth viciously into one of the vines that caught it again, and was promptly battered to death against the platform.

Cord felt a resurge of unreasoning hatred against Grandpa. Killing a bug was about equal to cutting a branch from a tree; they had almost no life-awareness. But the rider had aroused his partisanship because of its appearance of intelligent action— and it was in fact closer to the human scale in that feature than to the monstrous life-form that had, mechanically, but quite successfully, trapped both it and the human beings. Then his thoughts had drifted again; and he found himself speculating vaguely on the curious symbiosis in which the nerve systems of two creatures as dissimilar as the bugs and their riders could be linked so closely that they functioned as one organism.

Suddenly an expression of vast and stunned surprise appeared on his face.

Why—now he knew!

Cord stood up hurriedly, shaking with excitement, the whole plan complete in his mind. And a dozen long vines snaked instantly in the direction of his sudden motion, and groped for him, taut and stretching. They couldn't reach him, but their savagely alert reaction froze Cord briefly where he was. The platform was shuddering under his feet, as if in irritation at his inaccessibility; but it couldn't be tilted up suddenly here to throw him within the grasp of the vines, as it could around the edges.

Still, it was a warning! Cord sidled gingerly around the cone till he had gained the position he wanted, which was on the forward half of the raft. And then he waited. Waited long minutes, quite motionless, until his heart stopped pounding and the irregular angry shivering of the surface of the raft-thing died away, and the last vine tendril had stopped its blind groping. It might help a lot if, for a second or two after he next started moving, Grandpa wasn't too aware of his exact whereabouts!

He looked back once to check how far they had gone by now beyond the Straits Head Station. It couldn't, he decided, be even an hour behind them. Which was close enough, by the most pessimistic count—if everything else worked out all right! He didn't try to think out in detail what that "everything else" could include, because there were factors that simply couldn't be calculated in advance. And he had an uneasy feeling that speculating too vividly about them might make him almost incapable of carrying out his plan.

At last, moving carefully, Cord took the knife in his left hand but left the gun holstered. He raised the tightly knotted bundle of clothes slowly over his head, balanced in his right hand. With a long, smooth motion he tossed the bundle back across the cone, almost to the opposite edge of the platform.

It hit with a soggy thump. Almost immediately, the whole far edge of the raft buckled and flapped up to toss the strange object to the reaching vines.

Simultaneously, Cord was racing forward. For a moment, his attempt to divert Grandpa's attention seemed completely successful—then he was pitched to his knees as the platform came up.

He was within eight feet of the edge. As it slapped down again, he threw himself desperately forward.

An instant later, he was knifing down through cold, clear water, just ahead of the raft, then twisting and coming up again.

The raft was passing over him. Clouds of tiny sea creatures scattered through its dark jungle of feeding roots. Cord jerked back from a broad, wavering streak of glassy greenness, which was a stinger, and felt a burning jolt on his side, which meant he'd been touched lightly by another. He bumped on blindly through the slimy black tangles of hair roots that covered the bottom of the raft; then green half-light passed over him, and he burst up into the central bubble under the cone.

Half-light and foul, hot air. Water slapped around him, dragging him away again—nothing to hang on to here! Then above him, to his right, molded against the interior curve of the cone as if it had grown there from the start, the froglike, man-sized shape of the yellowhead.

The raft rider—

Cord reached up and caught Grandpa's symbiotic partner and guide by a flabby hind leg, pulled himself half out of the water and struck twice with the knife, fast while the pale-green eyes were still opening.

He'd thought the yellowhead might need a second or so to detach itself from its host, as the bug riders usually did, before it tried to defend itself. This one merely turned its head; the mouth slashed down and clamped on Cord's left arm above the elbow. His right hand sank the knife through one staring eye, and the yellowhead jerked away, pulling the knife from his grasp.

Sliding down, he wrapped both hands around the slimy leg and hauled with all his weight. For a moment more, the yellowhead hung on. Then the countless neural extensions that connected it now with the raft came free in a succession of sucking, tearing sounds; and Cord and the yellowhead splashed into the water together.

Black tangle of roots again—and two more electric burns suddenly across his back and legs! Strangling, Cord let go. Below him, for a moment, a body was turning over and over with oddly human motions; then a solid wall of water thrust him up and aside, as something big and white struck the turning body and went on.

Cord broke the surface twelve feet behind the raft. And that would have been that, if Grandpa hadn't already been slowing down.

After two tries, he floundered back up on the platform and lay there gasping and coughing awhile. There were no indications that his presence was resented now. A few vine tips twitched uneasily, as if trying to remember previous functions, when he came limping up presently to make sure his three companions were still breathing; but Cord never noticed that.

They were still breathing; and he knew better than to waste time trying to help them himself. He took Grayan's heat-gun from its holster. Grandpa had come to a full stop.

Cord hadn't had time to become completely sane again, or he might have worried now whether Grandpa, violently sundered from his controlling partner, was still capable of motion on his own. Instead, he determined the approximate direction of the Straits Head Station, selected a corresponding spot on the platform and gave Grandpa a light tap of heat.

Nothing happened immediately. Cord sighed patiently and stepped up the heat a little.

Grandpa shuddered gently. Cord stood up.

Slowly and hesitatingly at first, then with steadfast—though now again brainless—purpose, Grandpa began paddling back toward the Straits Head Station.

ISAAC ASIMOV

In accordance with my half of the Clarke-Asimov Treaty, concluded verbally some years ago in a cab proceeding down Park Avenue, I hereby declare that Isaac Asimov, Esquire, is (*a*) the best science writer and (*b*) the second-best science-*fiction* writer in the world.

In both categories, he is one of the most prolific, being practically the Simenon of science writing. At last count, his output was around sixty books—and some of them have hardly been slim volumes. His monumental *Intelligent Man's Guide to Science* strikes awe into the heart of a dilettante such as myself, and the sheer range of the subjects he has covered is equally impressive. Mathematics, linguistics, biochemistry (he was for some years Associate Professor of Biochemistry at the Boston University School of Medicine), astronomy, chemistry, physiology, history—Ike has tackled them all. He is also the only person I know who has written a short story while actually appearing on a TV show. (And, of course, got it published.)

The fictional Asimov is famous for the Three Laws of Robotics, and Toynbeean studies of the rise and fall of galactic civilizations. But he has written murder mysteries, and I fully expect that one day he will do a Western just for fun. (Probably a robot Western.)

This chilling little piece about the greatest planet in the solar system is perhaps even more topical than when it appeared in 1941. The idea that there might be life of some form on Jupiter, despite its enormous size and alien atmosphere, has gained considerable ground in the last few years. We now know that even *terrestrial* life-forms can flourish in the poisonous, oxygen-free Jovian environment; we are also fairly sure that the temperature a few miles below the visible cloud layer may be quite moderate—perhaps high enough for water to exist in the liquid state. As Asimov has remarked elsewhere, if there are seas on Jupiter, with its surface area greater than a hundred Earths, just think of the fishing. . . .

Since this story appeared a quarter of a century ago, we have learned the surprising fact that Jupiter emits extremely powerful bursts of radio waves, apparently associated with a few definite points on the hidden surface. They are pure noise, showing no sign of intelligent modulation, and no one really imagines that they are of artificial origin. Still—

What I particularly like about this story is its reminder that there is no such thing as finality in science, or in technology. It is a lesson which, after many shocks, the world is slowly beginning to learn.

Not Final!

Nicholas Orloff inserted a monocle in his left eye with all the incorruptible Britishness of a Russian educated at Oxford, and said reproachfully, "But, my dear Mr. Secretary! Half a billion dollars!"

Leo Birnam shrugged his shoulders wearily and allowed his lank body to cramp up still farther in the chair. "The appropriation must go through, Commissioner. The Dominion government here at Ganymede is becoming desperate. So far I've been holding them off, but as secretary of scientific affairs, my powers are small."

"I know, but—" And Orloff spread his hands helplessly.

"I suppose so," agreed Birnam. "The Empire government finds it easier to look the other way. They've done it consistently up to now. I've tried for a year now to have them understand the nature of the danger that hangs over the entire System, but it seems that it can't be done. But I'm appealing to you, Mr. Commissioner. You're new in your post and can approach this Jovian affair with an unjaundiced eye."

Orloff coughed and eyed the tips of his boots. In the three months since he had succeeded Gridley as colonial commissioner he had tabled unread everything relating to "these damned Jovian D.T.'s." That had been according to the established cabinet policy which had labeled the Jovian affair as "deadwood" long before he had entered office.

But now that Ganymede was becoming nasty, he found himself sent out to Jovopolis with instructions to hold the "blasted provincials" down. It was a nasty spot.

Birnam was speaking. "The Dominion government has reached the point where it needs the money so badly, in fact, that if they don't get it, they're going to publicize everything."

Orloff's phlegm broke completely, and he snatched at the monocle as it dropped. "My dear fellow!"

"I know what it would mean. I've advised against, but they're justified. Once the inside of the Jovian affair is out, once the people know about it, the Empire government won't stay in power a week. And when the Technocrats come in, they'll give us whatever we ask. Public opinion will see to that."

"But you'll also create a panic and hysteria—"

"Surely! That is why we hesitate. But you might call this an ultimatum. We want secrecy, we *need* secrecy; but we need money more."

"I see." Orloff was thinking rapidly, and the conclusions he came to were not pleasant. "In that case, it would be advisable to investigate the case further. If you have the papers concerning the communications with the planet Jupiter—"

"I have them," replied Birnam dryly, "and so has the Empire government at Washington. That won't do, Commissioner. It's the same cud that's been chewed by Earth officials for the last year, and it's gotten us nowhere. I want you to come to Ether Station with me."

The Ganymedan had risen from his chair, and he glowered down upon Orloff from his six and a half feet of height.

Orloff flushed. "Are you ordering me?"

"In a way, yes. I tell you there is no time. If you intend acting, you must act quickly or not at all." Birnam paused, then added, "You don't mind walking, I hope. Power vehicles aren't allowed to approach Ether Station ordinarily, and I can use the walk to explain a few of the facts. It's only two miles off."

"I'll walk," was the brusque reply.

The trip upward to subground level was made in silence, which was broken by Orloff when they stepped into the dimly lit anteroom.

"It's chilly here."

"I know. It's difficult to keep the temperature up to norm this near the surface. But it will be colder outside. Here!"

Birnam had kicked open a closet door and was indicating the garments suspended from the ceiling. "Put them on. You'll need them."

Orloff fingered them doubtfully. "Are they heavy enough?"

Birnam was pouring into his own costume as he spoke. "They're electrically heated. You'll find them plenty warm. That's it! Tuck the trouser legs inside the boots and lace them tight."

He turned then and, with a grunt, brought out a double compressed-gas cylinder from its rack in one corner of the closet. He glanced at the dial reading and then turned the stopcock. There was a thin wheeze of escaping gas, at which Birnam sniffed with satisfaction.

"Do you know how to work one of these?" he asked, as he screwed onto the jet a flexible tube of metal mesh, at the other end of which was a curiously curved object of thick, clear glass.

"What is it?"

"Oxygen nosepiece! What there is of Ganymede's atmosphere is argon and nitrogen, just about half and half. It isn't particularly breathable." He heaved the double cylinder into position and tightened it in its harness on Orloff's back.

Orloff staggered, "It's heavy. I can't walk two miles with this."

"It won't be heavy out there." Birnam nodded carelessly upward and lowered the glass nosepiece over Orloff's head.

"Just remember to breathe in through the nose and out through the mouth, and you won't have any trouble. By the way, did you eat recently?"

"I lunched before I came to your place."

Birnam sniffed dubiously. "Well, that's a little awkward." He drew a small metal container from one of his pockets and tossed it to the commissioner. "Put one of those pills in your mouth and keep sucking on it."

Orloff worked clumsily with gloved fingers and finally managed to get a brown spheroid out of the tin and into his mouth. He followed Birnam up a gently sloped ramp. The blind-alley ending of the corridor slid aside smoothly when they reached it, and there was a faint soughing as air slipped out into the thinner atmosphere of Ganymede.

Birnam caught the other's elbow and fairly dragged him out.

"I've turned your air tank on full," he shouted. "Breathe deeply and keep sucking at that pill."

Gravity had flicked to Ganymedan normality as they crossed the threshold, and Orloff, after one horrible moment of apparent levitation, felt his stomach turn a somersault and explode.

He gagged, and fumbled the pill with his tongue in a desperate attempt at self-control. The oxygen-rich mixture from the air cylinders burned his throat, and gradually Ganymede steadied. His stomach shuddered back into place. He tried walking.

"Take it easy, now," came Birnam's soothing voice. "It gets you that way the first few times you change gravity fields quickly. Walk slowly and get the rhythm, or you'll take a tumble That's right, you're getting it."

The ground seemed resilient. Orloff could feel the pressure of the other's arm holding him down at each step to keep him from springing too high. Steps were longer now—and flatter, as he got the rhythm. Birnam continued speaking, a voice a little muffled from behind the leather flap drawn loosely across mouth and chin.

"Each to his own world," he grinned. "I visited Earth a few years back, with my wife, and had a hell of a time. I couldn't get myself to learn to walk on a planet's surface without a nosepiece. I kept choking—I really did. The sunlight was too bright and the sky was too blue and the grass was too green. And the buildings were right out on the surface. I'll never forget the time they tried to get me to sleep in a room twenty stories up in the air, with the window wide open and the moon shining in.

"I went back on the first spaceship going my way and don't ever intend returning. How are you feeling now?"

"Fine! Splendid!" Now that the first discomfort had gone, Orloff found the low gravity exhilarating. He looked about him. The broken, hilly ground, bathed in a drenching yellow light, was covered with ground-hugging broad-leaved shrubs that showed the orderly arrangement of careful cultivation.

Birnam answered the unspoken question. "There's enough carbon dioxide in the air to keep the plants alive, and they all have the power to fix atmospheric nitrogen. That's what makes agriculture Ganymede's greatest industry. Those plants are worth their weight in gold as fertilizers back on Earth and worth double or triple that as sources for half a hundred alkaloids that can't be gotten anywhere else in the System. And, of course, everyone knows that Ganymedan green-leaf has Terrestrial tobacco beat hollow."

There was the drone of a strato-rocket overhead, shrill in the thin atmosphere, and Orloff looked up.

He stopped—stopped dead—and forgot to breathe!

It was his first glimpse of Jupiter in the sky.

It is one thing to see Jupiter, coldly harsh, against the ebony backdrop of space. At six hundred thousand miles, it is majestic enough. But on Ganymede, barely topping the hills, its outlines softened and ever so faintly hazed by the thin atmosphere, shining mellowly from a purple sky in which only a few fugitive stars dare compete with the Jovian giant—it can be described by no conceivable combination of words.

At first, Orloff absorbed the gibbous disk in silence. It was gigantic, thirty-two times the apparent diameter of the sun as seen from Earth. Its stripes stood out in faint washes of color against the yellowness beneath; around the Great Red Spot was an oval splotch of orange near the western rim.

And finally Orloff murmured weakly, "It's beautiful!"

Leo Birnam stared, too, but there was no awe in his eyes.

There was the mechanical weariness of viewing a sight often seen, and besides that, an expression of sick revulsion. The chin flap hid his twitching smile, but his grasp upon Orloff's arm left bruises through the tough fabric of the surface suit.

He said slowly, "It's the most horrible sight in the System."

Orloff turned reluctant attention to his companion. "Eh?" Then, disagreeably, "Oh, yes, those mysterious Jovians."

At that, the Ganymedan turned away angrily and broke into swinging, fifteen-foot strides. Orloff followed clumsily after, keeping his balance with difficulty.

"Here, now," he gasped.

But Birnam wasn't listening. He was speaking coldly, bitterly. "You on Earth can afford to ignore Jupiter. You know nothing of it. It's a little pinprick in your sky, a little flyspeck. You don't live here on Ganymede, watching that damned colossus gloating over you. Up and over fifteen hours—hiding God knows what on its surface. Hiding something that's waiting and waiting and *trying to get out*. Like a giant bomb just waiting to explode!"

"Nonsense!" Orloff managed to jerk out. "*Will* you slow down. I can't keep up."

Birnam cut his strides in half and said tensely, "Everyone knows that Jupiter is inhabited, but practically no one ever stops to realize what that means. I tell you that those Jovians, whatever they are, are born to the purple. *They are the natural rulers of the Solar System.*"

"Pure hysteria," muttered Orloff. "The Empire government has been hearing nothing else from your Dominion for a year."

"And you've shrugged it off. Well, listen! Jupiter, discounting the thickness of its colossal atmosphere, is eighty thousand miles in diameter. That means it possesses a surface one hundred times that of Earth, and more than fifty times that of the entire Terrestrial Empire. Its population, its resources, its war potential are in proportion."

"Mere numbers—"

"I know what you mean," Birnam drove on passionately. "Wars are not fought with numbers but with science and with organization. The Jovians have both. In the quarter of a century during which we have communicated with them, we've learned a bit. They have atomic power and they have radio. And in a world of ammonia under great pressure—a world, in other words, in which almost none of the metals can exist *as* metals for any length of time because of the tendency to form soluble ammonia complexes—they have managed to build up a complicated civilization. That means they have had to work through plastics, glasses, silicates, and synthetic building materials of one sort or another. *That* means a chemistry developed just as far as ours is, and I'd put odds on its having developed further."

Orloff waited long before answering. And then, "But how certain are you people about the Jovians' last message? We on Earth are inclined to doubt that the Jovians can possibly be as unreasonably belligerent as they have been described."

The Ganymedan laughed shortly. "They broke off all communication after that last message, didn't they? That doesn't sound friendly on their part, does it? I assure you that we've all but stood on our ears trying to contact them.

"Here, now, don't talk. Let me explain something to you. For twenty-five years here on Ganymede a little group of men have worked their hearts out trying to make sense out of a static-ridden, gravity-distorted set of variable clicks in our radio apparatus, for those clicks were our only connection with living intelligence upon Jupiter. It was a job for a world of scientists, but we never had more than two dozen at the Station at any one time. I was one of them from the very beginning and, as a philologist, did my part in helping construct and interpret the code that developed between ourselves and the Jovians, so that you can see I am speaking from the real inside.

"It was a devil of a heartbreaking job. It was five years before we got past the elementary clicks of arithmetic: three and four are seven; the square root of twenty-five is five; factorial six is seven hundred and twenty. After that, months sometimes passed before we could work out and check by further communication a single new fragment of thought.

"*But*—and this is the point—by the time the Jovians broke off relations, we understood them *thoroughly*. There was no more chance of a mistake in comprehension than there was of

Ganymede's suddenly cutting loose from Jupiter. And their last message was a threat and a promise of destruction. Oh, there's no doubt—there's no doubt!"

They were walking through a shallow pass in which the yellow Jupiter light gave way to a clammy darkness.

Orloff was disturbed. He had never had the case presented to him in this fashion before. He said, "But the reason, man. What reason did we give them—"

"No reason! It was simply this: the Jovians had finally discovered from our messages—just where and how I don't know—that *we* are *not* Jovians."

"Well, of course."

"It wasn't 'of course' to them. In their experiences they had never come across intelligences that were not Jovian. Why should they make an exception in favor of those from outer space?"

"You say they were scientists." Orloff's voice had assumed a wary frigidity. "Wouldn't they realize that alien environments would breed alien life? *We* knew it. We never thought the Jovians were Earthmen, though we had never met intelligences other than those of Earth."

They were back in the drenching wash of Jupiter light again, and a spreading region of ice glimmered amberly in a depression to the right.

Birnam answered, "I said they were chemists and physicists—but I never said they were astronomers. Jupiter, my dear Commissioner, has an atmosphere three thousand miles or more thick, and those miles of gas block off everything but the Sun and the four largest of Jupiter's moons. The Jovians know nothing of alien environments."

Orloff considered. "And so they decided we were aliens. What next?"

"If we weren't Jovians, then in their eyes, we weren't people. It turned out that a non-Jovian was 'vermin' by definition."

Orloff's automatic protest was cut off sharply by Birnam. "In their eyes, I said, vermin we were; and vermin we are. Moreover, we were vermin with the peculiar audacity of having dared to attempt to treat with Jovians—with *human beings*. Their last message was this, word for word—'Jovians are the masters.

There is no room for vermin. We will destroy you immediately.' I doubt if there was any animosity in that message—simply a cold statement of fact. But they meant it."

"But why?"

"Why did man exterminate the housefly?"

"Come, sir. You're not seriously presenting an analogy of that nature?"

"Why not, since it is certain that the Jovian considers us a sort of housefly—an insufferable type of housefly that dares aspire to intelligence."

Orloff made a last attempt. "But truly, Mr. Secretary, it seems impossible for intelligent life to adopt such an attitude."

"Do you possess much of an acquaintance with any other type of intelligent life than our own?" came with immediate sarcasm. "Do you feel competent to pass on Jovian psychology? Do you know just *how* alien Jovians must be physically? Just think of their world, with its gravity at two and one-half Earth normal; with its ammonia oceans—oceans that you might throw all Earth into without raising a respectable splash; with its three-thousand-mile atmosphere, dragged down by the colossal gravity into densities and pressures in its surface layers that make the sea bottoms of Earth resemble a medium-thick vacuum. I tell you, we've tried to figure out what sort of life could exist under those conditions and we've given up. It's thoroughly incomprehensible. Do you expect their mentality, then, to be any more understandable? Never! Accept it as it is. They intend destroying us. That's all we know and all we need to know."

He lifted a gloved hand as he finished, and one finger pointed. "There's Ether Station just ahead."

Orloff's head swiveled. "Underground?"

"Certainly! All except the Observatory. That's that steel-and-quartz dome to the right—the small one."

They had stopped before two large boulders that flanked an earthy embankment, and from behind either one a nosepieced, suited soldier in Ganymedan orange, with blasters ready, advanced upon the two.

Birnam lifted his face into Jupiter's light, and the soldiers saluted and stepped aside. A short word was barked into the wrist mike of one of them, and the camouflaged opening between the boulders fell into two and Orloff followed the secretary into the yawning airlock.

The Earthman caught one last glimpse of sprawling Jupiter before the closing door cut off the surface altogether.

It was no longer quite so beautiful.

Orloff did not feel quite normal again until he had seated himself in the overstuffed chair in Dr. Edward Prosser's private office. With a sigh of utter relaxation he propped his monocle under his eyebrow.

"Would Dr. Prosser mind if I smoked in here while we're waiting?" he asked.

"Go ahead," replied Birnam carelessly. "My own idea would be to drag Prosser away from whatever he's fooling with just now, but he's a queer chap. We'll get more out of him if we wait until he's ready for us." He withdrew a gnarled stick of greenish tobacco from its case and bit off the edge viciously.

Orloff smiled through the smoke of his own cigarette. "I don't mind waiting. I shall have something to say. You see, for the moment, Mr. Secretary, you gave me the jitters, but, after all, granted that the Jovians intend mischief once they get at us, it remains a fact," and here he spaced his words emphatically, "that they can't get at us."

"A bomb without a fuse, hey?"

"Exactly! It's simplicity itself, and not really worth discussing. You will admit, I suppose, that under no circumstances can the Jovians get away from Jupiter."

"Under *no* circumstances?" There was a quizzical tinge to Birnam's slow reply. "Shall we analyze that?"

He stared hard at the purple flame of his cigar. "It's an old trite saying that the Jovians can't leave Jupiter. The fact has been highly publicized by the sensation-mongers of Earth and Ganymede, and a great deal of sentiment has been driveled about the unfortunate intelligences who are irrevocably surface-bound and must forever stare into the Universe without, watching, watching, wondering, and never attaining.

"But, after all, what holds the Jovians to their planet? Two factors! That's all! The first is the immense gravity field of the planet. Two and a half Earth normal."

Orloff nodded. "Pretty bad!" he agreed.

"And Jupiter's gravitational potential is even worse, for, because of its greater diameter, the intensity of its gravitational field decreases with distance only one-tenth as rapidly as Earth's field does. It's a terrible problem—*but it's been solved*."

"Hey?" Orloff straightened.

"They've got atomic power. Gravity—even Jupiter's—means nothing once you've put unstable atomic nuclei to work for you."

Orloff crushed his cigarette to extinction with a nervous gesture. "But their atmosphere—"

"Yes, that's what's stopping them. They're living at the bottom of a three-thousand-mile-deep ocean of it, where the hydrogen of which it is composed is collapsed by sheer pressure to something approaching the density of *solid* hydrogen. It stays a gas because the temperature of Jupiter is above the critical point of hydrogen, but you just try to figure out the pressure that can make hydrogen *gas* half as heavy as water. You'll be surprised at the number of zeros you'll have to put down.

"No spaceship of metal or of any kind of matter can stand that pressure. No Terrestrial spaceship can land on Jupiter without smashing like an eggshell, and no Jovian spaceship can leave Jupiter without exploding like a soap bubble. That problem has not yet been solved, but it will be some day. Maybe tomorrow, maybe not for a hundred years, or a thousand. We don't know, but when it is solved, the Jovians will be on top of us. And it can be solved in a specific way."

"I don't see how—"

"Force fields! We've got them now, you know."

"Force fields!" Orloff seemed genuinely astonished, and he chewed the word over and over to himself for a few moments. "They're used as meteor shields for ships in the asteroid zone—but I don't see the application to the Jovian problem."

"The ordinary force field," explained Birnam, "is a feeble rarefied zone of energy extending over a hundred miles or more outside the ship. It'll stop meteors, but it's just so much empty ether to an object like a gas molecule. *But* what if you took that same zone of energy and compressed it to a thickness of a tenth of an inch. Molecules would bounce off it like this—ping-g-g-g!

And if you used stronger generators, and compressed the field to a hundredth of an inch, molecules would bounce off even when driven by the unthinkable pressure of Jupiter's atmosphere —and then if you build a ship inside—" He left the sentence dangling.

Orloff was pale. "You're not saying it can be done?"

"I'll bet you anything you like that the Jovians are *trying* to do it. And *we're* trying to do it right here at Ether Station."

The colonial commissioner jerked his chair closer to Birnam and grabbed the Ganymedan's wrist. "Why can't we bombard Jupiter with atomic bombs? Give it a thorough going over, I mean! With her gravity and her surface area, we can't miss."

Birnam smiled faintly. "We've thought of that. But atomite bombs would merely tear holes in the atmosphere. And even if you could penetrate, just divide the surface of Jupiter by the area of damage of a single bomb and find how many years we must bombard Jupiter at the rate of a bomb a minute before we begin to do significant damage. Jupiter's *big!* Don't ever forget that!"

His cigar had gone out, but he did not pause to relight. He continued in a low, tense voice. "No, we can't attack the Jovians as long as they're on Jupiter. We must wait for them to come out—and once they do, they're going to have the edge on us in numbers. A terrific, heartbreaking edge—so we'll just have to have the edge on them in science."

"But," Orloff broke in, and there was a note of fascinated horror in his voice, "how can we tell in advance what they'll have?"

"We can't. We've got to scrape up everything we can lay our hands on and hope for the best. But there's one thing we *do* know they'll have, and that's force fields. They can't get out without them. And if they have them, we must, too, and that's the problem we're trying to solve here. They will not ensure us victory, but without them we will suffer certain defeat. And now you know why we need money—and more than that. We want Earth itself to get to work. It's got to start a drive for scientific armaments and subordinate everything to that. You see?"

Orloff was on his feet. "Birnam, I'm with you—a hundred per cent with you. You can count on me back in Washington."

There was no mistaking his sincerity. Birnam gripped the hand outstretched toward him and wrung it—and at that moment the door flew open and a little pixie of a man hurtled in.

The newcomer spoke in rapid jerks, and exclusively to Birnam. "Where'd you come from? Been trying to get in touch with you. Secretary said you weren't in. Then five minutes later you show up on your own. Can't understand it." He busied himself furiously at his desk.

Birnam grinned. "If you'll take time out, Doc, you might say hello to Colonial Commissioner Orloff."

Dr. Edward Prosser turned on his toe like a ballet dancer and looked the Earthman up and down twice. "The new un, hey? We getting any money? We ought to. Been working on a shoestring ever since. At that we might not be needing any. It depends." He was back at the desk.

Orloff seemed a trifle disconcerted, but Birnam winked impressively, and he contented himself with a glassy stare through the monocle.

Prosser pounced upon a black leather booklet in the recesses of a pigeonhole, threw himself into his swivel chair, and wheeled about.

"Glad you came, Birnam," he said, leafing through the booklet. "Got something to show you. Commissioner Orloff, too."

"What were you keeping us waiting for?" demanded Birnam. "Where were you?"

"Busy! Busy as a pig! No sleep for three nights." He looked up and his small puckered face fairly flushed with delight. "Everything fell into place of a sudden. Like a jigsaw puzzle. Never saw anything like it. Kept us hopping, I tell you."

"You've gotten the dense force fields you're after?" asked Orloff in sudden excitement.

Prosser seemed annoyed. "No, not that. Something else. Come on." He glared at his watch and jumped out of his seat. "We've got half an hour. Let's go."

An electric-motored flivver waited outside, and Prosser spoke excitedly as he sped the purring vehicle down the ramps into the depths of the Station.

"Theory!" he said. "Theory! Damned important, that. You set a technician on a problem. He'll fool around. Waste lifetimes. Get nowhere. Just putter about at random. A true scientist works with theory. Lets math solve his problems." He overflowed with self-satisfaction.

The flivver stopped on a dime before a huge double door, and Prosser tumbled out, followed by the other two at a more leisurely pace.

"Through here! Through here!" he said. He shoved the door open and led them down the corridor and up a narrow flight of stairs onto a well-hugging passageway that circled a huge three-level room. Orloff recognized the gleaming quartz-and-steel pipe-sprouting ellipsoid two levels below as an atomic generator.

He adjusted his monocle and watched the scurrying activity below. An earphoned man on a high stool before a control board studded with dials looked up and waved. Prosser waved back and grinned.

Orloff said, "You create your force fields here?"

"That's right! Ever see one?"

"No." The commissioner smiled ruefully. "I don't even know what one *is*, except that it can be used as a meteor shield."

Prosser said, "It's very simple. Elementary matter. All matter is composed of atoms. Atoms are held together by interatomic forces. Take away atoms. Leave interatomic forces behind. *That's* a force field."

Orloff looked blank, and Birnam chuckled deep in his throat and scratched the back of his ear.

"That explanation reminds me of our Ganymedan method of suspending an egg a mile high in the air. It goes like this. You find a mountain just a mile high and put the egg on top. Then, keeping the egg where it is, you take the mountain away. That's all."

The colonial commissioner threw his head back to laugh, and the irascible Dr. Prosser puckered his lips into a pursed symbol of disapproval.

"Come, come. No joke, you know. Force fields most important. Got to be ready for the Jovians when they come."

A sudden rasping burr from below sent Prosser back from the railing.

"Get behind screen here," he babbled. "The twenty-millimeter field is going up. Bad radiation."

The burr muted almost into silence, and the three walked out onto the passageway again. There was no apparent change, but Prosser shoved his hand out over the railing and said, "Feel!"

Orloff extended a cautious finger, gasped, and slapped out with the palm of his hand. It was like pushing against very soft sponge rubber or superresilient steel springs.

Birnam tried, too. "That's better than anything we've done yet, isn't it?" He explained to Orloff, "A twenty-millimeter screen is one that can hold an atmosphere of a pressure of twenty millimeters of mercury against a vacuum without appreciable leakage."

The commissioner nodded. "I see! You'd need a seven-hundred-sixty-millimeter screen to hold Earth's atmosphere, then."

"Yes! That would be a unit atmosphere screen. Well, Prosser, is this what got you excited?"

"This twenty-millimeter screen. Of course not. I can go up to two hundred fifty millimeters using the activated vanadium pentasulphide in the praseodymium breakdown. But it's not necessary. Technician would do it and blow up the place. Scientist checks on theory and goes slow." He winked. "We're hardening the field now. Watch!"

"Shall we get behind the screen?"

"Not necessary now. Radiation bad only at beginning."

The burring waxed again, but not as loudly as before. Prosser shouted to the man at the control board, and a spreading wave of the hand was the only reply.

Then the control man waved a clenched fist and Prosser cried, "We've passed fifty millimeters! Feel the field!"

Orloff extended his hand and poked it curiously. The sponge rubber had hardened! He tried to pinch it between finger and thumb, so perfect was the illusion, but here the "rubber" faded to unresisting air.

Prosser tch-tched impatiently. "No resistance at right angles to force. Elementary mechanics that is."

The control man was gesturing again. "Past seventy," explained Prosser. "We're slowing down now. Critical point is 83.42."

He hung over the railing and kicked out with his feet at the other two. "Stay away! Dangerous!"

And then he yelled, "Careful! The generator's bucking!"

The burr had risen to a hoarse maximum and the control man worked frantically at his switches. From within the quartz heart of the central atomic generator the sullen red glow of the busting atoms had brightened dangerously.

There was a break in the burr, a reverberant roar, and a blast of air that threw Orloff hard against the wall.

Prosser dashed up. There was a cut over his eye. "Hurt? No? Good, good! I was expecting something of the sort. Should have warned you. Let's go down. Where's Birnam?"

The tall Ganymedan picked himself up off the floor and brushed at his clothes. "Here I am. What blew up?"

"Nothing blew up. Something buckled. Come on, down we go." He dabbed at his forehead with a handkerchief and led the way downward.

The control man removed his earphones as he approached, and got off his stool. He looked tired, and his dirt-smeared face was greasy with perspiration.

"The damn thing started going at 82.8, boss. It almost caught me."

"It did, did it?" growled Prosser. "Within limits of error, isn't it? How's the generator? Hey, Stoddard!"

The technician addressed replied from his station at the generator, "Tube Five died. It'll take two days to replace."

Prosser turned in satisfaction and said, "It worked. Went exactly as presumed. Problem solved, gentlemen. Trouble over. Let's get back to my office. I want to eat. And then I want to sleep."

He did not refer to the subject again until once more behind the desk in his office, and then he spoke between huge bites of a liver-and-onion sandwich.

He addressed Birnam. "Remember the work on space strain last June? It flopped, but we kept at it. Finch got a lead last week and I developed it. Everything fell into place. Slick as goose grease. Never saw anything like it."

"Go ahead," said Birnam calmly. He knew Prosser sufficiently well to avoid showing impatience.

"You saw what happened. When a field tops 83.42 millimeters, it becomes unstable. Space won't stand the strain. It buckles and the field blows. Boom!"

Birnam's mouth dropped open, and the arms of Orloff's chair creaked under sudden pressure. Silence for a while, and then Birnam said unsteadily, "You mean force fields stronger than that are impossible?"

"They're possible. You can create them. But the denser they are, the more unstable they are. If I had turned on the two-hundred-and-fifty-millimeter field, it would have lasted one-tenth of a second. Then, blooie! Would have blown up the Station! *And* myself! Technician would have done it. Scientist is warned by theory. Works carefully, the way I did. No harm done."

Orloff tucked his monocle into his vest pocket and said tremulously, "But if a force field is the same thing as interatomic forces, why is it that steel has such a strong interatomic binding force without bucking space? There's a flaw there."

Prosser eyed him in annoyance. "No flaw. Critical strength depends on number of generators. In steel, each atom is a force-field generator. That means about three hundred billion trillion generators for every ounce of matter. If we could use that many —As it is, one hundred generators would be the practical limit. That only raises the critical point to ninety-seven or thereabouts."

He got to his feet and continued with sudden fervor, "No, problem's over, I tell you. Absolutely impossible to create a force field capable of holding Earth's atmosphere for more than a hundredth of a second. Jovian atmosphere entirely out of question. Cold figures say that; backed by experiment. *Space won't stand it!*

"Let the Jovians do their damnedest. They can't get out! That's final! That's final! *That's final!*"

Orloff said, "Mr. Secretary, can I send a spacegram anywhere in the Station? I want to tell Earth that I'm returning by the next ship and that the Jovian problem is liquidated—entirely and for good."

Birnam said nothing, but the relief on his face as he shook hands with the colonial commissioner transfigured its gaunt homeliness unbelievably.

And Dr. Prosser repeated, with a birdlike jerk of his head, "That's *final!*"

Hal Tuttle looked up as Captain Everett, of the spaceship *Transparent*, newest ship of the Comet Space Lines, entered his private observation room in the nose of the ship.

The captain said, "A spacegram has just reached me from the home offices at Tucson. We're to pick up Colonial Commissioner Orloff at Jovopolis, Ganymede, and take him back to Earth."

"Good. We haven't sighted any ships?"

"No, no! We're way off the regular space lanes. The first the System will know of us will be the landing of the *Transparent* on Ganymede. It will be the greatest thing in space travel since the first trip to the Moon." His voice softened suddenly. "What's wrong, Hal? This is *your* triumph, after all."

Hal Tuttle looked up and out into the blackness of space. "I suppose it is. Ten years of work, Sam. I lost an arm and an eye in that first explosion, but I don't regret them. It's the reaction that's got me. The problem is solved; my lifework is finished."

"So is every steel-hulled ship in the System."

Tuttle smiled. "Yes. It's hard to realize, isn't it?" He gestured outward. "You see the stars? Part of the time there's nothing between them and us. It gives us a queasy feeling." His voice brooded, "Nine years I worked for nothing. I wasn't a theoretician, and never really knew where I was headed—just tried everything. I tried a little too hard, and space wouldn't stand it. I paid an arm and an eye and started fresh."

Captain Everett balled his fist and pounded the hull—the hull through which the stars shone unobstructed. There was the muffled thud of flesh striking an unyielding surface—but no response whatever from the invisible wall.

Tuttle nodded. "It's solid enough, now—though it flicks on and off eight hundred thousand times a second. I got the idea from the stroboscopic lamp. You know them—they flash on and off so rapidly that it gives all the impression of steady illumination.

"And so it is with the hull. It's not on long enough to buckle space. It's not off long enough to allow appreciable leakage of the atmosphere. And the net effect is a strength better than steel."

He paused and added slowly, "And there's no telling how far we can go. Speed up the intermission effect. Have the field flick off and on millions of times per second—billions of times. You can get fields strong enough to hold an atomic explosion. My lifework!"

Captain Everett pounded the other's shoulder. "Snap out of it, man. Think of the landing on Ganymede. The devil! It will be great publicity. Think of Orloff's face, for instance, when he finds he is to be the first passenger in history ever to travel in a spaceship with a force-field hull. How do you suppose he'll feel?"

Hal Tuttle shrugged. "I imagine he'll be rather pleased."

CYRIL KORNBLUTH

When Cyril Kornbluth died in 1958, at the age of thirty-four, he had been selling stories for half of his tragically short lifetime—scores of stories, under at least a dozen names. Yet despite his vast output, some of his work was the best that the field has ever seen. With Frederik Pohl, he coauthored *The Space Merchants,* the most celebrated anti-Utopia since *Brave New World.* His University of Chicago lecture "The Failure of the Science-Fiction Novel as Social Criticism" [1] is a brilliant analysis of such stories; by his own example, he did much to disprove the title of his thesis.

Kornbluth, like all thoughtful writers, frequently took a pessimistic view of the future—as is proved by such tales as "The Marching Morons" and "The Only Thing We Learn." The story that follows would not have endeared him to the medical profession, or those convinced of the inevitable perfectibility of mankind. But it is a horribly plausible glimpse of a future society, and a future science; you will not forget it in a hurry.

[1] Reprinted in *The Science-Fiction Novel* (Chicago: Advent Publishers, 1964).

The Little Black Bag

Old Dr. Full felt the winter in his bones as he limped down the alley. It was the alley and the back door he had chosen rather than the sidewalk and the front door because of the brown paper bag under his arm. He knew perfectly well that the flat-faced, stringy-haired women of his street and their gap-toothed, sour-smelling husbands did not notice if he brought a bottle of cheap wine to his room. They all but lived on the stuff themselves, varied with whiskey when pay checks were boosted by overtime. But Dr. Full, unlike them, was ashamed. A complicated disaster occurred as he limped down the littered alley. One of the neighborhood dogs—a mean little black one he knew and hated, with its teeth always bared and always snarling with menace—hurled at his legs through a hole in the board fence that lined his path. Dr. Full flinched, then swung his leg in what was to have been a satisfying kick to the animal's gaunt ribs. But the winter in his bones weighed down the leg. His foot failed to clear a half-buried brick, and he sat down abruptly, cursing. When he smelled unbottled wine and realized his brown paper package had slipped from under his arm and smashed, his curses died on his lips. The snarling black dog was circling him at a yard's distance, tensely stalking, but he ignored it in the greater disaster.

With stiff fingers as he sat on the filth of the alley, Dr. Full unfolded the brown paper bag's top, which had been crimped over, grocer-wise. The early autumnal dusk had come; he could not see plainly what was left. He lifted out the jug-handled top of his half gallon, and some fragments, and then the bottom of the bottle. Dr. Full was far too occupied to exult as he noted that there was a good pint left. He had a problem, and emotions could be deferred until the fitting time.

The dog closed in, its snarl rising in pitch. He set down the bottom of the bottle and pelted the dog with the curved triangular glass fragments of its top. One of them connected, and the dog ducked back through the fence, howling. Dr. Full then placed a razor-like edge of the half-gallon bottle's foundation to his lips and drank from it as though it were a giant's cup. Twice he had to put it down to rest his arms, but in one minute he had swallowed the pint of wine.

He thought of rising to his feet and walking through the alley to his room, but a flood of well-being drowned the notion. It was, after all, inexpressibly pleasant to sit there and feel the frost-hardened mud of the alley turn soft, or seem to, and to feel the winter evaporating from his bones under a warmth which spread from his stomach through his limbs.

A three-year-old girl in a cut-down winter coat squeezed through the same hole in the board fence from which the black dog had sprung its ambush. Gravely she toddled up to Dr. Full and inspected him with her dirty forefinger in her mouth. Dr. Full's happiness had been providentially made complete; he had been supplied with an audience.

"Ah, my dear," he said hoarsely. And then: "Preposserous accusation. 'If that's what you call evidence,' I should have told them, 'you better stick to your doctoring.' I should have told them: 'I was here before your County Medical Society. And the License Commissioner never proved a thing on me. So, gennulmen, doesn't it stand to reason? I appeal to you as fellow memmers of a great profession—' "

The little girl, bored, moved away, picking up one of the triangular pieces of glass to play with as she left. Dr. Full forgot her immediately, and continued to himself earnestly: "But so help me, they *couldn't* prove a thing. Hasn't a man got any *rights?*" He brooded over the question, of whose answer he was so sure, but on which the Committee on Ethics of the County Medical Society had been equally certain. The winter was

creeping into his bones again, and he had no money and no
more wine.

Dr. Full pretended to himself that there was a bottle of
whiskey somewhere in the fearful litter of his room. It was an
old and cruel trick he played on himself when he simply had to
be galvanized into getting up and going home. He might freeze
there in the alley. In his room he would be bitten by bugs and
would cough at the moldy reek from his sink, but he would not
freeze and be cheated of the hundreds of bottles of wine that
he still might drink, the thousands of hours of glowing content
he still might feel. He thought about that bottle of whiskey—
was it back of a mounded heap of medical journals? No; he
had looked there last time. Was it under the sink, shoved well
to the rear, behind the rusty drain? The cruel trick began to
play itself out again. Yes, he told himself with mounting excitement, yes, it might be! Your memory isn't so good nowadays,
he told himself with rueful good-fellowship. You know perfectly
well you might have bought a bottle of whiskey and shoved it
behind the sink drain for a moment just like this.

The amber bottle, the crisp snap of the sealing as he cut it,
the pleasurable exertion of starting the screw cap on its threads,
and then the refreshing tangs in his throat, the warmth in his
stomach, the dark, dull happy oblivion of drunkenness—they
became real to him. You *could* have, you know! You *could* have!
he told himself. With the blessed conviction growing in his
mind—It *could* have happened, you know! It *could* have!—he
struggled to his right knee. As he did, he heard a yelp behind
him, and curiously craned his neck around while resting. It was
the little girl, who had cut her hand quite badly on her toy, the
piece of glass. Dr. Full could see the rilling bright blood down
her coat, pooling at her feet.

He almost felt inclined to defer the image of the amber
bottle for her, but not seriously. He knew that it was there,
shoved well to the rear under the sink, behind the rusty drain
where he had hidden it. He would have a drink and then magnanimously return to help the child. Dr. Full got to his other
knee and then his feet, and proceeded at a rapid totter down
the littered alley toward his room, where he would hunt with
calm optimism at first for the bottle that was not there, then

with anxiety, and then with frantic violence. He would hurl books and dishes about before he was done looking for the amber bottle of whiskey, and finally would beat his swollen knuckles against the brick wall until old scars on them opened and his thick old blood oozed over his hands. Last of all, he would sit down somewhere on the floor, whimpering, and would plunge into the abyss of purgative nightmare that was his sleep.

After twenty generations of shilly-shallying and "we'll cross that bridge when we come to it," genus homo had bred itself into an impasse. Dogged biometricians had pointed out with irrefutable logic that mental subnormals were outbreeding mental normals and supernormals, and that the process was occurring on an exponential curve. Every fact that could be mustered in the argument proved the biometricians' case, and led inevitably to the conclusion that genus homo was going to wind up in a preposterous jam quite soon. If you think that had any effect on breeding practices, you do not know genus homo.

There was, of course, a sort of masking effect produced by that other exponential function, the accumulation of technological devices. A moron trained to punch an adding machine seems to be a more skillful computer than a medieval mathematician trained to count on his fingers. A moron trained to operate the twenty-first century equivalent of a linotype seems to be a better typographer than a Renaissance printer limited to a few fonts of movable type. This is also true of medical practice.

It was a complicated affair of many factors. The supernormals "improved the product" at greater speed than the subnormals degraded it, but in smaller quantity because elaborate training of their children was practiced on a custom-made basis. The fetish of higher education had some weird avatars by the twentieth generation: "colleges" where not a member of the student body could read words of three syllables; "universities" where such degrees as "Bachelor of Typewriting," "Master of Shorthand" and "Doctor of Philosophy (Card Filing)" were conferred with the traditional pomp. The handful of supernormals used such devices in order that the vast majority might keep some semblance of a social order going.

Some day the supernormals would mercilessly cross the bridge; at the twentieth generation they were standing irresolutely at its approaches wondering what had hit them. And the ghosts of twenty generations of biometricians chuckled malignantly.

It is a certain Doctor of Medicine of this twentieth generation that we are concerned with. His name was Hemingway—John Hemingway, B.Sc., M.D. He was a general practitioner, and did not hold with running to specialists with every trifling ailment. He often said as much, in approximately these words: "Now, uh, what I mean is you got a good old G.P. See what I mean? Well, uh, now a good old G.P. don't claim he knows all about lungs and glands and them things, get me? But you got a G.P., you got, uh, you got a, well, you got a . . . *all-around man!* That's what you got when you got a G.P.—you got a all-around man."

But from this, do not imagine that Dr. Hemingway was a poor doctor. He could remove tonsils or appendixes, assist at practically any confinement and deliver a living, uninjured infant, correctly diagnose hundreds of ailments, and prescribe and administer the correct medication or treatment for each. There was, in fact, only one thing he could not do in the medical line, and that was, violate the ancient canons of medical ethics. And Dr. Hemingway knew better than to try.

Dr. Hemingway and a few friends were chatting one evening when the event occurred that precipitates him into our story. He had been through a hard day at the clinic, and he wished his physicist friend Walter Gillis, B.Sc., M.Sc., Ph.D., would shut up so he could tell everybody about it. But Gillis kept rambling on, in his stilted fashion: "You got to hand it to old Mike; he don't have what we call the scientific method, but you got to hand it to him. There this poor little dope is, puttering around with some glassware, and I come up and I ask him, kidding of course, 'How's about a time-travel machine, Mike?'"

Dr. Gillis was not aware of it, but "Mike" had an I.Q. six times his own and was—to be blunt—his keeper. "Mike" rode herd on the pseudo-physicists in the pseudo-laboratory, in the guise of a bottle-washer. It was a social waste—but as has been mentioned before, the supernormals were still standing at the

approaches to a bridge. Their irresolution led to many such preposterous situations. And it happens that "Mike," having grown
frantically bored with his task, was malevolent enough to—but
let Dr. Gillis tell it:

"So he gives me these here tube numbers and says, 'Series
circuit. Now stop bothering me. Build your time machine, sit
down at it and turn on the switch. That's all I ask, Dr. Gillis—
that's all I ask.' "

"Say," marveled a brittle and lovely blond guest, "you remember real good, don't you, doc?" She gave him a melting
smile.

"Heck," said Gillis modestly, "I always remember good. It's
what you call an inherent facility. And besides I told it quick to
my secretary, so she wrote it down. I don't read so good, but I
sure remember good, all right. Now, where was I?"

Everybody thought hard, and there were various suggestions:
"Something about bottles, doc?"

"You was starting a fight. You said 'time somebody was
traveling.' "

"Yeah—you called somebody a swish. Who did you call a
swish?"

"Not swish—*switch!*"

Dr. Gillis' noble brow grooved with thought, and he declared:
"Switch is right. It was about time travel. What we call travel
through time. So I took the tube numbers he gave me and I put
them into the circuit-builder; I set it for 'series' and there it is—
my time-traveling machine. It travels things through time real
good." He displayed a box.

"What's in the box?" asked the lovely blonde.

Dr. Hemingway told her: "Time travel. It travels things
through time."

"Look," said Gillis, the physicist. He took Dr. Hemingway's
little black bag and put it on the box. He turned on the switch
and the little black bag vanished.

"Say," said Dr. Hemingway, "that was, uh, swell. Now bring
it back."

"Huh?"

"Bring back my little black bag."

"Well," said Dr. Gillis, "they don't come back. I tried it

backwards and they don't come back. I guess maybe that dummy Mike give me a bum steer."

There was wholesale condemnation of "Mike" but Dr. Hemingway took no part in it. He was nagged by a vague feeling that there was something he would have to do. He reasoned: "I am a doctor, and a doctor has got to have a little black bag. I ain't got a little black bag—so ain't I a doctor no more?" He decided that this was absurd. He *knew* he was a doctor. So it must be the bag's fault for not being there. It was no good, and he would get another one tomorrow from that dummy Al, at the clinic. Al could find things good, but he was a dummy—never liked to talk sociable to you.

So the next day Dr. Hemingway remembered to get another little black bag from his keeper—another little black bag with which he could perform tonsillectomies, appendectomies and the most difficult confinements, and with which he could diagnose and cure his kind until the day when the supernormals could bring themselves to cross that bridge. Al was kinda nasty about the missing little black bag, but Dr. Hemingway didn't exactly remember what had happened, so no tracer was sent out, so—

Old Dr. Full awoke from the horrors of the night to the horrors of the day. His gummy eyelashes pulled apart convulsively. He was propped against a corner of his room, and something was making a little drumming noise. He felt very cold and cramped. As his eyes focused on his lower body, he croaked out a laugh. The drumming noise was being made by his left heel, agitated by fine tremors against the bare floor. It was going to be the D.T.'s again, he decided dispassionately. He wiped his mouth with his bloody knuckles, and the fine tremor coarsened; the snare-drum beat became louder and slower. He was getting a break this fine morning, he decided sardonically. You didn't get the horrors until you had been tightened like a violin string, just to the breaking point. He had a reprieve, if a reprieve into his old body with the blazing, endless headache just back of the eyes and the screaming stiffness in the joints were anything to be thankful for.

There was something or other about a kid, he thought

vaguely. He was going to doctor some kid. His eyes rested on a little black bag in the center of the room, and he forgot about the kid. "I could have sworn," said Dr. Full, "I hocked that two years ago!" He hitched over and reached the bag, and then realized it was some stranger's kit, arriving here he did not know how. He tentatively touched the lock and it snapped open and lay flat, rows and rows of instruments and medications tucked into loops in its four walls. It seemed vastly larger open than closed. He didn't see how it could possibly fold up into that compact size again, but decided it was some stunt of the instrument makers. Since his time—that made it worth more at the hock shop, he thought with satisfaction.

Just for old times' sake, he let his eyes and fingers rove over the instruments before he snapped the bag shut and headed for Uncle's. More than a few were a little hard to recognize—exactly that is. You could see the things with blades for cutting, the forceps for holding and pulling, the retractors for holding fast, the needles and gut for suturing, the hypos—a fleeting thought crossed his mind that he could peddle the hypos separately to drug addicts.

Let's go, he decided, and tried to fold up the case. It didn't fold until he happened to touch the lock, and then it folded all at once into a little black bag. Sure have forged ahead, he thought, almost able to forget that what he was primarily interested in was its pawn value.

With a definite objective, it was not too hard for him to get to his feet. He decided to go down the front steps, out the front door and down the sidewalk. But first—

He snapped the bag open again on his kitchen table, and pored through the medication tubes. "Anything to sock the autonomic nervous system good and hard," he mumbled. The tubes were numbered, and there was a plastic card which seemed to list them. The left margin of the card was a run-down of the systems—vascular, muscular, nervous. He followed the last entry across to the right. There were columns for "stimulant," "depressant," and so on. Under "nervous system" and "depressant" he found the number 17, and shakily located the little glass tube which bore it. It was full of pretty blue pills and he took one.

It was like being struck by a thunderbolt.

Dr. Full had so long lacked any sense of well-being except the brief glow of alcohol that he had forgotten its very nature. He was panic-stricken for a long moment at the sensation that spread through him slowly, finally tingling in his fingertips. He straightened up, his pains gone and his leg tremor stilled.

That was great, he thought. He'd be able to *run* to the hock shop, pawn the little black bag and get some booze. He started down the stairs. Not even the street, bright with mid-morning sun, into which he emerged made him quail. The little black bag in his left hand had a satisfying, authoritative weight. He was walking erect, he noted, and not in the somewhat furtive crouch that had grown on him in recent years. A little self-respect, he told himself, that's what I need. Just because a man's down doesn't mean—

"Docta, please-a come wit'!" somebody yelled at him, tugging his arm. "Da litt-la girl, she's-a burn' up!" It was one of the slum's innumerable flat-faced, stringy-haired women, in a slovenly wrapper.

"Ah, I happen to be retired from practice—" he began hoarsely, but she would not be put off.

"In by here, Docta!" she urged, tugging him to a doorway. "You come look-a da litt-la girl. I got two dolla, you come look!" That put a different complexion on the matter. He allowed himself to be towed through the doorway into a mussy, cabbage-smelling flat. He knew the woman now, or rather knew who she must be—a new arrival who had moved in the other night. These people moved at night, in motorcades of battered cars supplied by friends and relations, with furniture lashed to the tops, swearing and drinking until the small hours. It explained why she had stopped him: she did not yet know he was old Dr. Full, a drunken reprobate whom nobody would trust. The little black bag had been his guarantee, outweighing his whiskery face and stained black suit.

He was looking down on a three-year-old girl who had, he rather suspected, just been placed in the mathematical center of a freshly changed double bed. God knew what sour and dirty mattress she usually slept on. He seemed to recognize her as he noted a crusted bandage on her right hand. Two dollars, he thought. An ugly flush had spread up her pipe-stem arm. He poked a finger into the socket of her elbow, and felt little spheres like marbles under the skin and ligaments roll apart. The child began to squall thinly; beside him, the woman gasped and began to weep herself.

"Out," he gestured briskly at her, and she thudded away, still sobbing.

Two dollars, he thought. Give her some mumbo jumbo, take the money and tell her to go to a clinic. Strep, I guess, from that stinking alley. It's a wonder any of them grow up. He put down the little black bag and forgetfully fumbled for his key, then remembered and touched the lock. It flew open, and he selected a bandage shears, with a blunt wafer for the lower jaw. He fitted the lower jaw under the bandage, trying not to hurt the kid by its pressure on the infection, and began to cut. It was amazing how easily and swiftly the shining shears snipped through the crusty rag around the wound. He hardly seemed to be driving the shears with fingers at all. It almost seemed as though the shears were driving his fingers instead as they scissored a clean, light line through the bandage.

Certainly have forged ahead since my time, he thought—sharper than a microtome knife. He replaced the shears in their loop on the extraordinarily big board that the little black bag turned into when it unfolded, and leaned over the wound. He whistled at the ugly gash, and the violent infection which had taken immediate root in the sickly child's thin body. Now what can you do with a thing like that? He pawed over the contents of the little black bag, nervously. If he lanced it and let some of the pus out, the old woman would think he'd done something for her and he'd get the two dollars. But at the clinic they'd want to know who did it and if they got sore enough they might send a cop around. Maybe there was something in the kit—

He ran down the left edge of the card to "lymphatic" and read across to the column under "infection." It didn't sound right at all to him; he checked again, but it still said that. In the square to which the line and column led were the symbols: "IV-g-3cc." He couldn't find any bottles marked with Roman numerals, and then noticed that that was how the hypodermic needles were designated. He lifted number IV from its loop, noting that it was fitted with a needle already and even seemed

to be charged. What a way to carry those things around! So—
three cc. of whatever was in hypo number IV ought to do something or other about infections settled in the lymphatic system
—which, God knows, this one was. What did the lower-case "g"
mean, though? He studied the glass hypo and saw letters engraved on what looked like a rotating disk at the top of the barrel. They ran from "a" to "i," and there was an index line
engraved on the barrel on the opposite side from the calibrations.

Shrugging, old Dr. Full turned the disk until "g" coincided
with the index line, and lifted the hypo to eye level. As he
pressed in the plunger he did not see the tiny thread of fluid
squirt from the tip of the needle. There was a sort of dark mist
for a moment about the tip. A closer inspection showed that
the needle was not even pierced at the tip. It had the usual
slanting cut across the bias of the shaft, but the cut did not
expose an oval hole. Baffled, he tried pressing the plunger again.
Again *something* appeared around the tip and vanished. "We'll
settle this," said the doctor. He slipped the needle into the skin
of his forearm. He thought at first that he had missed—that the
point had glided over the top of his skin instead of catching and
slipping under it. But he saw a tiny blood-spot and realized that
somehow he just hadn't felt the puncture. Whatever was in the
barrel, he decided, couldn't do him any harm if it lived up to
its billing—and if it could come out through a needle that had
no hole. He gave himself three cc. and twitched the needle out.
There was the swelling—painless, but otherwise typical.

Dr. Full decided it was his eyes or something, and gave three
cc. of "g" from hypodermic IV to the feverish child. There was
no interruption to her wailing as the needle went in and the
swelling rose. But a long instant later, she gave a final gasp and
was silent.

Well, he told himself, cold with horror, you did it that time.
You killed her with that stuff.

Then the child sat up and said: "Where's my mommy?"

Incredulously, the doctor seized her arm and palpated the
elbow. The gland infection was zero, and the temperature
seemed normal. The blood-congested tissues surrounding the
wound were subsiding as he watched. The child's pulse was
stronger and no faster than a child's should be. In the sudden

silence of the room he could hear the little girl's mother sobbing in her kitchen, outside. And he also heard a girl's insinuating voice:

"She gonna be OK, doc?"

He turned and saw a gaunt-faced, dirty-blond sloven of perhaps eighteen leaning in the doorway and eying him with amused contempt. She continued: "I heard about you, *Doc-tor* Full. So don't go try and put the bite on the old lady. You couldn't doctor up a sick cat."

"Indeed?" he rumbled. This young person was going to get a lesson she richly deserved. "Perhaps you would care to look at my patient?"

"Where's my mommy?" insisted the little girl, and the blond's jaw fell. She went to the bed and cautiously asked: "You OK now, Teresa? You all fixed up?"

"Where's my mommy?" demanded Teresa. Then, accusingly, she gestured with her wounded hand at the doctor. "You *poke* me!" she complained, and giggled pointlessly.

"Well—" said the blond girl, "I guess I got to hand it to you, doc. These loud-mouth women around here said you didn't know your . . . I mean, didn't know how to cure people. They said you ain't a real doctor."

"I *have* retired from practice," he said. "But I happened to be taking this case to a colleague as a favor, your good mother noticed me, and—" a deprecating smile. He touched the lock of the case and it folded up into the little black bag again.

"You stole it," the girl said flatly.

He sputtered.

"Nobody'd trust you with a thing like that. It must be worth plenty. You stole that case. I was going to stop you when I come in and saw you working over Teresa, but it looked like you wasn't doing her any harm. But when you give me that line about taking that case to a colleague I know you stole it. You gimme a cut or I go to the cops. A thing like that must be worth twenty-thirty dollars."

The mother came timidly in, her eyes red. But she let out a whoop of joy when she saw the little girl sitting up and babbling to herself, embraced her madly, fell on her knees for a quick prayer, hopped up to kiss the doctor's hand, and then dragged him into the kitchen, all the while rattling in her native language while the blond girl let her eyes go cold with disgust. Dr. Full allowed himself to be towed into the kitchen, but flatly declined a cup of coffee and a plate of anise cakes and St.-John's-bread.

"Try him on some wine, ma," said the girl sardonically.

"Hyass! Hyass!" breathed the woman delightedly. "You like-a wine, docta?" She had a carafe of purplish liquid before him in an instant, and the blond girl snickered as the doctor's hand twitched out at it. He drew his hand back, while there grew in his head the old image of how it would smell and then taste and then warm his stomach and limbs. He made the kind of calculation at which he was practiced; the delighted woman would not notice as he downed two tumblers, and he could overawe her through two tumblers more with his tale of Teresa's narrow brush with the Destroying Angel, and then—why, then it would not matter. He would be drunk.

But for the first time in years, there was a sort of counterimage: a blend of the rage he felt at the blond girl to whom he was so transparent, and of pride at the cure he had just effected. Much to his own surprise, he drew back his hand from the carafe and said, luxuriating in the words: 'No, thank you. I don't believe I'd care for any so early in the day." He covertly watched the blond girl's face, and was gratified at her surprise. Then the mother was shyly handing him two bills and saying: "Is no much-a money, docta—but you come again, see Teresa?"

"I shall be glad to follow the case through," he said. "But now excuse me—I really must be running along." He grasped the little black bag firmly and got up; he wanted very much to get away from the wine and the older girl.

"Wait up, doc," said she, "I'm going your way." She followed him out and down the street. He ignored her until he felt her hand on the black bag. Then old Dr. Full stopped and tried to reason with her:

"Look, my dear. Perhaps you're right. I might have stolen it. To be perfectly frank, I don't remember how I got it. But you're young and you can earn your own money—"

"Fifty-fifty," she said, "or I go to the cops. And if I get another word outta you, it's sixty-forty. And you know who gets the short end, don't you, doc?"

Defeated, he marched to the pawnshop, her impudent hand still on the handle with his, and her heels beating out a tattoo against his stately tread.

In the pawnshop, they both got a shock.

"It ain't stendard," said Uncle, unimpressed by the ingenious lock. "I ain't nevva seen one like it. Some cheap Jap stuff, maybe? Try down the street. This I nevva could sell."

Down the street they got an offer of one dollar. The same complaint was made: "I ain't a collecta, mista—I buy stuff that got resale value. Who could I sell this to, a Chinaman who don't know medical instruments? Every one of them looks funny. You sure you didn't make these yourself?" They didn't take the one-dollar offer.

The girl was baffled and angry; the doctor was baffled too, but triumphant. He had two dollars, and the girl had a half-interest in something nobody wanted. But, he suddenly marveled, the thing had been all right to cure the kid, hadn't it?

"Well," he asked her, "do you give up? As you see, the kit is practically valueless."

She was thinking hard. "Don't fly off the handle, doc. I don't get this but something's going on all right . . . would those guys know good stuff if they saw it?"

"They would. They make a living from it. Wherever this kit came from—"

She seized on that, with a devilish faculty she seemed to have of eliciting answers without asking questions. "I thought so. You don't know either, huh? Well, maybe I can find out for you. C'mon in here. I ain't letting go of that thing. There's money in it—some way, I don't know how, there's money in it." He followed her into a cafeteria and to an almost empty corner. She was oblivious to stares and snickers from the other customers as she opened the little black bag—it almost covered a cafeteria table—and ferreted through it. She picked out a retractor from a loop, scrutinized it, contemptuously threw it down, picked out a speculum, threw it down, picked out the lower half of an O.B. forceps, turned it over, close to her sharp young eyes—and saw what the doctor's dim old ones could not have seen.

All old Dr. Full knew was that she was peering at the neck of the forceps and then turned white. Very carefully, she placed the half of the forceps back in its loop of cloth and then replaced the retractor and the speculum. "Well?" he asked. "What did you see?"

" 'Made in U.S.A.,' " she quoted hoarsely. " 'Patent Applied for July 2450.' "

He wanted to tell her she must have misread the inscription, that it must be a practical joke, that—

But he knew she had read correctly. Those bandage shears: they *had* driven his fingers, rather than his fingers driving them. The hypo needle that had no hole. The pretty blue pill that had struck him like a thunderbolt.

"You know what I'm going to do?" asked the girl, with sudden animation. "I'm going to go to charm school. You'll like that, won't ya, doc? Because we're sure going to be seeing a lot of each other."

Old Dr. Full didn't answer. His hands had been playing idly with that plastic card from the kit on which had been printed the rows and columns that had guided him twice before. The card had a slight convexity; you could snap the convexity back and forth from one side to the other. He noted, in a daze, that with each snap a different text appeared on the cards. *Snap.* "The knife with the blue dot in the handle is for tumors only. Diagnose tumors with your Instrument Seven, the Swelling Tester. Place the Swelling Tester—" *Snap.* "An overdose of the pink pills in Bottle 3 can be fixed with one white pill from Bottle—" *Snap.* "Hold the suture needle by the end without the hole in it. Touch it to one end of the wound you want to close and let go. After it has made the knot, touch it—" *Snap.* "Place the top half of the O.B. Forceps near the opening. Let go. After it has entered and conformed to the shape of—" *Snap.*

The slot man saw "FLANNERY 1—MEDICAL" in the upper left corner of the hunk of copy. He automatically scribbled "trim to .75" on it and skimmed it across the horseshoe-shaped copy desk to Piper, who had been handling Edna Flannery's quack-exposé series. She was a nice youngster, he thought, but like all youngsters she overwrote. Hence, the "trim."

Piper dealt back a city hall story to the slot, pinned down Flannery's feature with one hand and began to tap his pencil across it, one tap to a word, at the same steady beat as a teletype carriage traveling across the roller. He wasn't exactly reading it this first time. He was just looking at the letters and words to find out whether, as letters and words, they conformed to *Herald* style. The steady tap of his pencil ceased at intervals as it drew a black line ending with a stylized letter "d" through the word "breast" and scribbled in "chest" instead, or knocked down the capital "E" in "East" to lower case with a diagonal, or closed up a split word—in whose middle Flannery had bumped the space bar of her typewriter—with two curved lines like parentheses rotated through ninety degrees. The thick black pencil zipped a ring around the "30" which, like all youngsters, she put at the end of her stories. He turned back to the first page for the second reading. This time the pencil drew lines with the stylized "d's" at the end of them through adjectives and whole phrases, printed big "L's" to mark paragraphs, hooked some of Flannery's own paragraphs together with swooping recurved lines.

At the bottom of "FLANNERY ADD 2—MEDICAL" the pencil slowed down and stopped. The slot man, sensitive to the rhythm of his beloved copy desk, looked up almost at once. He saw Piper squinting at the story, at a loss. Without wasting words, the copy reader skimmed it back across the masonite horseshoe to the chief, caught a police story in return and buckled down, his pencil tapping. The slot man read as far as the fourth add, barked at Howard, on the rim: "Sit in for me," and stumped through the clattering city room toward the alcove where the managing editor presided over his own bedlam.

The copy chief waited his turn while the makeup editor, the pressroom foreman and the chief photographer had words with the M.E. When his turn came, he dropped Flannery's copy on his desk and said: "She says this one isn't a quack."

The M.E. read:

"FLANNERY 1—MEDICAL, by Edna Flannery, *Herald* Staff Writer.

"The sordid tale of medical quackery which the *Herald* has exposed in this series of articles undergoes a change of pace today which the reporter found a welcome surprise. Her quest for the facts in the case of today's subject started just the same way that her exposure of one dozen shyster M.D.'s and faith-

healing phonies did. But she can report for a change that Dr.
Bayard Full is, despite unorthodox practices which have drawn
the suspicion of the rightly hypersensitive medical associations,
a true healer living up to the highest ideals of his profession.

"Dr. Full's name was given to the *Herald's* reporter by the
ethical committee of a county medical association, which reported that he had been expelled from the association on July 18,
1941 for allegedly 'milking' several patients suffering from trivial
complaints. According to sworn statements in the committee's
files, Dr. Full had told them they suffered from cancer, and that
he had a treatment which would prolong their lives. After his
expulsion from the association, Dr. Full dropped out of their
sight—until he opened a midtown 'sanitarium' in a brownstone
front which had for years served as a rooming house.

"The *Herald's* reporter went to that sanitarium, on East 89th
Street, with the full expectation of having numerous imaginary
ailments diagnosed and of being promised a sure cure for a flat
sum of money. She expected to find unkempt quarters, dirty
instruments and the mumbo-jumbo paraphernalia of the shyster
M.D. which she had seen a dozen times before.

"She was wrong.

"Dr. Full's sanitarium is spotlessly clean, from its tastefully
furnished entrance hall to its shining, white treatment rooms.
The attractive, blond receptionist who greeted the reporter was
soft-spoken and correct, asking only the reporter's name, address
and the general nature of her complaint. This was given, as usual,
as 'nagging backache.' The receptionist asked the *Herald's* reporter to be seated, and a short while later conducted her to a
second-floor treatment room and introduced her to Dr. Full.

"Dr. Full's alleged past, as described by the medical society
spokesman, is hard to reconcile with his present appearance. He
is a clear-eyed, white-haired man in his sixties, to judge by his
appearance—a little above middle height and apparently in good
physical condition. His voice was firm and friendly, untainted by
the ingratiating whine of the shyster M.D. which the reporter
has come to know too well.

"The receptionist did not leave the room as he began his
examination after a few questions as to the nature and location
of the pain. As the reporter lay face down on a treatment table

the doctor pressed some instrument to the small of her back. In about one minute he made this astounding statement: 'Young woman, there is no reason for you to have any pain where you say you do. I understand they're saying nowadays that emotional upsets cause pains like that. You'd better go to a psychologist or psychiatrist if the pain keeps up. There is no physical cause for it, so I can do nothing for you.'

"His frankness took the reporter's breath away. Had he guessed she was, so to speak, a spy in his camp? She tried again: 'Well, doctor, perhaps you'd give me a physical checkup, I feel rundown all the time, besides the pains. Maybe I need a tonic.' This is never-failing bait to shyster M.D.'s—an invitation for them to find all sorts of mysterious conditions wrong with a patient, each of which 'requires' an expensive treatment. As explained in the first article of this series, of course, the reporter underwent a thorough physical checkup before she embarked on her quack-hunt, and was found to be in one hundred percent perfect condition, with the exception of a 'scarred' area at the bottom tip of her left lung resulting from a childhood attack of tuberculosis and a tendency toward 'hyperthyroidism'—over-activity of the thyroid gland which makes it difficult to put on weight and sometimes causes a slight shortness of breath.

"Dr. Full consented to perform the examination, and took a number of shining, spotlessly clean instruments from loops in a large board literally covered with instruments—most of them unfamiliar to the reporter. The instrument with which he approached first was a tube with a curved dial in its surface and two wires that ended on flat disks growing from its ends. He placed one of the disks on the back of the reporter's right hand and the other on the back of her left. 'Reading the meter,' he called out some number which the attentive receptionist took down on a ruled form. The same procedure was repeated several times, thoroughly covering the reporter's anatomy and thoroughly convincing her that the doctor was a complete quack. The reporter had never seen any such diagnostic procedure practiced during the weeks she put in preparing for this series.

"The doctor then took the ruled sheet from the receptionist, conferred with her in low tones and said: 'You have a slightly overactive thyroid, young woman. And there's something wrong with your left lung—not seriously, but I'd like to take a closer look.'

"He selected an instrument from the board which, the reporter knew, is called a 'speculum'—a scissorlike device which spreads apart body openings such as the orifice of the ear, the nostril and so on, so that a doctor can look in during an examination. The instrument was, however, too large to be an aural or nasal speculum but too small to be anything else. As the *Herald's* reporter was about to ask further questions, the attending receptionist told her: 'It's customary for us to blindfold our patients during lung examinations—do you mind?' The reporter, bewildered, allowed her to tie a spotlessly clean bandage over her eyes, and waited nervously for what would come next.

"She still cannot say exactly what happened while she was blindfolded—but X rays confirm her suspicions. She felt a cold sensation at her ribs on the left side—a cold that seemed to enter inside her body. Then there was a snapping feeling, and the cold sensation was gone. She heard Dr. Full say in a matter-of-fact voice: 'You have an old tubercular scar down there. It isn't doing any particular harm, but an active person like you needs all the oxygen she can get. Lie still and I'll fix it for you.'

"Then there was a repetition of the cold sensation, lasting for a longer time. 'Another batch of alveoli and some more vascular glue,' the *Herald's* reporter heard Dr. Full say, and the receptionist's crisp response to the order. Then the strange sensation departed and the eye-bandage was removed. The reporter saw no scar on her ribs, and yet the doctor assured her: 'That did it. We took out the fibrosis—and a good fibrosis it was, too; it walled off the infection so you're still alive to tell the tale. Then we planted a few clumps of alveoli—they're the little gadgets that get the oxygen from the air you breathe into your blood. I won't monkey with your thyroxin supply. You've got used to being the kind of person you are, and if you suddenly found yourself easygoing and all the rest of it, chances are you'd only be upset. About the backache: just check with the county medical society for the name of a good psychologist or psychiatrist. And look out for quacks; the woods are full of them.'

"The doctor's self-assurance took the reporter's breath away. She asked what the charge woud be, and was told to pay the receptionist fifty dollars. As usual, the reporter delayed paying until she got a receipt signed by the doctor himself, detailing the services for which it paid. Unlike most, the doctor cheerfully wrote: 'For removal of fibrosis from left lung and restoration of alveoli,' and signed it.

"The reporter's first move when she left the sanitarium was to head for the chest specialist who had examined her in preparation for this series. A comparison of X rays taken on the day of the 'operation' and those taken previously would, the *Herald's* reporter then thought, expose Dr. Full as a prince of shyster M.D.'s and quacks.

"The chest specialist made time on his crowded schedule for the reporter, in whose series he has shown a lively interest from the planning stage on. He laughed uproariously in his staid Park Avenue examining room as she described the weird procedure to which she had been subjected. But he did not laugh when he took a chest X ray of the reporter, developed it, dried it, and compared it with the ones he had taken earlier. The chest specialist took six more X rays that afternoon, but finally admitted that they all told the same story. The *Herald's* reporter has it on his authority that the scar she had eighteen days ago from her tuberculosis is now gone and has been replaced by healthy lung-tissue. He declares that this is a happening unparalleled in medical history. He does not go along with the reporter in her firm conviction that Dr. Full is responsible for the change.

"The *Herald's* reporter, however, sees no two ways about it. She concludes that Dr. Bayard Full—whatever his alleged past may have been—is now an unorthodox but highly successful practitioner of medicine, to whose hands the reporter would trust herself in any emergency.

"Not so is the case of 'Rev.' Annie Dimsworth—a female harpy who, under the guise of 'faith,' preys on the ignorant and suffering who come to her sordid 'healing parlor' for help and remain to feed 'Rev.' Annie's bank account, which now totals up to $53,238.64. Tomorrow's article will show, with photostats of bank statements and sworn testimony, that—"

The managing editor turned down "FLANNERY LAST ADD—MEDICAL" and tapped his front teeth with a pencil, trying to think straight. He finally told the copy chief: "Kill the story. Run the teaser as a box." He tore off the last paragraph —the "teaser" about "Rev." Annie—and handed it to the desk man, who stumped back to his masonite horseshoe.

The makeup editor was back, dancing with impatience as he tried to catch the M.E.'s eye. The interphone buzzed with the red light which indicated that the editor and publisher wanted to talk to him. The M.E. thought briefly of a special series on this Dr. Full, decided nobody would believe it and that he probably was a phony anyway. He spiked the story on the "dead" hook and answered his interphone.

Dr. Full had become almost fond of Angie. As his practice had grown to engross the neighborhood illnesses, and then to a corner suite in an uptown taxpayer building, and finally to the sanitarium, she seemed to have grown with it. Oh, he thought, we have our little disputes—

The girl, for instance, was too much interested in money. She had wanted to specialize in cosmetic surgery—removing wrinkles from wealthy old women and whatnot. She didn't realize, at first, that a thing like this was in their trust, that they were the stewards and not the owners of the little black bag and its fabulous contents.

He had tried, ever so cautiously, to analyze them, but without success. All the instruments were slightly radioactive, for instance, but not quite so. They would make a Geiger-Mueller counter indicate, but they would not collapse the leaves of an electroscope. He didn't pretend to be up on the latest developments, but as he understood it, that was just plain *wrong*. Under the highest magnification there were lines on the instruments' superfinished surfaces: incredibly fine lines, engraved in random hatchments which made no particular sense. Their magnetic properties were preposterous. Sometimes the instruments were strongly attracted to magnets, sometimes less so, and sometimes not at all.

Dr. Full had taken X rays in fear and trembling lest he disrupt whatever delicate machinery worked in them. He was *sure* they were not solid, that the handles and perhaps the blades must be mere shells filled with busy little watchworks—but the X rays showed nothing of the sort. Oh, yes—and they were always sterile, and they wouldn't rust. Dust *fell* off them if you shook them: now, that was something he understood. They ionized the dust, or were ionized themselves, or something of the sort. At any rate, he had read of something similar that had to do with phonograph records.

She wouldn't know about that, he proudly thought. She kept the books well enough, and perhaps she gave him a useful prod now and then when he was inclined to settle down. The move from the neighborhood slum to the uptown quarters had been her idea, and so had the sanitarium. Good, good, it enlarged his sphere of usefulness. Let the child have her mink coats and her convertible, as they seemed to be calling roadsters nowadays. He himself was too busy and too old. He had so much to make up for.

Dr. Full thought happily of his Master Plan. She would not like it much, but she would have to see the logic of it. This marvelous thing that had happened to them must be handed on. She was herself no doctor; even though the instruments practically ran themselves, there was more to doctoring than skill. There were the ancient canons of the healing art. And so, having seen the logic of it, Angie would yield; she would assent to his turning over the little black bag to all humanity.

He would probably present it to the College of Surgeons, with as little fuss as possible—well, perhaps a *small* ceremony, and he would like a souvenir of the occasion, a cup or a framed testimonial. It would be a relief to have the thing out of his hands, in a way; let the giants of the healing art decide who was to have its benefits. No, Angie would understand. She was a goodhearted girl.

It was nice that she had been showing so much interest in the surgical side lately—asking about the instruments, reading the instruction card for hours, even practicing on guinea pigs. If something of his love for humanity had been communicated to her, old Dr. Full sentimentally thought, his life would not have been in vain. Surely she would realize that a greater good would be served by surrendering the instruments to wiser hands than theirs, and by throwing aside the cloak of secrecy necessary to work on their small scale.

Dr. Full was in the treatment room that had been the brown-stone's front parlor; through the window he saw Angie's yellow convertible roll to a stop before the stoop. He liked the way she looked as she climbed the stairs; neat, not flashy, he thought. A sensible girl like her, she'd understand. There was somebody with her—a fat woman, puffing up the steps, overdressed and petulant. Now, what could she want?

Angie let herself in and went into the treatment room, followed by the fat woman. "Doctor," said the blond girl gravely, "may I present Mrs. Coleman?" Charm school had not taught her everything, but Mrs. Coleman, evidently *nouveau riche*, thought the doctor, did not notice the blunder.

"Miss Aquella told me *so* much about you, doctor, and your remarkable system!" she gushed.

Before he could answer, Angie smoothly interposed: "Would you excuse us for just a moment, Mrs. Coleman?"

She took the doctor's arm and led him into the reception hall. "Listen," she said swiftly, "I know this goes against your grain, but I couldn't pass it up. I met this old thing in the exercise class at Elizabeth Barton's. Nobody else'll talk to her there. She's a widow. I guess her husband was a black marketeer or something, and she has a pile of dough. I gave her a line about how you had a system of massaging wrinkles out. My idea is, you blindfold her, cut her neck open with the Cutaneous Series knife, shoot some Firmol into the muscles, spoon out some of that blubber with an Adipose Series curette and spray it all with Skintite. When you take the blindfold off she's got rid of a wrinkle and doesn't know what happened. She'll pay five hundred dollars. Now, don't say 'no,' doc. Just this once, let's do it my way, can't you? I've been working on this deal all along too, haven't I?"

"Oh," said the doctor, "very well." He was going to have to tell her about the Master Plan before long anyway. He would let her have it her way this time.

Back in the treatment room, Mrs. Coleman had been thinking things over. She told the doctor sternly as he entered: "Of course, your system is permanent, isn't it?"

"It is, madam," he said shortly. "Would you please lie down there? Miss Aquella, get a sterile three-inch bandage for Mrs. Coleman's eyes." He turned his back on the fat woman to avoid conversation, and pretended to be adjusting the lights. Angie blindfolded the woman, and the doctor selected the instruments he would need. He handed the blond girl a pair of retractors, and told her: "Just slip the corners of the blades in as I cut—" She gave him an alarmed look, and gestured at the reclining woman. He lowered his voice: "Very well. Slip in the corners and rock them along the incision. I'll tell you when to pull them out."

Dr. Full held the Cutaneous Series knife to his eyes as he adjusted the little slide for three centimeters' depth. He sighed a little as he recalled that its last use had been in the extirpation of an "inoperable" tumor of the throat.

"Very well," he said, bending over the woman. He tried a tentative pass through her tissues. The blade dipped in and flowed through them, like a finger through quicksilver, with no wound left in the wake. Only the retractors could hold the edges of the incision apart.

Mrs. Coleman stirred and jabbered: "Doctor, that felt so peculiar! Are you sure you're rubbing the right way?"

"Quite sure, madam," said the doctor wearily. "Would you please try not to talk during the massage?"

He nodded at Angie, who stood ready with the retractors. The blade sank in to its three centimeters, miraculously cutting only the dead horny tissues of the epidermis and the live tissue of the dermis, pushing aside mysteriously all major and minor blood vessels and muscular tissue, declining to affect any system or organ except the one it was—tuned to, could you say? The doctor didn't know the answer, but he felt tired and bitter at this prostitution. Angie slipped in the retractor blades and rocked them as he withdrew the knife, then pulled to separate the lips of the incision. It bloodlessly exposed an unhealthy string of muscle, sagging in a dead-looking loop from blue-gray ligaments. The doctor took a hypo, Number IX, preset to "g," and raised it to his eye level. The mist came and went; there probably was no possibility of an embolus with one of these gadgets, but why take chances? He shot one cc. of "g"—identified as "Firmol" by the card—into the muscle. He and Angie watched as it tightened up against the pharynx.

He took the Adipose Series curette, a small one, and spooned out yellowish tissue, dropping it into the incinerator box, and then nodded to Angie. She eased out the retractors and the gaping incision slipped together into unbroken skin, sagging now. The doctor had the atomizer—dialed to "Skintite"—ready. He sprayed, and the skin shrank up into the new firm throat line.

As he replaced the instruments, Angie removed Mrs. Coleman's bandage and gaily announced: "We're finished! And there's a mirror in the reception hall—"

Mrs. Coleman didn't need to be invited twice. With incredulous fingers she felt her chin, and then dashed for the hall. The doctor grimaced as he heard her yelp of delight, and Angie turned to him with a tight smile. "I'll get the money and get her out," she said. "You won't have to be bothered with her any more."

He was grateful for that much.

She followed Mrs. Coleman into the reception hall, and the doctor dreamed over the case of instruments. A ceremony, certainly—he was *entitled* to one. Not everybody, he thought, would turn such a sure source of money over to the good of humanity. But you reached an age when money mattered less, and when you thought of these things you had done that *might* be open to misunderstanding if, just if, there chanced to be any of that, well, that judgment business. The doctor wasn't a religious man, but you certainly found yourself thinking hard about some things when your time drew near—

Angie was back, with a bit of paper in her hands. "Five hundred dollars," she said matter-of-factly. "And you realize, don't you, that we could go over her an inch at a time—at five hundred dollars an inch?"

"I've been meaning to talk to you about that," he said.

There was bright fear in her eyes, he thought—but why?

"Angie, you've been a good girl and an understanding girl, but we can't keep this up forever, you know."

"Let's talk about it some other time," she said flatly. "I'm tired now."

"No—I really feel we've gone far enough on our own. The instruments—"

"Don't say it, doc!" she hissed. "Don't say it, or you'll be sorry!" In her face there was a look that reminded him of the hollow-eyed, gaunt-faced, dirty-blond creature she had been. From under the charm-school finish there burned the guttersnipe whose infancy had been spent on a sour and filthy mattress, whose childhood had been play in the littered alley and whose adolescence had been the sweatshops and the aimless gatherings at night under the glaring street lamps.

He shook his head to dispel the puzzling notion. "It's this way," he patiently began. "I told you about the family that invented the O.B. forceps and kept them a secret for so many generations, how they could have given them to the world but didn't?"

"They knew what they were doing," said the guttersnipe flatly.

"Well, that's neither here nor there," said the doctor, irritated. "My mind is made up about it. I'm going to turn the instruments over to the College of Surgeons. We have enough money to be comfortable. You can even have the house. I've been thinking of going to a warmer climate, myself." He felt peeved with her for making the unpleasant scene. He was unprepared for what happened next.

Angie snatched the little black bag and dashed for the door, with panic in her eyes. He scrambled after her, catching her arm, twisting it in a sudden rage. She clawed at his face with her free hand, babbling curses. Somehow, somebody's finger touched the little black bag, and it opened grotesquely into the enormous board, covered with shining instruments, large and small. Half a dozen of them joggled loose and fell to the floor.

"*Now* see what you've done!" roared the doctor, unreasonably. Her hand was still viselike on the handle, but she was standing still, trembling with choked-up rage. The doctor bent stiffly to pick up the fallen instruments. Unreasonable girl! he thought bitterly. Making a scene—

Pain drove in between his shoulderblades and he fell face down. The light ebbed. "Unreasonable girl!" he tried to croak. And then: "They'll know I tried, anyway—"

Angie looked down on his prone body, with the handle of the Number Six Cautery Series knife protruding from it. "—will cut through all tissues. Use for amputations before you spread on the Re-Gro. Extreme caution should be used in the vicinity of vital organs and major blood vessels or nerve trunks—"

"I didn't mean to do that," said Angie, dully, cold with horror. Now the detective would come, the implacable detective who would reconstruct the crime from the dust in the room. She would run and turn and twist, but the detective would find her out and she would be tried in a courtroom before a judge and jury; the lawyer would make speeches, but the jury would convict her anyway, and the headlines would scream: "BLOND KILLER GUILTY!" and she'd maybe get the chair, walking down a plain corridor where a beam of sunlight struck through the dusty air, with an iron door at the end of it. Her mink, her convertible, her dresses, the handsome man she was going to meet and marry—

The mist of cinematic clichés cleared, and she knew what she would do next. Quite steadily, she picked the incinerator box from its loop in the board—a metal cube with a different-textured spot on one side. "—to dispose of fibroses or other unwanted matter, simply touch the disk—" You dropped something in and touched the disk. There was a sort of soundless whistle, very powerful and unpleasant if you were too close, and a sort of lightless flash. When you opened the box again, the contents were gone. Angie took another of the Cautery Series knives and went grimly to work. Good thing there wasn't any blood to speak of— She finished the awful task in three hours.

She slept heavily that night, totally exhausted by the wringing emotional demands of the slaying and the subsequent horror. But in the morning, it was as though the doctor had never been there. She ate breakfast, dressed with unusual care—and then undid the unusual care. Nothing out of the ordinary, she told herself. Don't do one thing different from the way you would have done it before. After a day or two, you can phone the cops. Say he walked out spoiling for a drunk, and you're worried. But don't rush it, baby—*don't rush it.*

Mrs. Coleman was due at ten A.M. Angie had counted on being able to talk the doctor into at least one more five-hundred-dollar session. She'd have to do it herself now—but she'd have to start sooner or later.

The woman arrived early. Angie explained smoothly: "The doctor asked me to take care of the massage today. Now that he has the tissue-firming process beginning, it only requires somebody trained in his methods—" As she spoke, her eyes swiveled to the instrument case—open! She cursed herself for the single flaw as the woman followed her gaze and recoiled.

"What are those things!" she demanded. "Are you going to cut me with them? I *thought* there was something fishy—"

"Please, Mrs. Coleman," said Angie, "please, *dear* Mrs. Coleman—you don't understand about the . . . the massage instruments!"

"Massage instruments, my foot!" squabbled the woman shrilly. "That doctor *operated* on me. Why, he might have killed me!"

Angie wordlessly took one of the smaller Cutaneous Series knives and passed it through her forearm. The blade flowed like a finger through quicksilver, leaving no wound in its wake. *That* should convince the old cow!

It didn't convince her, but it did startle her. "What did you do with it? The blade folds up into the handle—that's it!"

"Now look closely, Mrs. Coleman," said Angie, thinking desperately of the five hundred dollars. "Look very closely and you'll see that the, uh, the sub-skin massager simply slips beneath the tissues without doing any harm, tightening and firming the muscles themselves instead of having to work through layers of skin and adipose tissue. It's the secret of the doctor's method. Now, how can outside massage have the effect that we got last night?"

Mrs. Coleman was beginning to calm down. "It *did* work, all right," she admitted, stroking the new line of her neck. "But your arm's one thing and my neck's another! Let me see you do that with your neck!"

Angie smiled—

Al returned to the clinic after an excellent lunch that had almost reconciled him to three more months he would have to spend on duty. And then, he thought, and then a blessed year at the blessedly supernormal South Pole working on his specialty —which happened to be telekinesis exercises for ages three to six. Meanwhile, of course, the world had to go on and of course he had to shoulder his share in the running of it.

Before settling down to desk work he gave a routine glance at the bag board. What he saw made him stiffen with shocked

surprise. A red light was on next to one of the numbers—the first
since he couldn't think when. He read off the number and murmured "OK, 674101. That fixes *you*." He put the number on a
card sorter and in a moment the record was in his hand. Oh, yes
—Hemingway's bag. The big dummy didn't remember how or
where he had lost it; none of them ever did. There were hundreds of them floating around.

Al's policy in such cases was to leave the bag turned on. The
things practically ran themselves, it was practically impossible
to do harm with them, so whoever found a lost one might as
well be allowed to use it. You turn it off, you have a social loss
—you leave it on, it may do some good. As he understood it,
and not very well at that, the stuff wasn't "used up." A temporalist had tried to explain it to him with little success that the
prototypes in the transmitter *had been transducted* through a
series of point-events of transfinite cardinality. Al had innocently
asked whether that meant prototypes had been stretched, so to
speak, through all time, and the temporalist had thought he was
joking and left in a huff.

"Like to see him do this," thought Al darkly, as he telekinized
himself to the combox, after a cautious look to see that there
were no medics around. To the box he said: "Police chief," and
then to the police chief: "There's been a homicide committed
with Medical Instrument Kit 674101. It was lost some months
ago by one of my people, Dr. John Hemingway. He didn't have
a clear account of the circumstances."

The police chief groaned and said: "I'll call him in and question him." He was to be astonished by the answers, and was to
learn that the homicide was well out of his jurisdiction.

Al stood for a moment at the bag board by the glowing red
light that had been sparked into life by a departing vital force
giving, as its last act, the warning that Kit 674101 was in homi-
cidal hands. With a sigh, Al pulled the plug and the light went
out.

"Yah," jeered the woman. "You'd fool around with my neck,
but you wouldn't risk your own with that thing!"

Angie smiled with serene confidence a smile that was to shock
hardened morgue attendants. She set the Cutaneous Series knife

to three centimeters before drawing it across her neck. Smiling, knowing the blade would cut only the dead horny tissue of the epidermis and the live tissue of the dermis, mysteriously push aside all major and minor blood vessels and muscular tissue—

Smiling, the knife plunging in and its microtomesharp metal shearing through major and minor blood vessels and muscular tissue and pharynx, Angie cut her throat.

In the few minutes it took the police, summoned by the shrieking Mrs. Coleman, to arrive, the instruments had become crusted with rust, and the flasks which had held vascular glue and clumps of pink, rubbery alveoli and spare gray cells and coils of receptor nerves held only black slime, and from them when opened gushed the foul gases of decomposition.

PHILIP LATHAM

This story is a perfectly fascinating example of the way in which a writer who is also a first-rate scientist can combine pleasure with business. It is no secret that "Philip Latham" is actually Dr. Robert S. Richardson, for many years on the staff of the Mount Wilson and Palomar Observatories, and coauthor of textbooks on astronomy and symposia on astronautics. He was one of the first professional astronomers to become seriously interested in space flight and publicly enthusiastic about it.

Besides numerous popular articles, Dr. Richardson has written several apocalyptic short stories on the Doomsday theme; the one that follows, however, shows him in a slightly more benign mood.

"The Blindness" contains so many elements of interest that it is hard to know which to discuss first. It opens with an exciting event which will—repeat, *will*—occur in 1987, as it has occurred every seventy-seven years since the beginning of history. With any luck, most of us should witness it.

Dr. Richardson deserves no great credit for predicting the return of Halley's comet, but his account of its first sighting has the ring of absolute authenticity. In fact, very soon after he published this story, he was himself involved in a similar situation—the discovery of the asteroid Icarus by Baade on June 26, 1949. It is almost uncanny to compare the opening events in this work of fiction with what actually happened to Dr. Richardson only three years later: here are a few quotations from his article, "The Discovery of Icarus," in *Scientific American* for April, 1965:

"When Baade returned to the Mount Wilson and Palomar office at Pasadena, he asked Seth B. Nicholson and me if we would like to compute an orbit for the new body. . . . Nicholson had become an expert at tracking down minor members of the Solar System and determining their orbits. As a graduate student at the Lick Observatory in 1914, he had discovered the ninth satellite of Jupiter (J IX) and later at Mount Wilson he had found J X, J XI and J XII. I had become familiar with orbit work by helping him keep track of his satellites, which were always getting lost."

The passage of some twenty years has also made this little story even more timely in other respects. Dr. Richardson's account of the chaotic state of nuclear theory in the 1960's is only too near the truth. (At the moment, as far as I can gather, there are rather more "fundamental" particles than elements.) And the vital importance of the ozone layer to life on this planet has recently become a matter of great concern, for some experts believe that the hundreds of tons of burned propellants our giant rockets will soon be dumping in the upper atmosphere may destroy this protective umbrella.

If they are right, we will not have to wait until 1987. . . .

The Blindness

It must have taken all of Blakeslee's self-control to leave the plate in the developer for the full eleven minutes.

If it had been my plate, I think I might have cheated a little on that eleventh minute, especially with an energetic developer like DQ-17. But Blakeslee rocked the tray methodically back and forth, up and down, with no more visible impatience than if it had been a snapshot of his Aunt Mable. And then, after the plate was in the hypo, he waited another full eleven minutes before removing and rinsing.

"Now, Latham, if we may have the lights, please."

I snapped on the switch, revealing the immaculate interior of the 300-inch darkroom. Blakeslee tapped the eight-by-ten plate gently to detach a few lingering drops of water, then held it up before the blank white rectangle of the viewer. I caught my breath at the sight. A perfect negative! Exposure time, seeing, guiding, development—everything exactly right. The star trails were as sharp as if they had been etched by an engraver. But where was the object we were seeking? Of that I was unable to detect a trace.

Blakeslee was examining the region around 20 Geminorum with a low-power eyepiece. After several minutes of close scrutiny he handed the plate and eyepiece to me without a word. At first I could discern only the multitude of black and gray star trails with here and there a defect due to irregular clustering of silver grains. Then I found it! A hazy smudge. The merest trace of faint nebulosity with a tiny nucleus buried in the center.

A wave of emotion welled up within me such as I had never experienced before in my whole life. A sudden realization of the transientness of human existence and the eternity of space and time.

I returned the plate to Blakeslee with trembling hands. "It's back again," I whispered.

He smiled faintly. "Yes, back again. Halley's comet—back again after three-quarters of a century."

Blakeslee, having finished his second cup of coffee, lighted his old briar pipe and subsided into the battered armchair that faces the library windows toward the south. The discovery plate of Halley's comet was in the drying cabinet from where it would soon be transferred to the measuring machine upstairs. In the meantime, with the comet safely trapped, we could afford to relax in the luxurious contemplation of two years' work brought to a triumphant conclusion. Gazing out through the library windows at the dim lights of the Horological Laboratory below us, I wondered how many others in the teeming scientific line of the Nucleus dared snatch a moment of quiet satisfaction.

When in 1951, the Congress of the United States passed an Act to "establish in the state of Arizona an institution for the investigation, exploration, and general inquiry into the fundamental nature of matter and energy, with special emphasis upon the structure of the atom," the Nucleus was born. Consisting at first of a physics building, a cyclotron, and chemistry laboratory, hastily constructed, inadequately staffed, and miserably financed, under the leadership of a series of vigorous directors, gradually every type of instrument was assembled that might contribute to our knowledge of the atom. The central collection of laboratories and machine shops came to be known as the Nucleus, after the old Bohr atom; and the lines of dwellings surrounding it, the Shell. The 300-inch telescope, with its mirror cast from a single block of obsidian from Iceland, was a comparatively recent addition. Many of the scientists had lived within the Nucleus during their entire residence. I still felt like a stranger in my bachelor headquarters at the edge of the Shell, where the inhabitants are regarded as loosely attached, or valence, electrons.

I doubt if atomic theory can ever hope again to reach the state of perfection that it attained back in the early years of the feverish '50s. The wave theory of Schrodinger and the quantum mechanics of Heisenberg reigned supreme. As far as one could see in 4 pi directions nothing met the eye but a gleaming expanse of beautifully explained observations.

Then in 1957 Sondelius discovered the planetron, the nuclear particle that in a sense put the second dimension into atomic physics. Previously our concept of the fine structure of matter had been essentially linear or one-dimensional, like a straight line. In the middle was the neutron without charge. To the right were the proton and positron with unit positive charge; on the left, the electron with unit negative charge. You could think of them as beads strung upon a wire. By combining them in the proper way the whole periodic table of the elements could be built up.

Trouble with the planetron is that it stubbornly refuses to fit into this neat little scheme of things. For it is neither positive nor negative, nor yet is it neutral. A particle of mass 1111e. Unquestionably it is endowed with a charge of *some* kind, of that we are very sure. But just as we cannot comprehend a fourth dimension in space, no more can we comprehend a charge that departs from the straight line of plus and minus quantities. What is the planetron? That is the question science has been straining to answer for the last thirty years.

Following the collapse of the wave theory, there ensued a chaotic period of about five years when physicists had no atom whatever to guide them. Gradually there arose the idea of what has been termed the "psychological atom," an intangible mass endowed with virtually human powers of instinct and perception. It is as hopeless to try to describe or make a model of this atom as it is to draw a diagram of the character of a man. Yet we all have a fairly clear idea of what is meant by character, and from experience can predict with assurance how an individual would behave in a certain situation. In somewhat the same way, from a knowledge of the facts of observations concerning the different atoms, we can predict rather accurately how they will react under various temperatures, pressures, electrical excitation, et cetera.

Are you surprised to find that scientists, after shaking the world with the atomic bomb in 1945, chose to seclude themselves within the sanctuary of the Nucleus, instead of taking an active part in political affairs? Brother, you don't know scientists. They scurried back to their former jobs like the introvert rabbits they are, content to nibble again upon the meager rations which an indifferent population grudgingly allowed them.

But then according to Murdock, our cynical young astrophysicist and chief ticket-taker on visitors' night at the observatory, men generally get precisely what they deserve in this life. Perhaps he is right at that. Come to think of it, Murdock generally is right. Which reminds me that I owe him two dollars since that big sunspot last week failed to create a magnetic storm— something that looked like a cinch bet at the time if I ever saw one.

So much for the scientific life on Julian Date 2447045, or September 5, 1987, in ordinary terms.

Dreaming of the manifold projects going on night and day within the Nucleus, I had nearly dozed off when Blakeslee yanked me out of my reverie.

"Ever think of the heavenly bodies as living things, Latham?"

Now this is not the type of question that the director of an observatory is likely to hurl at his assistants early on every morning. Consequently, I had to ponder for some time before hazarding a reply.

"Why, yes, subconsciously I believe I have. The Sun with its family of planets and Jupiter with his thirteen satellites naturally remind one of masterful dominating parents. The Moon is a cold white goddess." I paused to think some more. "Uranus and Neptune are great beasts prowling in semidarkness. Sirius is a sparkling lady with a glass of champagne." I laughed nervously to cover my embarrassment at thus waxing poetic. "I guess that's as far as I can go along that line."

To my surprise, Blakeslee's deep-set eyes showed no amusement. Instead his face was deadly serious.

"I've often wondered how this world would appear to Halley's comet, if that flimsy conglomeration of gas and stone were endowed with super-radionic vision. What would such a creature, forced to pass this way every seventy-seven years, think of this little planet of ours?"

As if to answer his own question, he strolled over to the reference books by the fireplace and without even stretching his lanky frame, easily removed the worn copy of Sherwood's *Guide to World History* from the topmost shelf.

"This afternoon I jotted down the dates of all the returns of Halley's comet. Let's look up a few at random. I'm curious to know what it would have seen as it came this way."

Blakeslee turned the pages near the front of the volume. "Now here's the return of 66 A.D. and first persecution of Christians begins by Nero. Doesn't sound like a very auspicious start, does it?"

He turned some more leaves. "Suppose we try 374 A.D. The Huns advanced into central Europe. The Visigoths, expelled by the Huns, are allowed by Valerius to settle in Thrace. Very considerate of him. Wonder what his motive was?

"Let's go on to the next return. Here we are in 452 A.D. 'Attila ravages Italy. Rome is saved by its bishop, Leo the Great.'"

Blakeslee was talking more to himself than to me. "Now comes the most famous return of them all—1066 A.D.: 'Harold II elected king; killed at the Battle of Hastings. 1146: Thebes and Corinth plundered by the Sicilians. 1455: Outbreak of the War of the Roses. 1608: Henry IV plans downfall of Hapsburgs. 1683: France invades the Spanish Netherlands, siege of Rome by the Turks.'

"Now we're getting down to modern times. The pace quickens. What have we here? 'Invasion of Canada in 1759. Death of Wolfe. Quebec taken. Russians and Austrians defeat Frederick the Great. 1836: Massacre of the Alamo and defeat of the Mexicans at San Jacinto.'"

He paused and drew a deep breath. "And finally the last return in 1910. The world must have looked pretty good for a change. Everything pretty peaceful. Only a hint here and there of the holocaust to come."

"Anything about 1987?" I inquired.

Blakeslee closed the book grimly and replaced it upon the shelf.

"Remember the end of World War III, in 1968? How the delegates from each country solemnly vowed that never again would such destruction be set free. In less than twelve hours they had seen one of the most powerful nations on earth destroyed, wiped out, utterly and completely obliterated as if it had never existed. Those honorable men were never more serious than when they pledged their sacred word to keep the peace."

He laughed bitterly. "And today it's merely a matter of weeks or days till World War IV."

Suddenly he turned on me as if I had dared to challenge his statement. "Right after a war a nation is like a man coming out of a drunk. How awful he feels! How can a man live and feel so awful? It's never, never going to happen again. And he means it—*then!*

"But wait till he's sobered up and back on his feet. The old urge returns, the old restlessness, the old lust for exhibitionism and power, that will not down or be put aside.

"Do you know what I would do if I were Halley's comet?" he blazed. "I would destroy this world and myself along with it in one grand and glorious smashup. So that never again would I be condemned to return century after century to witness such suffering and stupidity."

The mood left him as suddenly as it had come and he was

Blakeslee once more, cold, aloof, objective. He glanced at his watch.

"Our plate should be dry by this time. I'm anxious to see how closely the comet is following our predicted path. That close brush with Saturn could have had serious consequences. It wouldn't have taken much to make a big difference in the eccentricity and the longitude of the node." He looked at me quizzically.

I got it without being told. "Murdock said he'd be glad to help with the measurements. I've had the astrographic zone and the comparison stars selected for a week. With good luck we should have the position by morning."

"Excellent," said Blakeslee. "In that case, I'll leave it entirely in your hands. Don't hesitate to wake me when you've got the answer."

"If you say so," I told him, getting up and stretching.

I was mildly surprised to find Murdock in the measuring room seated before one of the computing machines. From the pile of cigarette stubs in the ashtray I judged he was at grips with the praseodymium atom again.

"How's the spectrum analysis coming?" I greeted.

"Not so good," he muttered, his dark face flushed. "Trying to find combination differences in praseodymium VII is like trying to work a crossword puzzle in three dimensions blindfolded."

"Well, suppose you exert your talents on this plate for a while," I said, extracting our precious photograph from its envelope.

Murdock regarded it without enthusiasm. "One of those rush jobs, I'll bet."

"Just the discovery plate of Halley's comet is all."

He whistled. "Don't tell me the rest. Blakeslee is champing at the bit wondering if it fits his ephemeris or not. OK. Let's get going."

He switched on the light behind the big Reuchlin measuring machine, swept some papers in the wastebasket, and began adjusting the eyepiece. "I feel wide awake now. Suppose I measure and you record."

"Suits me," I agreed, handing him the plate. He held it up

to the light inspecting the star images critically. There was very little evidence of coma thanks to the zero-power correcting lens we use at the Newtonian focus of the 300-inch. I had already drawn ink lines around the stars I wished to use for comparison.

Murdock opened the astrographic catalogue to the page I had marked. Fortunately we were working in a zone assigned to the reliable Observatoire de Bordeaux, so that I had every confidence in their results.

"First star to be measured will be number 56 on cliché 1003," he announced. "Zone plus fifteen degrees and six hours twenty-eight minutes." He bent over to read the fine print at the bottom of the page. "Measured by Mesdemoiselles E. Chatenay and G. Vedrome."

"All I want is the astronomical part," I retorted. "You can leave out the sex."

Chuckling, he moved his head from side to side testing the optical system for parallax. After a few more minor adjustments he turned the horizontal dial slowly from left to right.

"I'll give you the setting in X first." He brought the cross-hairs up until they bisected the image of the star. "It is ten point one two seven four."

"Ten point one two seven four," I repeated, writing it down.

He reversed the dial, approached the setting from left to right again. "Ten point one two six eight."

"Point one two six eight."

With the approach of dawn the Nucleus had grown very still. But for us the long grind had only begun.

Blakeslee opened his door so promptly that I suspect he was sitting up waiting for me. Taking the measures, he opened a loose-leaf notebook with "H. C." stamped on the cover in large letters, and turned to the last page where the ephemeris was typed. After a few minutes' work he jotted down the predicted right ascension and declination interpolated for our position that night. We stared at them in awe.

"Why they're almost identical!" I exclaimed.

Blakeslee frowned. "This is the true mean place of Halley's comet referred to the equator and equinox of 1987.0, isn't it?" he asked, indicating my figures.

"That's right," I responded.

"Hm-m-m!" he sighed, still frowning.

Again I realized I was confronted by one of the curious quirks of the scientific mind. Nothing worries some scientists so much as having their predictions agree precisely with their observations. It recalled the first job assigned to me of making some thermocouple measures on the Moon. The astronomer for whom I worked didn't give me the least hint of the results I was to get. He simply told me how to operate the apparatus and turned me loose. When I showed him my galvanometer deflections he was dumfounded. They gave temperatures for the Moon's subsolar point that agreed exactly with his computations! So immediately he got busy trying to find out what was the matter with them!

Now Blakeslee looked as glum as a navigator who had plotted his wind in backward. Finally after much figuring he shoved the paper reluctantly back at me.

"Well, you might as well get this off to Harvard. Need the code? That I.A.U. handbook should be around here some place."

"No. I think I can do it from memory. It's very simple."

While I was toiling over the message in the measuring room, Murdock came in for his praseodymium notes.

"Well, do tell," he said, "is Halley's comet following that high-powered path you fellows laid down for it, or does it have ideas of its own?"

"The agreement is almost exact," I said rather complacently.

"How's Blakeslee taking it?"

"Pretty hard." We both grinned.

First I wrote out the telegram in everyday language.

COMET HALLEY HAS BEEN OBSERVED ON SEPTEMBER 4, 1987, BY BLAKESLEE AND LATHAM AT 10 HOURS 50.1 MINUTES UNIVERSAL TIME AT RIGHT ASCENSION (1987.0) 6 HOURS 28 MINUTES 31.3 SECONDS DECLINATION (1987.0) PLUS 17 DEGREES 11 MINUTES 30 SECONDS. MAGNITUDE 15. DIFFUSE WITH CENTRAL NUCLEUS.

After scanning this with the utmost care word for word I proceeded to condense it into the official code adopted by the International Astronomical Union.

1987 September 5

The Nucleus, Arizona
COMET HALLEY 04157 SEPTEMBER 10501 06283 21711
81330 23982 BLAKESLEE LATHAM

When I had this on the wire, Murdock deigned to read it over.

"By the way, how close is Halley's comet coming this trip?"

"It will be slightly under a million and a quarter miles on May 1, 1988," I said. "This is closer than any comet has ever come before. The previous record-holder was Lexell's comet 'way back in 1770 that came within a million and a half miles."

Murdock looked a trifle less bored if possible. "So we may expect some excitement along about May Day, eh? Lots of little people running around getting panicky, and all that." He yawned. "Wake me up when it happens."

I was dead tired myself, and lost no time in getting to bed in my room at the observatory. Although I had not slept for twenty-four hours, yet my mind was racing so that I tossed restlessly for half an hour. At last I got up, took half a grain of phyllonal, and climbed back under the covers. Faintly from down the hall I could hear Murdock's radio giving the seven-o'clock news report, something about war tension rises in Turkestan and Persia. Five minutes later I was sound asleep.

The days that followed found me on the go every moment, photographing Halley's comet after midnight and measuring and reducing plates in the afternoon. Also, I tried to keep our regular program going in the forepart of the night of high-dispersion spectrograms on emission-type B stars. Since Congress had failed to come through with an appropriation for an extra night assistant, I got it in the neck, as usual. There were times when I had to drive myself pretty hard. The comet returned to follow Blakeslee's calculated path with uncanny precision, like a high-frequency controlled rocket.

About the middle of February Halley's comet became visible to the unaided eye if you knew exactly where to look. People began calling up by the dozen wanting to know when it would be nearest the Earth, if there was likely to be a collision, would we all be suffocated by poison gas, et cetera, et cetera? In fact, people grew so agitated about the comet that sometimes it actually edged the war news off the front page. Murdock wrote down the answers to questions people asked most frequently, so that when called to the phone he could reel off long numbers without a second's hesitation, thus acquiring a wholly unmerited reputation as a cometary expert.

Waiting in the early morning for Halley's comet to rise over the dark pines in the northeast, watching its soft filmy structure come up in the developer, following it against the glittering background of stars, night after night for weeks, gradually a strange feeling took possession of me such as I had never felt toward an inanimate object before. I can best express it as a conviction that Halley's comet and I existed for each other alone. One must remember the strained unnatural conditions under which we all were working. I was absorbed in Halley's comet. I lived with it. There was not a waking moment when it was entirely out of my mind.

Speeding sunward the comet behaved like a living thing, changing erratically in form and brightness, as unpredictable as a woman. Now it would die down in luminosity, then flare up again as brilliant jets streamed from the nucleus in gracefully rounded envelopes. On nights when Murdock or Blakeslee had the exclusive use of the telescope I felt acutely jealous. Wasn't it Balzac who wrote a story about a fellow who fell in love with a tiger?[1] Well, I won't go so far as to say I fell in love with Halley's comet, but I must confess that I came to regard it—very secretly—with a deep sense of personal possession and attachment.

By April, Halley's comet was within one hundred twenty million miles of the Earth and fifty-four million miles of the Sun. Have you ever had a nightmare in which a huge ghostly figure towers menacingly above you, threatening you with some horrible fate, so awful as to be beyond the power of words to express or the mind to contemplate? That was the feeling Halley's comet inspired as it rose in the morning sky. People stood facing the dawn huddled close together, as if afraid to view the intruder from outer space alone. At first they watched in hushed silence, speaking to one another only in whispers. But as the

[1]Yes. "A Passion in the Desert." Ed.

pale specter loomed larger and larger in the heavens, a sort of uneasy restlessness would occasionally run through the assemblage, marked by excited mutterings and outcries. Women were frequently overcome, partly by persons jostling roughly against them but more often purely from dread engendered by contemplation of the comet itself. Many cases of trance, somnambulism, and paralysis were reported which psychiatrists claimed were entirely hysterical in origin.

Naturally all sorts of rumors and predictions spread about the comet, and the wilder they were the more ready people were to believe them. Despite repeated assurances from the highest authorities that no possible evil could be associated with the approach of Halley's comet, nevertheless there developed in the public mind the firm conviction that it foretold the final destruction of mankind, the "death, and mourning, and famine," prophesied in the Book of Revelation. Those of us in the Nucleus never ceased to marvel at the hold superstition has upon the human race. Here we had flattered ourselves that we lived in a rational scientific age when objects such as comets were thoroughly understood. Yet I doubt if the darkest hours of the Middle Ages ever beheld scenes such as we witnessed in Anno Domini 1988.

Gradually a form of mania for destruction and revelry seized people which even presumably sane and well-educated individuals were unable to resist. So-called comet orgies occurred all over the globe in which hundreds were killed and property damage ran into the millions. In Lisbon a mob ranged unchecked for three days before troops were able to restore some semblance of order.

Then, just as people were becoming partially reassured that Halley's comet was indeed merely a "harmless bag of nothing," as Professor Challis of the University of Illinois characterized it, the very worst thing imaginable happened. The old premier of China, Ts'ai Lun, certainly one of the most influential men in the world, was delivering an address in which he implored the people to come to their senses and quit pointing to Halley's comet as an evil omen in the sky. Just as he was ridiculing the notion that the comet could possibly harm anyone, he was stricken by coronary thrombosis and died on the platform before help could reach him. Riots immediately flared anew with increased violence and now no appeal to reason made the slightest impression.

Scientists—especially astronomers—came in for plenty of abuse. People associated us with the comet and in some obscure way felt that we should get busy and do something about it. Twice on Saturday evenings when the telescope is thrown open to visitors members of the staff were attacked by cranks; and one night a rock came hurtling through the opening in the dome, narrowly missing the big mirror and laying Murdock out cold for a couple of minutes. Eventually the situation grew so serious that the authorities were forced to erect a high barb-wire fence around the entire Shell. Sentries were posted at all the gates and everyone rigorously excluded except the scientific personnel.

Despite the unsettled times we managed to keep our observing program going pretty much according to plan. Probably never again would astronomers have an opportunity to study a large comet at such close range, and we were determined that posterity should not find us wanting.

Apart from its sensational aspect, the most interesting feature about Halley's comet as it neared perihelion was the extraordinary development of the carbon spectrum. Murdock and I got a complete series of overlapping spectra from 12.000 angstroms in the infrared down to the beginning of the ozone absorption of 2900 in the ultraviolet. The cynogen band heads at wavelengths 3596, 3883 and 4216 were always conspicuous, while the Swan band system of carbon grew in strength until it dominated the whole spectrum in the blue, green and yellow. The region around the (1.0) 4737 band was particularly interesting. We had no trouble in detecting the faint isotope band at 4744.5 due to the carbon molecule $C_{13}C_{12}$. In addition, Murdock was highly elated over what he believes to be a new band system of CO for which he has been able to make a tentative vibrational analysis.

One evening near the summer solstice I had strolled out on the railing that surrounds the 300-inch dome to watch the sunset. The weather had been oppressively warm during the past week, and now a hot dry wind had risen, rendering the air electric with tension, and sending up clouds of brown dust and leaves. If we had been in Haiti instead of Arizona, I would have said there would be voodoo going on before the night was over.

Whether it was because of the dust or whether it was my overwrought imagination, the whole landscape seemed lit up by an unnatural bluish-red tint, as if seen through a lens poorly corrected for chromatic aberration. The curious part was that when I looked at a distant bright object by averted vision it appeared vividly colored, but upon regarding it directly the effect vanished. I was experimenting to see if the light might possibly be polarized in some way when Blakeslee joined me. He was sucking on his briar pipe, as calm and unruffled as if the whole scene were created for his special benefit.

For probably some fifteen minutes we stood there watching the changing shape of the sun as it neared the horizon. Lights were beginning to come on in windows, people were scurrying for home, while others were already returning to desk or laboratory. Over in the Horological Laboratory the entire third floor was illuminated, where according to the local grapevine some high-powered experiment was in progress.

As the last trace of the oblate crimson sun disappeared behind the ventilators on Ballantyne Hall, I could not refrain from asking Blakeslee:

"Say, have you noticed anything peculiar about the appearance of the landscape lately?"

"A kind of prismatic effect?"

"You might describe it that way."

He nodded. "Yes, I've been aware of it for the last two weeks."

This was news to me. "Never noticed it until tonight. A peculiar meteorological condition, I suppose?"

Very deliberately he knocked the ashes from his pipe against the iron railing. "Let's take a look in the library. It's my experience you can find practically anything in the library."

The book-lined walls were a welcome relief from the dust and wind on the balcony. Blakeslee went to the shelves where the *Astrophysical Journal* is kept and took out a faded volume.

Without hesitation he handed the book to me open at page
373.

"I rather think you'll find the answer to your question here,"
he said.

I glanced at the cover. It was Volume XXXIX, for the year
1914. The article to which Blakeslee had referred me was entitled, "Possible Effects of Halley's Comet on the Earth's Atmosphere," written by Edward Emerson Bernard, a name I
recognized as belonging to one of the most careful and astute
observers of the early part of the century. After the phenomena
I had witnessed that evening, his words might have been addressed to me directly across three quarters of a century.

. . . consisted of a peculiar iridescence and unnatural appearance
of the clouds near the Sun and of a bar of prismatic light on the
clouds in the south. This, combined with the general effect of the
sky and clouds—for the entire sky had a most unnatural and wild
look—would have attracted attention at any time than when one
was looking for something out of the ordinary.

The most suggestive phenomenon, however, was apparent later
on in June and for at least a year afterward. It was first noticed
here on the night of June 7, 1910, and consisted of slowly moving
stripes and masses of self-luminous haze which were not confined
to any one part of the sky. It is true that these peculiarities might
in some way have been of auroral origin, but this I do not think
probable, for they do not seem to resemble in any way, either in
position or in appearance, any auroral phenomenon with which I
am familiar.

I read the brief article through several times before laying
it aside. "So it's Halley's comet that's responsible," I said.

"Don't think there can be much doubt about it," Blakeslee
replied. "We are probably immersed in that portion of the
tail near the head, if indeed we are not in the coma itself. For
the past month I have had two junior astronomers making
naked-eye observations, as well as taking exposures on the night
sky with a one-prism spectrograph."

Blakeslee worked faster sometimes than one would expect
from his indolent attitude. "By the way," I remarked, "how is
Halley's comet following your predicted path? I've been too
busy recently to keep track of it."

Blakeslee hauled out his pipe from the patch pocket of his threadbare observing jacket, crammed the bowl with rough-cut, and took several reflective puffs before answering.

"I don't see any reason why you shouldn't know," he said at length. "However, I'd advise you to keep it quiet for a while. As a matter of fact, the nucleus of the comet, upon which I have based my orbit, is now nearly two degrees in declination from my computed position."

"Two degrees!" I exclaimed. "Why that's four times the diameter of the full moon! What on earth has gone wrong?"

Blakeslee studied the glowing bowl of his pipe with a critical eye. "I'm sure I haven't the ghost of an idea what on earth has gone wrong," he said.

It was at precisely 0212 Mountain Time that I heard a commotion outside the dome that night as if something unusual had happened. I recall the time distinctly because I had just started an hour exposure on H.D. 218393 and was entering it in the record book. Living in a place constantly you become extraordinarily sensitive to deviations from the norm. Pretty soon Blakeslee came in looking very grim.

"Something up?" I inquired.

He snapped on the television set we keep in a cabinet over the plane grating Cassegrain spectrograph. "They say Pittsburgh and Seattle are being destroyed—if they aren't destroyed already."

He fiddled with the dials on our old Vane-Hanlon set. "What's the matter with this thing anyhow?"

"We had the same trouble with it last night. There—it's coming in now."

But the image kept fading in and out and the static was so bad that after a few minutes Blakeslee gave it up.

"I don't see how they could get through so easily," I puzzled. "What about our highly vaunted hydromagnetic wave defense? Thought it was supposed to form a kind of canopy over the country. Detonate anything that got within a thousand miles of us."

"That's what they're trying to figure out now," said Blakeslee. "Apparently it worked perfectly on two rockets that exploded in the North Atlantic near Greenland. But half a dozen others seem to have come through according to schedule."

I went back to the telescope and took a look at the bloated H.D. 218393 hopping about on the slit. The seeing was terrible.

"What shall we do?" I asked.

Blakeslee rose wearily and started for the stairs. "Keep going," he replied. "Keep going as usual. We don't know how soon they'll hit us, but until they do let no one say we faltered in our task."

At the head of the stairway he paused. "Besides—what else can we do?"

After Blakeslee left, the seeing became so much worse I had to lengthen the exposure time by thirty minutes to compensate. Incredible as it sounds, I was not nearly so concerned over the fact that another war had started as I was over my photograph. This was the first chance I had had to try out my new all-mirror concave grating spectrograph that is particularly fast in the ultraviolet of the second order. We had all been anticipating the war for so long that when it finally came we were resigned in a dull, apathetic way. The human animal is peculiar in that it will persist in its routine activities up till the very end, when the ground is crumbling beneath its feet.

Waiting for the plate to develop down in the darkroom, I noticed that my eyes burned as if I had not slept for days, and the skin over my cheeks felt tight and dry. The interval timer aroused me with a jerk.

"This had better be good," I muttered to myself. "I don't think I can last out another exposure."

The plate was good all right. At least, there was plenty of spectrum there. But I had trouble in recognizing it at first. Then slowly I began to identify the old familiar landmarks: H beta with a bright hydrogen core, H gamma with a distinctly bright edge on the red, 4471 of helium, and the ionized silicon lines at 4128 and 4131. The puzzling feature was the long, irregular extension of lines and bands far into the ultraviolet, ending with a big black blob at the edge of the plate.

Studying the spectrum further, a tingling sensation began creeping up my spine, a wild excitement, that snapped me out of my lethargy like a shot of benzedrine. If this was what I thought it was, it was the biggest thing in astrophysics since Janssen observed helium in the sun without an eclipse. No use getting excited until I had confirmation first, though.

Dashing upstairs, I found Murdock in the dome tinkering with the television set.

"You're a spectroscopic expert," I told him. "Come down to the darkroom and tell me what I've got on the plate I just took."

Murdock looked as puzzled as myself when he examined the strip of spectrum with his ocular.

"Its a ninety-minute exposure on H.D. 218393," I explained, "taken with my new ultraviolet spectrograph. The star's a peculiar B-type variable with hydrogen emission lines. What I don't understand is all this spectrum south of 2900."

Murdock was studying each line in turn. "What's your dispersion?" he asked.

"Fourteen angstroms to the millimeter."

He took out a little millimeter scale and made some measurements on the various lines. Next he did some figuring on the back of an envelope, checking each result by repeating his measures on the plate.

"Well, there's only one answer that I can see," he said finally, tapping the scale against his fingertips. "Apparently the ozone layer in the Earth's upper atmosphere has ceased to function. Looks as if the oxygen bands are lying down on the job, too. At any rate, the thin layer of molecules that we depend upon to shield us from the Sun's ultraviolet light has gone on a strike.

"As a result, my dear Latham, you have obtained the first stellar spectrogram of that distinguished head of the hydrogen family, Lyman alpha at 1216." He indicated that black blob at the end of the plate. "Congratulations."

"Let's go tell Blakeslee," I said.

We routed Blakeslee out of the library, where he was going over some tables in an old copy of the *Astronomische Gesellschaft*.

He inspected the plate closely and listened silently to Murdock's interpretation of the spectrum.

"This may explain a lot of things," he said slowly. "We can tell definitely when the sun comes up tomorrow morning."

"Yeah, providing we're still here to see it," Murdock added.

I didn't wake up till nearly noon next day. The first thought that popped into my head was that spectrogram of H.D. 218393. The plate should be dry by now so that I could put it on the measuring machine and really find out what I had.

When I reached the darkroom, to my chagrin the "Busy" sign was hanging outside.

"Open up," I called, pounding on the door. "It's Latham."

"Hello, Latham," Murdock called back cheerily, "How are you this morning?"

"I'm all right. I want to get that plate."

"What plate is that?"

"You know what plate I mean. Come on—open up."

Murdock looked like a wild man. He was unshaven, his black hair was standing straight up, and there was an excited gleam in his eye. He thrust a dripping plate into my hands.

"The solar spectrum down to 600 angstroms!" he cried.

From the looks of the place he must have been up for hours. There were a dozen plates in the drying rack and a dozen more in the hypo.

"Six hundred angstroms!" I gasped. "Man, you're crazy. There ain't no sunlight left at six hundred angstroms."

"And still going strong!" he enthused. "Why, there's apparently no limit to the Sun's ultraviolet spectrum. If anything, it's picking up instead of petering out."

One glance at the plate was enough to confirm his assertion.

"Way back in 1937," Murdock said, lighting a cigarette, "astrophysicists began to suspicion that the Sun didn't radiate like a black body at six thousand absolute. Half a dozen different lines of evidence all agreed in indicating that the ultraviolet spectrum of the sun corresponded to that of a black body at around twenty thousand absolute. Of course, they couldn't be sure. Then when the coronal lines were identified with atoms of iron and nickel ionized a dozen times, they realized there must be energy loose equivalent to a temperature of a hundred thousand, maybe a million, degrees."

He was so excited he kept walking around the darkroom, taking plates out of the wash, examining them with his eyepiece, putting them back in the wash again.

"Trouble was, nobody could figure out how you could get such high-frequency radiation from a yellow dwarf like the Sun. Saha suggested some process akin to uranium fission might be the answer. It sounded kind of farfetched at the time. Now it looks as if we had been too conservative, as usual."

He crushed out his half-smoked cigarette and reached for another.

"Reports come in from anywhere else on this?"

Murdock shook his head. "Electronic communication all over the globe's tied up in a hard knot. Ionosphere's been knocked to hell and gone. Have to rely on carrier pigeon and pony express from now on."

"How's the war coming?"

He shrugged. "Search me. We're still here, aren't we?"

All the rest of the afternoon we banged away at the coudé focus of the 300-inch, taking plates as fast as we could, so that by sunset we had a complete record of the solar spectrum down to 100 A with calibrations, enough to keep a corps of assistants busy measuring till 2000 A.D. When the last plate was photometered and developed, we heaved a sigh of relief and for the first time began to think of food. Murdock had a can of coffee and some cheese and crackers in his room, and I contributed a couple of chocolate bars. While the coffee was boiling we had our first chance to talk things over.

"Murdock, what's happened, anyhow?"

He reached for a sheet of paper and pencil. "Well, here's the way I dope it," he said. "You can fill in the details later, but essentially the story must be something like this.

"There's no doubt but that the molecular equilibrium of the upper atmosphere has been completely upset. Now the fundamental process of ozone formation is the photolysis of the oxygen molecule, like so."

And he wrote down the equation $O_2 + hw = o + o$, in his bold irregular handwriting.

"That is, each photon absorbed by an oxygen molecule produces two oxygen atoms. At moderate altitudes where there are still plenty of other molecules handy, we get three-body collisions of the type, $o, o + M = o_2 + M$, where M can be any old collision partner, say another nitrogen molecule, for instance.

"Ozone is a highly unstable molecule, so that we also have the reverse processes going on continually, of ozone back to oxygen again. Therefore, the concentration of ozone at any instant will depend upon the relative rates at which these various reactions proceed."

He paused long enough to examine the concentration of coffee in the coffee pot before returning to the ozone problem.

"But now Halley's comet comes along and so what happens? We know from observations of its spectrum that it's loaded to the guards with carbon. Carbon and oxygen have a powerful affection for each other, so that whenever possible they immediately proceed to unite with great exultation. Result is that the oxygen of the upper atmosphere, instead of forming ozone and other compounds, is busy forming stable carbon compounds. This opens the door for your far ultraviolet light for the first time, which comes blasting through a layer that previously had stopped it like a stone wall."

He poured out the coffee in beakers we use for mixing developer.

"Wait a minute," I objected. "Sounds to me as if there's a fatal flaw in your theory. Carbon monoxide and carbon dioxide also absorb strongly in the ultraviolet if I remember correctly."

"Right," Murdock agreed. "But not so effectively as ozone and oxygen. As a matter of fact, your objection furnished me with a conclusive proof of the theory."

He selected a plate from the drying rack and passed it across the table to me. "Take a look at that exposure over on your left there. Notice that heavily absorbed region between 1150 and 690 angstroms. Know what that is? It's the strongest band of the carbon-dioxide molecule. See how they've been stuffing themselves on the ultraviolet of our sunlight."

In the days that followed we learned what life is like on the surface of a planet such as Mercury or the Moon that is exposed to the shortwave end of the solar spectrum. Never before had I the faintest conception of how delicate is the balance between contending forces that makes our existence possible. For ages man has strutted about utterly oblivious of the death that forever threatens him from above, his sole protection a shifting, unstable mass of molecules. Talk about the Sword of Damocles! It was no laughing matter when it fell, believe me.

Within the Nucleus, scientists grasped the seriousness of the situation at once, and by taking suitable precautions were able to manage without difficulty. Not so with those outside. Although people were warned of the danger and informed how to guard against it, yet just as in the case of Halley's comet, through perversity or plain stupidity they refused to make the necessary adjustments. This was due in part to the fact that superficially everything *seemed* about the same as before. The sunlight looked somewhat bluer but the effect was not particularly striking. The trouble is, you can't see or smell or taste an X ray.

As Murdock said, communication was tied up in a hard knot, but after sunset fragmentary reports occasionally filtered through of the havoc outside the Nucleus. People were going blind by the thousands. Even with glasses, enough diffuse radiation could enter the eye to produce severe injury. Almost overnight men were reduced from clearly seeing, upright individuals to helpless, groping creatures. The pandemic of ophthalmic conjunctivitis came to be known simply as The Blindness, a term which aptly described it from several points of view.

The injury to the eye had, of course, been anticipated and to some extent discounted in advance. What was wholly unforeseen was the startling increase in certain other maladies which developed at a rate beyond any possible control. Among the most serious was the appalling outbreak of skin cancer—lupus erythematodes discoides—among infants and the aged. Apparently this variety of cancer is latent in all of us, waiting only suitable stimulation to flare into being. Radiologists determined that a narrow band of radiation from 2670 to 3200 is the activating cause of skin cancer. Ordinarily, only the rays between 2900 and 3200 can get through, so that skin cancer develops chiefly in those who undergo prolonged exposure to the sky, such as sailors and farmers.

As if the uncontrolled growth in cancer were not bad enough, gradually through the heavily censored news reports there spread terrifying rumors of other diseases, rendered all the more fearful because of what was left untold and only suggested. Of the effects of ultraviolet light upon the central nervous system due to overradiation and heating of the skull, producing shock, convulsions, and in extreme cases, insanity and suicide.

As for the war, it was stopped almost before it was well under way. Electronically controlled rockets went careening wildly, often destroying the very ones who had launched them. Technicians working far underground sat helpless before elaborate instrument panels, impotent when their sense of sight was dead. And so peace was forced upon a reluctant world, that accepted it only when stricken by a plague worse than one of its own devising.

Slowly the return to normal began. Recovery was by lysis rather than crisis. But each day as Halley's comet receded from the Earth we watched our photographs shrink in the ultraviolet, until they terminated at 2900 as before.

It was on an evening in August, about a week after peace was proclaimed, that Blakeslee, Murdock, and I were engaged in our favorite occupation of watching the sunset from the balcony of the 300-inch. As the light faded, we were able to discern Halley's comet in the western sky in the constellation of Sextans, where it was moving slowly south into Hydra. Now more than three hundred million miles from the Earth it retained little of its former splendor, a thin ghost dissolving into the sunset.

I thought of the long journey that lay ahead of it, out into the region of perpetual twilight between the orbits of Uranus and Neptune, before turning sunward again. And what kind of a world would it find at the next return? That I would never know.

I said to Blakeslee, "Did you ever find out what caused Halley's comet to deviate from your calculated course?"

He was gazing off at the comet probably with much the same thoughts as my own. "No, I never did," he said. "I checked my integration series over every step from the last perihelion passage on April 19, 1910, to that night last August when we secured our first photographs, without finding a single error large enough to affect my positions appreciably. The whole thing seems incomprehensible by the law of gravitation."

He paused to reload his pipe. "This anomalous behavior of Halley's comet is not without precedent, however. At the previous return, Cowell and Crommelin at Greenwich did a magnificent piece of work on the motions of Halley's comet from perihelion in 1759 to 1910. When the Gold Medal of the Royal Society was presented to Cowell, the statement was made that he had rigorously taken into account distances along the comet's path of less than five feet. Yet Halley's comet passed perihelion in 1910 three whole days before the predicted time. That discrepancy of three days has never been explained."

Murdock shifted his position against the railing. "There's one conceivable explanation that occurs to me. It sounds fantastic, I'll admit. Still it's not incompatible with current atomic theory.

"There is evidence that inorganic matter possesses a certain degree of sentience; that is, the atom may have consciousness and will, and therefore in a limited sense the power to control its own destiny. We got our first intimation of this power more than half a century ago when the famous physicist Pauli announced his so-called exclusion principle. The exclusion principle says that inside the atom one and the same quantum state can be occupied only by one electron. It is forbidden for any two electrons in an atom to have the same values for all four of the quantum numbers necessary to specify a particular electronic state.

"The catch comes in trying to figure out how in heck the electrons can be aware of the quantum positions that are to be occupied, so that they never transgress Pauli's exclusion principle. It was never adequately explained by the old wave mechanics, and today it is still one of the most mysterious and fundamental properties of the atom.

"Whether atomic sentience can be invoked to explain the misbehavior of a comet I don't know. Maybe Halley's comet likes to stray by the wayside once in a while like the rest of us. Maybe it gets tired at having to look at us every seventy-five years, or whatever it is." He paused.

"Maybe we'll find the answer next time when Halley's comet comes back about 2065," I suggested.

Murdock laughed. "Well, there's no predicting what Halley's comet may find then. Have you heard the big military secret that everybody in the Nucleus is talking about? Dillon over in the Horological Laboratory has cracked the time problem. Went forward in time last Friday night after five years of experimentation."

"How far?" I asked.

"About three-thousandths of a second. But I got it straight from MacIntire, who is Dillon's chief assistant, and he claims that with their technique they can easily measure a millionth of that amount. So it looks like the goods, all right. The Army's been swarming all over the place."

"So Halley's comet may find us fighting a Time War next trip?"

"It could be," Murdock said.

Blakeslee had been gazing moodily off toward Halley's comet apparently indifferent to Murdock's remarks. "There isn't going to be a next trip," he said quietly.

Murdock and I both turned in astonishment. "Why, what do you mean?" we demanded.

"I mean that this is the last visit Halley's comet will ever pay Earth," he replied. "During the past month the eccentricity of its orbit has definitely turned from an elongated ellipse to a hyperbola.

"Take a good look now, for this is the last time anyone will ever see Halley's comet again."

A hyperbola! A curve that begins and ends at infinity. And Halley's comet was heading for infinity. Surely, it couldn't be! I tried to protest but somehow my throat was all choked up so that the words refused to come. As if from a great distance I heard Murdock speaking.

"Funny how people always think of comets as evil omens," he mused. "It seems to me that Halley's comet has been a faithful companion and a mighty good friend of ours during all these years. It certainly stopped World War IV in a hurry. If it hadn't been for The Blindness we might not even be here tonight."

"Yes," said Blakeslee. "If it hadn't been for The Blindness."

ARTHUR C. CLARKE

It has always seemed to me that for an editor to anthologize his own works involves a certain conflict of interest. I've tried to minimize that conflict by using one of the shortest stories I have ever written. At the same time, it is the one in which I stuck my neck out the furthest.

Everybody *knows* that a man exposed to the vacuum of space will die instantly and horribly; there have been vivid descriptions of the fragile human body exploding into mist under the change of pressure. To the best of my knowledge, the first person to suggest that this was nonsense was the brilliant young writer Stanley Weinbaum, whose tragic death at the age of thirty-three robbed science fiction of one of its most promising talents. In a short story called "The Red Peri" (published in *Astounding Stories* for November, 1935, only a month before the author's death) Weinbaum gave logical reasons for thinking that a man could live and work in a complete vacuum for short periods of time.

My interest in this subject, undoubtedly, arose from my underwater activities, and my surprise at discovering the length of time that the human body can survive without breathing. (I did not take up diving until my mid-thirties, and never pushed my underwater endurance beyond three and a half minutes. A young man in good health can do much better than this; but if you're tempted, don't try it alone!) Lack of oxygen is not, therefore, a serious problem for periods of a few minutes; the real danger is lack of pressure.

The human body, however, is a pretty tough structure; it can stand an *increase* of pressure of at least thirty atmospheres (corresponding to a dive of a thousand feet), so why should it not stand a decrease of a mere *one* atmosphere?

That was the theory behind "Take a Deep Breath," which has aroused the ire of some conservative space-medics. They may yet be right, but we shall know the truth very soon. Not long ago, trained chimpanzees were depressurized to complete vacuum and continued working on their assigned tasks for some fifteen seconds, then they suddenly lost consciousness. On repressurization, they recovered completely.

Before long, some brave human will try this experiment— perhaps under controlled conditions, perhaps a desperate emergency. But it would be nice to know if it *can* be done, before we have to find out the hard way.

Volunteers can form a line on the right.

Take a Deep Breath

A long time ago I discovered that people who've never left Earth have certain fixed ideas about conditions in space. Everyone "knows," for example, that a man dies instantly and horribly when exposed to the vacuum that exists beyond the atmosphere. You'll find numerous gory descriptions of exploded space travelers in the popular literature, and I won't spoil your appetite by repeating them here. Many of those tales, indeed, are basically true. I've pulled men back through the air lock who were very poor advertisements for space flight.

Yet, at the same time, there are exceptions to every rule— even this one. I should know, for I learned the hard way.

We were on the last stages of building Communications Satellite Two; all the main units had been joined together, the living quarters had been pressurized, and the station had been given the slow spin around its axis that had restored the unfamiliar sensation of weight. I say "slow," but at its rim our two-hundred-foot-diameter wheel was turning at thirty miles an hour. We had, of course, no sense of motion, but the centrifugal force caused by this spin gave us about half the weight we would have possessed on Earth. That was enough to stop things from drifting around, yet not enough to make us feel uncomfortably sluggish after our weeks with no weight at all.

Four of us were sleeping in the small cylindrical cabin known as Bunkhouse Number 6 on the night that it happened. The bunkhouse was at the very rim of the station; if you imagine a bicycle wheel, with a string of sausages replacing the tire, you have a good idea of the layout. Bunkhouse Number 6 was one of these sausages, and we were slumbering peacefully inside it.

I was awakened by a sudden jolt that was not violent enough to cause me alarm, but which did make me sit up and wonder what had happened. Anything unusual in a space station demands instant attention, so I reached for the intercom switch by my bed. "Hello, Central," I called. "What was that?"

There was no reply; the line was dead.

Now thoroughly alarmed, I jumped out of bed—and had an even bigger shock. *There was no gravity.* I shot up to the ceiling before I was able to grab a stanchion and bring myself to a halt, at the cost of a sprained wrist.

It was impossible for the entire station to have suddenly stopped rotating. There was only one answer; the failure of the intercom and, as I quickly discovered, of the lighting circuit as well forced us to face the appalling truth. We were no longer part of the station; our little cabin had somehow come adrift, and had been slung off into space like a raindrop falling on a spinning flywheel.

There were no windows through which we could look out, but we were not in complete darkness, for the battery-powered emergency lights had come on. All the main air vents had closed automatically when the pressure dropped. For the time being, we could live in our own private atmosphere, even though it was not being renewed. Unfortunately, a steady whistling told us that the air we did have was escaping through a leak somewhere in the cabin.

There was no way of telling what had happened to the rest

of the station. For all we knew, the whole structure might have come to pieces, and all our colleagues might be dead or in the same predicament as we—drifting through space in leaking cans of air. Our one slim hope was the possibility that we were the only castaways, that the rest of the station was intact and had been able to send a rescue team to find us. After all, we were receding at no more than thirty miles an hour, and one of the rocket scooters could catch up to us in minutes.

It actually took an hour, though without the evidence of my watch I should never have believed that it was so short a time. We were now gasping for breath, and the gauge on our single emergency oxygen tank had dropped to one division above zero.

The banging on the wall seemed like a signal from another world. We banged back vigorously, and a moment later a muffled voice called to us through the wall. Someone outside was lying with his space-suit helmet pressed against the metal, and his shouted words were reaching us by direct conduction. Not as clear as radio—but it worked.

The oxygen gauge crept slowly down to zero while we had our council of war. We would be dead before we could be towed back to the station; yet the rescue ship was only a few feet away from us, with its air lock already open. Our little problem was to cross that few feet—*without* space suits.

We made our plans carefully, rehearsing our actions in the full knowledge that there could be no repeat performance. Then we each took a deep, final swig of oxygen, flushing out our lungs. When we were all ready, I banged on the wall to give the signal to our friends waiting outside.

There was a series of short, staccato raps as the power tools got to work on the thin hull. We clung tightly to the stanchions, as far away as possible from the point of entry, knowing just what would happen. When it came, it was so sudden that the mind couldn't record the sequence of events. The cabin seemed to explode, and a great wind tugged at me. The last trace of air gushed from my lungs, through my already-opened mouth. And then—utter silence, and the stars shining through the gaping hole that led to life.

Believe me, I didn't stop to analyze my sensations. I think—though I can never be sure that it wasn't imagination—that my eyes were smarting and there was a tingling feeling all over my body. And I felt very cold, perhaps because evaporation was already starting from my skin.

The only thing I can be certain of is that uncanny silence. It is never completely quiet in a space station, for there is always the sound of machinery or air pumps. But this was the absolute silence of the empty void, where there is no trace of air to carry sound.

Almost at once we launched ourselves out through the shattered wall, into the full blast of the sun. I was instantly blinded—but that didn't matter, because the men waiting in space suits grabbed me as soon as I emerged and hustled me into the air lock. And there, sound slowly returned as the air rushed in, and we remembered we could breathe again. The entire rescue, they told us later, had lasted just twenty seconds. . . .

Well, we were the founding members of the Vacuum-Breathers' Club. Since then, at least a dozen other men have done the same thing, in similar emergencies. The record time in space is now two minutes; after that, the blood begins to form bubbles as it boils at body temperature, and those bubbles soon get to the heart.

In my case, there was only one aftereffect. For maybe a quarter of a minute I had been exposed to *real* sunlight, not the feeble stuff that filters down through the atmosphere of Earth. Breathing space didn't hurt me at all—but I got the worst dose of sunburn I've ever had in my life.

JACK VANCE

There are some metals—gold is the prime example—that men have valued for their aesthetic qualities; only later have they discovered other uses. This story is about such a metal.

It is also about Beauty, which is one of the main ingredients of science but is not too common in science fiction. If you are looking for it, you cannot do better than study the writings of Jack Vance, whose command of language is found at its best in his splendid novel *The Dragon Masters*. Much of his work lies on the borderland of fantasy, and he is one of the few heirs to the mantle of Professor J. R. R. Tolkien.

A Californian, Jack Vance began writing science fiction while serving in the merchant marine during World War II. "The Potters of Firsk," though one of his earliest stories, already gives hints of imaginative things to come.

The Potters of Firsk

The yellow bowl on Thomm's desk stood about a foot high, flaring out from a width of eight inches at the base to a foot across the rim. The profile showed a simple curve, clean and sharp, with a full sense of completion: the body was thin without fragility; the whole piece gave an impression of ringing well-arched strength.

The craftsmanship of the body was matched by the beauty of the glaze—a glorious transparent yellow, luminescent like a hot summer afterglow. It was the essence of marigolds, a watery wavering saffron, a yellow as of transparent gold, a yellow glass that seemed to fabricate curtains of light within itself and fling them off, a yellow brilliant but mild, tart as lemon, sweet as quince jelly, soothing as sunlight.

Keselsky had been furtively eying the bowl during his interview with Thomm, personnel chief for the Department of Planetary Affairs. Now, with the interview over, he could not help but bend forward to examine the bowl more closely. He said with obvious sincerity: "This is the most beautiful piece I've ever seen."

Thomm, a man of early middle age with a brisk gray mustache, a sharp but tolerant eye, leaned back in his chair. "It's a souvenir. Souvenir's as good a name for it as anything else. I got it many years ago, when I was your age." He glanced at his desk clock. "Lunchtime."

Keselsky looked up, hastily reached for his briefcase. "Excuse me, I had no idea—"

Thomm raised his hand. "Not so fast. I'd like you to have lunch with me."

Keselsky muttered embarrassed excuses, but Thomm insisted.

"Sit down, by all means." A menu appeared on the screen. "Now—look that over."

Without further urging Keselsky made a selection, and Thomm spoke into the mesh. The wall opened, a table slid out with their lunch.

Even while eating Keselsky fondled the bowl with his eyes. Over coffee, Thomm handed it across the table. Keselsky hefted it, stroked the surface, looked deep into the glaze.

"Where on earth did you find such a marvelous piece?" He examined the bottom, frowned at the marks scratched in the clay.

"Not on Earth," said Thomm. "On the planet Firsk." He

sat back. "There's a story connected with that bowl." He paused inquiringly.

Keselsky hurriedly swore that nothing could please him more than to listen while Thomm spoke of all things under the sun. Thomm smiled faintly. After all, this was Keselsky's first job.

"As I've mentioned, I was about your age," said Thomm. "Perhaps a year or two older, but then I'd been out on the Channel Planet for nineteen months. When my transfer to Firsk came I was naturally very pleased, because Channel, as perhaps you know, is a bleak planet, full of ice and frost-fleas and the dullest aborigines in space—"

Thomm was entranced with Firsk. It was everything the Channel Planet had not been: warm, fragrant, the home of the Mi-Tuun, a graceful people of a rich, quaint and ancient culture. Firsk was by no means a large planet, though its gravity approached that of Earth. The land surface was small—a single equatorial continent in the shape of a dumbbell.

The Planetary Affairs Bureau was located at Penolpan, a few miles in from the South Sea, a city of fable and charm. The tinkle of music was always to be heard somewhere in the distance; the air was mellow with incense and a thousand flower scents. The low houses of reed, parchment and dark wood were arranged negligently, three-quarters hidden under the foliage of trees and vines. Canals of green water laced the city, arched over by wooden bridges trailing ivy and orange flowers, and here swam boats each decorated in an intricate, many-colored pattern.

The inhabitants of Penolpan, the amber-skinned Mi-Tuun, were a mild people devoted to the pleasures of life, sensuous without excess, relaxed and gay, guiding their lives by ritual. They fished in the South Sea, cultivated cereals and fruit, manufactured articles of wood, resin and paper. Metal was scarce on Firsk, and was replaced in many instances by tools and utensils of earthenware, fabricated so cleverly that the lack was never felt.

Thomm found his work at the Penolpan Bureau pleasant in the extreme, marred only by the personality of his superior. This was George Covill, a short ruddy man with prominent blue eyes, heavy wrinkled eyelids, sparse sandy hair. He had a habit, when he was displeased—which was often—of cocking his head sidewise and staring for a brittle five seconds. Then, if the offense was great, he exploded in wrath; if not, he stalked away.

On Penolpan Covill's duties were more of a technical than sociological nature, and even so, in line with the Bureau's policy of leaving well-balanced cultures undisturbed, there was little to occupy him. He imported silica yarn to replace the root fiber from which the Mi-Tuun wove their nets; he built a small cracking plant and converted the fish oil they burned in their lamps into a lighter, cleaner fluid. The varnished paper of Penolpan's houses had a tendency to absorb moisture and split after a few months of service. Covill brought in a plastic varnish which protected them indefinitely. Aside from these minor innovations Covill did little. The Bureau's policy was to improve the native standard of living within the framework of its own culture, introducing Earth methods, ideas, philosophy very gradually and only when the natives themselves felt the need.

Before long, however, Thomm came to feel that Covill paid only lip-service to the Bureau philosophy. Some of his actions seemed dense and arbitrary to the well-indoctrinated Thomm. He built an Earth-style office on Penolpan's main canal, and the concrete and glass made an inexcusable jar against Penolpan's mellow ivories and browns. He kept strict office hours and on a dozen occasions a delegation of Mi-Tuun, arriving in ceremonial regalia, had to be turned away with stammered excuses by Thomm, when in truth Covill, disliking the crispness of his linen suit, had stripped to the waist and was slumped in a wicker chair with a cigar, a quart of beer, watching girl-shows on his telescreen.

Thomm was assigned to Pest Control, a duty Covill considered beneath his dignity. On one of his rounds Thomm first heard mentioned the Potters of Firsk.

Laden with insect spray, with rat-poison cartridges dangling from his belt, he had wandered into the poorest outskirts of Penolpan, where the trees ended and the dry plain stretched out to the Kukmank Mountains. In this relatively drab location he came upon a long open shed, a pottery bazaar. Shelves and tables held ware of every description, from stoneware crocks for pickling fish to tiny vases thin as paper, lucent as milk. Here were

nd small, bowls of every size and shape, no two
tureens, demijohns, tankards. One rack held earth-
es, the clay vitrified till it rang like iron, the cutting
ed cleanly, sharper than any razor, from a thick drip-
aze.

m was astounded by the colors. Rare rich ruby, the
green of flowing river water, turquoise ten times deeper than
the sky. He saw metallic purples, browns shot with blond light,
pinks, violets, grays, dappled russets, blues of copper and cobalt,
the odd streaks and flows of rutilated glass. Certain glazes
bloomed with crystals like snowflakes, others held floating within
them tiny spangles of metal.

Thomm was delighted with his find. Here was beauty of form,
of material, of craftsmanship. The sound body, sturdy with
natural earthy strength given to wood and clay, the melts of
colored glass, the quick restless curves of the vases, the capacity
of the bowls, the expanse of the plates—they produced a tremendous enthusiasm in Thomm. And yet—there were puzzling
aspects to the bazaar. First—he looked up and down the shelves
—something was lacking. In the many-colored display he missed
—yellow. There were no yellow glazes of any sort. A cream, a
straw, an amber—but no full-bodied glowing yellow.

Perhaps the potters avoided the color through superstition,
Thomm speculated, or perhaps because of identification with
royalty, like the ancient Chinese of Earth, or perhaps because of
association with death or disease. The train of thought led to
the second puzzle: Who were the potters? There were no kilns
in Penolpan to fire ware such as this.

He approached the clerk, a girl just short of maturity, who
had been given an exquisite loveliness. She wore the *pareu* of
the Mi-Tuun, a flowered sash about the waist, and reed sandals.
Her skin glowed like one of the amber glazes at her back; she
was slender, quiet, friendly.

"This is all very beautiful," said Thomm. "For instance, what
is the price of this?" He touched a tall flagon glazed a light
green, streaked and shot with silver threads.

The price she mentioned, in spite of the beauty of the piece,
was higher than what he had expected. Observing his surprise,

the girl said, "They are our ancestors, and to sell them as cheaply as wood or glass would be irreverent."

Thomm raised his eyebrows, and decided to ignore what he considered a ceremonial personification.

"Where's the pottery made?" he asked. "In Penolpan?"

The girl hesitated and Thomm felt a sudden shade of restraint. She turned her head, looked out toward the Kukmank Range. "Back in the hills are the kilns; out there our ancestors go, and the pots are brought back. Aside from this I know nothing."

Thomm said carefully, "Do you prefer not to talk of it?"

She shrugged. "Indeed, there's no reason why I should. Except that we Mi-Tuun fear the Potters, and the thought of them oppresses us."

"But why is that?"

She grimaced. "No one knows what lies beyond the first hill. Sometimes we see the glow of furnaces, and then sometimes when there are no dead for the Potters they take the living."

Thomm thought that if so, here was a case for the interference of the Bureau, even to the extent of armed force.

"Who are these Potters?"

"There," she said, and pointed. "There is a Potter."

Following her finger, he saw a man riding out along the plain. He was taller, heavier than the Mi-Tuun. Thomm could not see him distinctly, wrapped as he was in a long gray burnoose, but he appeared to have a pale skin and reddish-brown hair. He noted the bulging panniers on the pack-beast. "What's he taking with him now?"

"Fish, paper, cloth, oil—goods he traded his pottery for."

Thomm picked up his pest-killing equipment. "I think I'll visit the Potters one of these days."

"No—" said the girl.

"Why not?"

"It's very dangerous. They're fierce, secretive—"

Thomm smiled. "I'll be careful."

Back at the Bureau he found Covill stretched out on a wicker chaise longue, half-asleep. At the sight of Thomm he roused himself, sat up.

"Where the devil have you been? I told you to get the estimates on that power plant ready today."

"I put them on your desk," replied Thomm politely. "If you've been out front at all, you couldn't have missed them."

Covill eyed him belligerently, but for once found himself at a loss for words. He subsided in his chair with a grunt. As a general rule Thomm paid little heed to Covill's sharpness, recognizing it as resentment against the main office. Covill felt his abilities deserved greater scope, a more important post.

Thomm sat down, helped himself to a glass of Covill's beer. "Do you know anything about the potteries back in the mountains?"

Covill grunted: "A tribe of bandits, something of the sort." He hunched forward, reached for the beer.

"I looked into the pottery bazaar today," said Thomm. "A clerk called the pots 'ancestors.' Seemed rather strange."

"The longer you knock around the planets," Covill stated, "the stranger the things you see. Nothing could surprise me any more—except maybe a transfer to the Main Office." He snorted bitterly, gulped at his beer. Refreshed, he went on in a less truculent voice, "I've heard odds and ends about these Potters, nothing definite, and I've never had time to look into 'em. I suppose it's religious ceremonial, rites of death. They take away the dead bodies, bury 'em for a fee or trade goods."

"The clerk said that when they don't get the dead, sometimes they take the living."

"Eh? What's that?" Covill's hard blue eyes stared bright from his red face. Thomm repeated his statement.

Covill scratched his chin, presently hoisted himself to his feet. "Let's fly out, just for the devilment of it, and see what these Potters are up to. Been wanting to go out a long time."

Thomm brought the copter out of the hangar, set down in front of the office, and Covill gingerly climbed in. Covill's sudden energy mystified Thomm, especially since it included a ride in the copter. Covill had an intense dislike of flying, and usually refused to set foot in an aircraft.

The blades sang, grabbed the air, the copter wafted high. Penolpan became a checkerboard of brown roofs and foliage. Thirty miles distant, across a dry sandy plain, rose the Kukmank

Range—barren shoulders and thrusts of gray rock. At first sight locating a settlement among the tumble appeared a task of futility.

Covill, peering down into the wastes, grumbled something to this effect; Thomm, however, pointed toward a column of smoke. "Potters need kilns. Kilns need heat—"

As they approached the smoke, they saw that it issued not from brick stacks but from a fissure at the peak of a conical dome.

"Volcano," said Covill, with an air of vindication. "Let's try out there along that ridge—then if there's nothing we'll go back."

Thomm had been peering intently below. "I think we've found them right here. Look close, you can see buildings."

He dropped the copter, and the rows of stone houses became plain.

"Should we land?" Thomm asked dubiously. "They're supposed to be fairly rough."

"Certainly, set down," snapped Covill. "We're official representatives of the System."

The fact might mean little to a tribe of mountaineers, reflected Thomm; nevertheless he let the copter drop onto a stony flat place in the center of the village.

The copter, if it had not alarmed the Potters, at least had made them cautious. For several minutes there was no sign of life. The stone cabins stood bleak and vacant as cairns.

Covill alighted, and Thomm, assuring himself that his gamma-gun was in easy reach, followed. Covill stood by the copter, looking up and down the line of houses. "Cagey set of beggars," he growled. "Well . . . we better stay here till someone makes a move."

To this plan Thomm agreed heartily, so they waited in the shadow of the copter. It was clearly the village of the Potters. Shards lay everywhere—brilliant bits of glazed ware glinting like lost jewels. Down the slope rose a heap of broken bisque, evidently meant for later use, and beyond was a long tile-roofed shed. Thomm sought in vain for a kiln. A fissure into the side of the mountain caught his eye, a fissure with a well-worn path leading into it. An intriguing hypothesis formed in his mind—but now three men had appeared, tall and erect in gray burnooses. The hoods were flung back, and they looked like monks of medieval Earth, except that instead of monkish tonsure, fuzzy red hair rose in a peaked mound above their heads.

The leader approached with a determined step, and Thomm stiffened, prepared for anything. Not so Covill: he appeared contemptuously at ease, a lord among serfs.

Ten feet away the leader halted—a man taller than Thomm, with a hook nose, hard intelligent eyes like gray pebbles. He waited an instant but Covill only watched him. At last the Potter spoke in a courteous tone.

"What brings strangers to the village of the Potters?"

"I'm Covill, of the Planetary Affairs Bureau in Penolpan, official representative of the System. This is merely a routine visit, to see how things are going with you."

"We make no complaints," replied the chief.

"I've heard reports of you Potters kidnaping Mi-Tuun," said Covill. "Is there any truth in that?"

"Kidnaping?" mused the chief. "What is that?"

Covill explained. The chief rubbed his chin, staring at Covill with eyes black as water.

"There is an ancient agreement," said the chief at last. "The Potters are granted the bodies of the dead: and occasionally when the need is great, we do anticipate nature by a year or two. But what matter? The soul lives forever in the pot it beautifies."

Covill brought out his pipe, and Thomm held his breath. Loading the pipe was sometimes a preliminary to the cold sidelong stares which occasionally ended in an explosion of wrath. For the moment, however, Covill held himself in check.

"Just what do you do with the corpses?"

The leader raised his eyebrows in surprise. "Is it not obvious? No? But then you are no potter. Our glazes require lead, sand, clay, alkali, spar and lime. All but the lime is at our hand, and this we extract from the bones of the dead."

Covill lit his pipe, puffed. Thomm relaxed. For the moment the danger was past.

"I see," said Covill. "Well, we don't want to interfere in any native customs, rites or practices, so long as the peace isn't disturbed. You'll have to understand there can't be any more kidnaping. The corpses—that's between you and whoever's responsible for the body, but lives are more important than pots. If you need lime, I can get you tons of it. There must be lime-stone beds somewhere on the planet. One of these days I'll send Thomm out prospecting and you'll have more lime than you'll know what to do with."

The chief shook his head, half amused. "Natural lime is a poor substitute for the fresh live lime of bones. There are certain other salts which act as fluxes, and then, of course, the spirit of the person is in the bones and this passes into the glaze and gives it an inner fire otherwise unobtainable."

Covill puffed, puffed, puffed, watching the chief with his hard blue eyes. "I don't care what you use," he said, "as long as there's no kidnaping, no murder. If you need lime, I'll help you find it; that's what I'm here for, to help you, and raise your standard of living; but I'm also here to protect the Mi-Tuun from raiding. I can do both—one about as good as the other."

The corners of the chief's mouth drew back. Thomm inter-posed a question before he spat out an angry reply. "Tell me, where are your kilns?"

The chief turned him a cool glance. "Our firing is done by the Great Monthly Burn. We stack our ware in the caves, and then, on the twenty-second day, the scorch rises from below. One entire day the heat roars up white and glowing, and two weeks later the caves have cooled for us to go after our ware."

"That sounds interesting," said Covill. "I'd like to look around your works. Where's your pottery, down there in that shed?"

The chief moved not a muscle. "No man may look inside that shed," he said slowly, "unless he is a Potter—and then only after he has proved his mastery of the clay."

"How does he go about that?" Covill asked lightly.

"At the age of fourteen he goes forth from his home with a hammer, a mortar, a pound of bone lime. He must mine clay, lead, sand, spar. He must find iron for brown, malachite for green, cobalt earth for blue, and he must grind a glaze in his mortar, shape and decorate a tile, and set it in the Mouth of the Great Burn. If the tile is successful, the body whole, the glaze good, then he is permitted to enter the long pottery and know the secrets of the craft."

Covill pulled the pipe from his mouth, asked quizzically, "And if the tile's no good?"

"We need no poor Potters," said the chief. "We always need bonelime."

Thomm had been glancing along the shards of colored pottery. "Why don't you use yellow glaze?"

The chief flung out his arms. "Yellow glaze? It is unknown, a secret no Potter has penetrated. Iron gives a dingy tan, silver a gray-yellow, chrome a green-yellow, and antimony burns out in the heat of the Great Burn. The pure rich yellow, the color of the sun . . . ah, that is a dream."

Covill was uninterested. "Well, we'll be flying back, since you don't dare to show us around. Remember, if there's any technical help you want, I can get it for you. I might even find how to make you your precious yellow—"

"Impossible," said the chief. "Have not we, the Potters of the Universe, sought for thousands of years?"

". . . But there must be no more taking of lives. If necessary, I'll put a stop to the potting altogether."

The chief's eyes blazed. "Your words are not friendly!"

"If you don't think I can do it, you're mistaken," said Covill. "I'll drop a bomb down the throat of your volcano and cave in the entire mountain. The System protects every man jack everywhere, and that means protecting the Mi-Tuun from a tribe of Potters who want their bones."

Thomm plucked him nervously by the sleeve. "Get back in the copter," he whispered. "They're getting ugly. In another minute they'll jump us."

Covill turned his back on the lowering chief, deliberately climbed into the copter. Thomm followed more warily. In his eyes the chief was teetering on the verge of attack, and Thomm had no inclination for fighting.

He flung in the clutch: the blades chewed at the air; the copter rose, leaving a knot of gray-burnoosed Potters silent below.

Covill settled back with an air of satisfaction. "There's only one way to handle people like that, and that is, get the upper hand on 'em; that's the only way they'll respect you. You act just a little uncertain, they sense it, sure as fate, and then you're a goner."

Thomm said nothing. Covill's methods might produce immediate results, but in the long run they seemed shortsighted, intolerant, unsympathetic. In Covill's place he would have stressed the Bureau's ability to provide substitutes for the bonelime, and possibly assist with any technical difficulties—though indeed, they seemed to be masters of their craft, completely sure of their ability. Yellow glaze, of course, still was lacking them. That evening he inserted a strip from the Bureau library into his portable viewer. The subject was pottery, and Thomm absorbed as much of the lore as he was able.

Covill's pet project—a small atomic power plant to electrify Penolpan—kept him busy the next few days, even though he worked reluctantly. Penolpan, with its canals softly lit by yellow lanterns, the gardens glowing to candles and rich with the fragrance of night blossoms, was a city from fairyland; electricity, motors, fluorescents, water pumps would surely dim the charm —Covill, however, was insistent that the world would benefit by a gradual integration into the tremendous industrial complex of the System.

Twice Thomm passed by the pottery bazaar and twice he turned in, both to marvel at the glistening ware and to speak with the girl who tended the shelves. She had a fascinating beauty, grace and charm, breathed into her soul by a lifetime in Penolpan: she was interested in everything Thomm had to tell her of the outside universe, and Thomm, young, softhearted and lonely, looked forward to his visits with increasing anticipation.

For a period Covill kept him furiously busy. Reports were due at the home office, and Covill assigned the task to Thomm, while he either dozed in his wicker chair or rode the canals of Penolpan in his special red and black boat.

At last, late one afternoon, Thomm threw aside his journals and set off down the street, under the shade of great kaotang trees. He crossed through the central market, where the shopkeepers were busy with late trade, turned down a path beside a turf-banked canal and presently came to the pottery bazaar.

But he looked in vain for the girl. A thin man in a black jacket stood quietly to the side, waiting his pleasure. At last Thomm turned to him. "Where's Su-then?"

The man hesitated, Thomm grew impatient.

"Well, where is she? Sick? Has she given up working here?"

"She has gone."

"Gone where?"

"Gone to her ancestors."

Thomm's skin froze to stiffness. "*What?*"

The clerk lowered his head.

"Is she dead?"

"Yes, she is dead."

"But—how? She was healthy a day or so ago."

The man of the Mi-Tuun hesitated once more. "There are many ways of dying, Earthman."

Thomm became angry. "Tell me now—what happened to her?"

Rather startled by Thomm's vehemence the man blurted, "The Potters have called her to the hills; she is gone, but soon she will live forever, her spirit wrapped in glorious glass—"

"Let me get this straight," said Thomm. 'The Potters took her —alive?"

"Yes—alive."

"And any others?"

"Three others."

"All alive?"

"All alive."

Thomm ran back to the Bureau.

Covill, by chance, was in the front office, checking Thomm's work. Thomm blurted: "The Potters have been raiding again— they took four Mi-Tuun in the last day or so."

Covill thrust his chin forward, cursed fluently. Thomm understood that his anger was not so much for the act itself, but the fact that the Potters had defied him, disobeyed his orders. Covill personally had been insulted; now there would be action.

"Get the copter out," said Covill shortly. "Bring it around in front."

When Thomm set the copter down, Covill was waiting with one of the three atom bombs in the Bureau armory—a long cylinder attached to a parachute. Covill snapped it in place on the copter, then stood back. "Take this over that blasted volcano," he said harshly. "Drop it down the crater. I'll teach those murdering devils a lesson they won't forget. Next time it'll be on their village."

Thomm, aware of Covill's dislike of flying, was not surprised by the assignment. Without further words he took off, rose above Penolpan, flew out toward the Kukmank Range.

His anger cooled. The Potters, caught in the rut of their customs, were unaware of evil. Covill's orders seemed ill-advised —headstrong, vindictive, overhasty. Suppose the Mi-Tuun were yet alive? Would it not be better to negotiate for their release? Instead of hovering over the volcano, he dropped his copter into the gray village, and assuring himself of his gamma-gun, he jumped out onto the dismal stony square.

This time he had only a moment to wait. The chief came striding up from the village, burnoose flapping back from powerful limbs, a grim smile on his face.

"So—it is the insolent lordling again. Good—we are in need of bonelime, and yours will suit us admirably. Prepare your soul for the Great Burn, and your next life will be the eternal glory of a perfect glaze."

Thomm felt fear, but he also felt a kind of desperate recklessness. He touched his gun. "I'll kill a lot of Potters, and you'll be the first," he said in a voice that sounded strange to him. "I've come for the four Mi-Tuun that you took from Penolpan. These raids have got to stop. You don't seem to understand that we can punish you."

The chief put his hands behind his back, apparently unimpressed. "You may fly like the birds, but birds can do no more than defile those below."

Thomm pulled out his gamma-gun, pointed to a boulder a quarter-mile away. "Watch that rock." And he blasted the granite to gravel with an explosive pellet.

The chief drew back, eyebrows raised. "In truth, you wield more sting than I believed. But—" he gestured to the ring of burnoosed Potters around Thomm— "we can kill you before you can do much damage. We Potters do not fear death, which is merely eternal meditation from the glass."

"Listen to me," said Thomm earnestly. "I came not to threaten, but to bargain. My superior, Covill, gave me orders to destroy the mountain, blast away your caves—and I can do it as easily as I blasted that rock."

A mutter arose from the Potters.

"If I'm harmed, be sure that you'll suffer. But, as I say, I've come down here, against my superior's orders, to make a bargain with you."

"What sort of bargain can interest us?" said the Chief Potter disdainfully. "We care for nothing but our craft." He gave a sign and, before Thomm could twitch, two burly Potters had gripped him, wrested the gun from his hand.

"I can give you the secret of the true yellow glaze," shouted Thomm desperately. "The royal fluorescent yellow that will stand the fire of your kiln!"

"Empty words," said the chief. Mockingly he asked: "And what do you want for your secret?"

"The return of the four Mi-Tuun you've just stolen from Penolpan, and your word never to raid again."

The chief listened intently, pondered a moment. "How then would we formulate our glaze?" He spoke with a patient air, like a man explaining a practical truth to a child. "Bonelime is one of our most necessary fluxes."

"As Covill told you, we can give you unlimited quantities of lime, with any properties you ask for. On Earth we have made pottery for thousands of years and we know a great deal of such things."

The Chief Potter tossed his head. "That is evidently untrue. Look—" he kicked Thomm's gamma-gun— "the substance of this is dull opaque metal. A people knowing clay and transparent glass would never use material of that sort."

"Perhaps it would be wise to let me demonstrate," suggested Thomm. "If I show you the yellow glaze, then will you bargain with me?"

The Chief Potter scrutinized Thomm almost a full minute. Grudgingly: "What sort of yellow can you make?"

Thomm said wryly: "I'm not a Potter, and I can't predict exactly—but the formula I have in mind can produce any shade from light luminous yellow to vivid orange."

The chief made a signal. "Release him. We will make him eat his words."

Thomm stretched his muscles, cramped under the grip of the Potters. He reached to the ground, picked up his gamma-gun, holstered it, under the sardonic eyes of the Chief Potter.

"Our bargain is this," said Thomm, "I show you how to make yellow glaze, and guarantee you a plentiful supply of lime. You will release the Mi-Tuun to me and undertake never to raid Penolpan for live men and women."

"The bargain is conditional on the yellow glaze," said the Chief Potter. "We ourselves can produce dingy yellows as often as we wish. If your yellow comes clear and true from the fire, I agree to your bargain. If not, we Potters hold you a charlatan and your spirit will be lodged forever in the basest sort of utensil."

Thomm went to the copter, unsnapped the atom bomb from the frame, discarded the parachute. Shouldering the long cylinder, he said: "Take me to your pottery. I'll see what I can do."

Without a word the Chief Potter took him down the slope to the long shed, and they entered through an arched stone doorway. To the right stood bins of clay, a row of wheels, twenty or thirty lined against one wall, and in the center a rack crowded with drying ware. To the left stood vats, further shelves and tables. From a doorway came a harsh grinding sound, evidently a mill of some sort. The Chief Potter led Thomm to the left, past the glazing tables and to the end of the shed. Here were shelves lined with various crocks, tubs and sacks, these marked in symbols strange to Thomm. And through a doorway nearby, apparently unguarded, Thomm glimpsed the Mi-Tuun, seated despondently, passively, on benches. The girl Su-then looked up, saw him, and her mouth fell open. She jumped to her feet, hesitated in the doorway, deterred by the stern form of the Chief Potter.

Thomm said to her: "You're a free woman—with a little luck." Then turning to the Chief Potter: "What kind of acid do you have?"

The Chief pointed to a row of stoneware flagons. "The acid of salt, the acid of vinegar, the acid of fluorspar, the acid of saltpeter, the acid of sulphur."

Thomm nodded, and laying the bomb on a table, opened the hinged door, withdrew one of the uranium slugs. Into five porcelain bowls he carved slivers of uranium with his pocket knife, and into each bowl he poured a quantity of acid, a different acid into each. Bubbles of gas fumed up from the metal.

The Chief Potter watched with folded arms. "What are you trying to do?"

Thomm stood back, studied his fuming beakers. "I want to precipitate a uranium salt. Get me soda and lye."

Finally a yellow powder settled in one of his beakers; this he seized upon and washed triumphantly.

"Now," he told the Chief Potter, "bring me clear glaze."

He poured out six trays of glaze and mixed into each a varying amount of his yellow salt. With tired and slumped shoulders he stood back, gestured. "There's your glaze. Test it."

The Chief gave an order; a Potter came up with a trayful of tiles. The Chief strode to the table, scrawled a number on the first bowl, dipped a tile into the glaze, numbered the tile correspondingly. This he did for each of the batches.

He stood back, and one of the Potters loaded the tiles in a small brick oven, closed the door, kindled a fire below.

"Now," said the Chief Potter, "you have twenty hours to question whether the burn will bring you life or death. You may as well spend the time in the company of your friends. You cannot leave, you will be well guarded." He turned abruptly, strode off down the central aisle.

Thomm turned to the nearby room, where Su-then stood in the doorway. She fell into his arms naturally, gladly.

The hours passed. Flame roared up past the oven and the bricks glowed red-hot—yellow-hot—yellow-white, and the fire was gradually drawn. Now the tiles lay cooling and behind the bricked-up door the colors were already set, and Thomm fought the impulse to tear open the brick. Darkness came; he fell into a fitful doze with Su-then's head resting on his shoulder.

Heavy footsteps aroused him; he went to the doorway. The Chief Potter was drawing aside the bricked-up door. Thomm approached, stood staring. It was dark inside; only the white gleam of the tiles could be seen, the sheen of colored glass on top. The Chief Potter reached into the kiln, pulled out the first tile. A muddy mustard-colored blotch crusted the top. Thomm swallowed hard. The Chief smiled at him sardonically. He reached for another. This was a mass of brownstone blisters. The Chief smiled again, reached in once more. A pad of mud.

The Chief's smile was broad. "Lordling, your glazes are worse than the feeblest attempts of our children."

He reached in again. A burst of brilliant yellow, and it seemed the whole room shone.

The Chief Potter gasped, the other Potters leaned forward, and Thomm sank back against the wall. "Yellow—"

When Thomm at last returned to the Bureau he found Covill in a fury. "Where in thunder have you been? I sent you out on business which should take you two hours and you stay two days."

Thomm said: "I got the four Mi-Tuun back and made a contract with the Potters. No more raiding."

Covill's mouth slackened. "You *what?*"

Thomm repeated his information.

"You didn't follow my instructions?"

"No," said Thomm. "I thought I had a better idea, and the way it turned out, I had."

Covill's eyes were hard blue fires. "Thomm, you're through here, through with Planetary Affairs. If a man can't be trusted to carry out his superior's orders, he's not worth a cent to the Bureau. Get your gear together, and leave on the next packet out."

"Just as you wish," said Thomm, turning away.

"You're on company time till four o'clock tonight," said Covill coldly. "Until then you'll obey my orders. Take the copter to the hangar, and bring the bomb back to the armory."

"You haven't any more bomb," said Thomm. "I gave the uranium to the Potters. That was one of the prices of the contract."

"*What?*" bellowed Covill, popeyed. "*What?*"

"You heard me," said Thomm. "And if you think you could have used it better by blasting away their livelihood, you're crazy."

"Thomm, you get in that copter, you go out and get that uranium. Don't come back without it. Why, you abysmal blasted imbecile, with that uranium, those Potters could tear Penolpan clear off the face of the planet."

"If you want that uranium," said Thomm, "you go out and get it. I'm fired, I'm through."

Covill stared, swelling like a toad in his rage. Words came thickly from his mouth.

Thomm said: "If I were you, I'd let sleeping dogs lie. I think it would be dangerous business trying to get that uranium back."

Covill turned, buckled a pair of gamma-guns about his waist, stalked out the door. Thomm heard the whirr of copter blades.

"There goes a brave man," Thomm said to himself. "And there goes a fool."

Three weeks later Su-then excitedly announced visitors, and Thomm, looking up, was astounded to see the Chief Potter, with two other Potters behind—stern, forbidding in their gray burnooses.

Thomm greeted them with courtesy, offered them seats, but they remained standing.

"I came down to the city," said the Chief Potter, "to inquire if the contract we made was still bound and good."

"So far as I am concerned," said Thomm.

"A madman came to the village of the Potters," said the Chief Potter. "He said that you had no authority, that our agreement was good enough, but he couldn't allow the Potters to keep the heavy metal that makes glass like the sunset."

Thomm said: "Then what happened?"

"There was violence," said the Chief Potter without accent. "He killed six good wheel-men. But that is no matter. I come to find whether our contract is good."

"Yes," said Thomm. "It is bound by my word and by the word of my great chief back on Earth. I have spoken to him and he says the contract is good."

The Chief Potter nodded. "In that case, I bring you a present." He gestured, and one of his men laid a large bowl on Thomm's desk, a bowl of marvelous yellow radiance.

"The madman is a lucky man indeed," said the Chief Potter, "for his spirit dwells in the brightest glass ever to come from the Great Burn."

Thomm's eyebrows shot up. "You mean that Covill's bones—"

"The fiery soul of the madman has given luster to an already glorious glaze," said the Chief Potter. "He lives forever in the entrancing shimmer—"

JULIAN HUXLEY

Sir Julian Huxley, F.R.S., has achieved equal fame as a scientist, a writer, and an administrator. It would take several pages of small print to list all his accomplishments, the earliest of which was contriving to be the grandson of the great T. H. Huxley, "Darwin's bulldog." Genes will out, as was also proved by the example of Sir Julian's late brother, Aldous—whose *Brave New World* still remains one of the most memorable of anti-utopias.

I suspect that a word count would prove that Sir Julian has published even more than his brother; his output includes poetry, essays, textbooks, and scientific popularizations (some with such notable collaborators as H. G. Wells and J. B. S. Haldane). He has been Secretary-General of UNESCO and, if the juxtaposition is not tactless, Secretary of the London Zoo. His countless honors include one that I am particularly happy to mention—the Kalinga Prize for science writing.

"The Tissue-Culture King" was written some forty years ago, but has dated in no essential detail; in fact, the recent staggering advances in molecular biology make it even more timely. While preparing this volume I came across the following headline in the *Los Angeles Times* (2 November 1964): "Experts Say Man May Reproduce Like Plants." Though to many this may not seem like the fulfillment of a long-felt want, the ability to grow complete organs—and perhaps complete individuals—from small pieces of tissue would be of immense value to medical research. It would also lead to the control of man's genetic future, and to much more besides.

Some of these possibilities are hinted at in Sir Julian's story. Read its concluding paragraphs with care—and remember that they were written almost twenty years before Hiroshima.

The Tissue-Culture King

We had been for three days engaged in crossing a swamp. At last we were out on dry ground, winding up a gentle slope. Near the top the brush grew thicker. The look of a rampart grew as we approached; it had the air of having been deliberately planted by men. We did not wish to have to hack our way through the spiky barricade, so turned to the right along the front of the green wall. After three or four hundred yards we came on a clearing which led into the bush, narrowing down to what seemed a regular passage or trackway. This made us a little suspicious. However, I thought we had better make all the progress we could, and so ordered the caravan to turn into the opening, myself taking second place behind the guide.

Suddenly the tracker stopped with a guttural exclamation. I looked, and there was one of the great African toads, hopping with a certain ponderosity across the path. But it had a second head growing upwards from its shoulders! I had never seen anything like this before, and wanted to secure such a remarkable monstrosity for our collections; but as I moved forward, the creature took a couple of hops into the shelter of the prickly scrub.

We pushed on, and I became convinced that the gap we were following was artificial. After a little, a droning sound came to our ears, which we very soon set down as that of a human voice. The party was halted, and I crept forward with the guide. Peeping through the last screen of brush we looked down into a hollow and were immeasurably startled at what we saw there. The voice proceeded from an enormous Negro man at least eight feet high, the biggest man I had ever seen outside a circus. He was squatting, from time to time prostrating the forepart of his body, and reciting some prayer or incantation. The object of his devotion was before him on the ground; it was a small flat piece of glass held on a little carved ebony stand. By his side was a huge spear, together with a painted basket with a lid.

After a minute or so, the giant bowed down in silence, then took up the ebony-and-glass object and placed it in the basket. Then to my utter amazement he drew out a two-headed toad like the first I had seen, but in a cage of woven grass, placed it on the ground, and proceeded to more genuflection and ritual murmurings. As soon as this was over, the toad was replaced, and the squatting giant tranquilly regarded the landscape.

Beyond the hollow or dell lay an undulating country, with clumps of bush. A sound in the middle distance attracted attention; glimpses of color moved through the scrub; and a party of three or four dozen men were seen approaching, most of them as gigantic as our first acquaintance. All marched in order, armed with great spears, and wearing colored loin straps with a sort of sporran, it seemed, in front. They were preceded by an intelligent-looking Negro of ordinary stature armed with a club, and accompanied by two figures more remarkable than the giants. They were undersized, almost dwarfish, with huge heads, and enormously fat and brawny both in face and body. They wore bright yellow cloaks over their black shoulders.

At sight of them, our giant rose and stood stiffly by the side of his basket. The party approached and halted. Some order was given, a giant stepped out from the ranks towards ours, picked up the basket, handed it stiffly to the newcomer, and fell into place in the little company. We were clearly witnessing some regular routine of relieving guard, and I was racking my brains to think what the whole thing might signify—guards, giants, dwarfs, toads—when to my dismay I heard an exclamation at my shoulder.

It was one of those damned porters, a confounded fellow who always liked to show his independence. Bored with waiting, I suppose, he had self-importantly crept up to see what it was all about, and the sudden sight of the company of giants had been too much for his nerves. I made a signal to lie quiet, but it was too late. The exclamation had been heard; the leader gave a quick command, and the giants rushed up and out in two groups to surround us.

Violence and resistance were clearly out of the question. With my heart in my mouth, but with as much dignity as I could muster, I jumped up and threw out my empty hands, at the same time telling the tracker not to shoot. A dozen spears seemed towering over me, but none were launched, the leader ran up the slope and gave a command. Two giants came up and put my hands through their arms. The tracker and the porter were herded in front at the spear point. The other porters now discovered there was something amiss, and began to shout and run away, with half the spearmen after them. We three were gently but firmly marched down and across the hollow.

I understood nothing of the language, and called to my tracker to try his hand. It turned out that there was some dialect of which he had a little understanding, and we could learn nothing save the fact that we were being taken to some superior authority.

For two days we were marched through pleasant park-like country, with villages at intervals. Every now and then some new monstrosity in the shape of a dwarf or an incredibly fat woman or a two-headed animal would be visible, until I thought I had stumbled on the original source of supply of circus freaks.

The country at last began to slope gently down to a pleasant river valley; and presently we neared the capital. It turned out to be a really large town for Africa, its mud walls of strangely impressive architectural form, with their heavy, slabby buttresses, and giants standing guard upon them. Seeing us approach, they shouted, and a crowd poured out of the nearest gate. My God, what a crowd! I was getting used to giants by this time, but here was a regular Barnum and Bailey show; more semi-dwarfs; others like them but more so—one could not tell whether the creatures were precociously mature children or horribly stunted adults; others portentously fat, with arms like sooty legs of mutton, and rolls and volutes of fat crisping out of their steatopygous posteriors; still others precociously senile and wizened, others hateful and imbecile in looks. Of course, there were plenty of ordinary Negroes too, but enough of the extraordinary to make one feel pretty queer. Soon after we got inside, I suddenly noted something else which appeared inexplicable—a telephone wire, with perfectly good insulators, running across from tree to tree. A telephone—in an unknown African town. I gave it up.

But another surprise was in store for me. I saw a figure pass across from one large building to another—a figure unmistakably that of a white man. In the first place, it was wearing white ducks and sun helmet; in the second, it had a pale face.

He turned at the sound of our cavalcade and stood looking a moment; then walked towards us.

"Halloa!" I shouted. "Do you speak English?"

"Yes," he answered, "but keep quiet a moment," and began talking quickly to our leaders, who treated him with the greatest deference. He dropped back to me and spoke rapidly: "You are to be taken into the council hall to be examined: but I will see to it that no harm comes to you. This is a forbidden land to strangers, and you must be prepared to be held up for a time. You will be sent down to see me in the temple buildings as soon as the formalities are over, and I'll explain things. They want a bit of explaining," he added with a dry laugh. "By the way, my name is Hascombe, lately research worker at Middlesex Hospital, now religious adviser to His Majesty King Mgobe." He laughed again and pushed ahead. He was an interesting figure—perhaps fifty years old, spare body, thin face, with a small beard, and rather sunken, hazel eyes. As for his expression, he looked cynical, but also as if he were interested in life.

By this time we were at the entrance to the hall. Our giants formed up outside, with my men behind them, and only I and the leader passed in. The examination was purely formal, and remarkable chiefly for the ritual and solemnity which characterized all the actions of the couple of dozen fine-looking men in long robes who were our examiners. My men were herded off to some compound. I was escorted down to a little hut, furnished with some attempt at European style, where I found Hascombe.

As soon as we were alone I was after him with my questions. "Now you can tell me. Where are we? What is the meaning of all this circus business and this menagerie of monstrosities? And how do you come here?" He cut me short. "It's a long story, so let me save time by telling it my own way."

I am not going to tell it as he told it; but will try to give a more connected account, the result of many later talks with him, and of my own observations.

Hascombe had been a medical student of great promise; and after his degree had launched out into research. He had first started on parasitic protozoa, but had given that up in favor of tissue culture; from these he had gone off to cancer research, and from that to a study of developmental physiology. Later a big Commission on sleeping sickness had been organized, and Hascombe, restless and eager for travel, had pulled wires and got himself appointed as one of the scientific staff sent to Africa. He was much impressed with the view that wild game acted as a reservoir for the *Trypanosoma gambiense*. When he learned of the extensive migrations of game, he saw here an important possible means of spreading the disease and asked leave to go up country to investigate the whole problem. When the Commission as a whole had finished its work, he was allowed to stay in Africa with one other white man and a company of porters to see what he could discover. His white companion was a laboratory technician, a taciturn, noncommissioned officer of science called Aggers.

There is no object in telling of their experiences here. Suffice it that they lost their way and fell into the hands of this same tribe. That was fifteen years ago: and Aggers was now long dead —as the result of a wound inflicted when he was caught, after a couple of years, trying to escape.

On their capture, they too had been examined in the council chamber, and Hascombe (who had interested himself in a dilettante way in anthropology as in most other subjects of scientific inquiry) was much impressed by what he described

as the exceedingly religious atmosphere. Everything was done
with an elaboration of ceremony; the chief seemed more priest
than king, and performed various rites at intervals, and priests
were busy at some sort of altar the whole time. Among other
things, he noticed that one of their rites was connected with
blood. First the chief and then the councillors were in turn
requisitioned for a drop of vital fluid pricked from their fingertips, and the mixture, held in a little vessel, was slowly evap-
orated over a flame.

Some of Hascombe's men spoke a dialect not unlike that of
their captors, and one was acting as interpreter. Things did not
look too favorable. The country was a "holy place," it seemed,
and the tribe a "holy race." Other Africans who trespassed there,
if not killed, were enslaved, but for the most part they let well
alone, and did not trespass. White men they had heard of, but
never seen till now, and the debate was what to do—to kill, let
go, or enslave? To let them go was contrary to all their principles:
the holy place would be defiled if the news of it were spread
abroad. To enslave them—yes; but what were they good for?
And the Council seemed to feel an instinctive dislike for these
other-colored creatures. Hascombe had an idea. He turned to
the interpreter. "Say this: 'You revere the blood. So do we white
men; but we do more—we can render visible the blood's hidden
nature and reality, and with permission I will show this great
magic.'" He beckoned to the bearer who carried his precious
microscope, set it up, drew a drop of blood from the tip of his
finger with his knife, and mounted it on a slide under a cover-
slip. The bigwigs were obviously interested. They whispered to
each other. At length, "Show us," commanded the chief.

Hascombe demonstrated his preparation with greater interest
than he had ever done to first-year medical students in the old
days. He explained that the blood was composed of little people
of various sorts, each with their own lives, and that to spy upon
them thus gave us new powers over them. The elders were more
or less impressed. At any rate the sight of these thousands of
corpuscles where they could see nothing before made them
think, made them realize that the white man had power which
might make him a desirable servant.

They would not ask to see their own blood for fear that the sight would put them into the power of those who saw it. But they had blood drawn from a slave. Hascombe asked too for a bird, and was able to create a certain interest by showing how different were the little people of its blood.

"Tell them," he said to the interpreter, "that I have many other powers and magics which I will show them if they will give me time."

The long and short of it was that he and his party were spared —He said he knew then what one felt when the magistrate said: "Remanded for a week."

He had been attracted by one of the elder statesmen of the tribe—a tall, powerful-looking man of middle-age; and was agreeably surprised when this man came round next day to see him. Hascombe later nicknamed him the Prince-Bishop, for his combination of the qualities of the statesman and the ecclesiastic: his real name was Bugala. He was anxious to discover more about Hascombe's mysterious powers and resources as Hascombe was to learn what he could of the people into whose hands he had fallen, and they met almost every evening and talked far into the night.

Bugala's inquiries were as little prompted as Hascombe's by a purely academic curiosity. Impressed himself by the microscope, and still more by the effect which it had had on his colleagues, he was anxious to find out whether by utilizing the powers of the white man he could not secure his own advancement. At length, they struck a bargain. Bugala would see to it that no harm befell Hascombe. But Hascombe must put his resources and powers at the disposal of the Council; and Bugala would take good care to arrange matters so that he himself benefited. So far as Hascombe could make out, Bugala imagined a radical change in the national religion, a sort of reformation based on Hascombe's conjuring tricks; and that he would emerge as the High Priest of this changed system.

Hascombe had a sense of humor, and it was tickled. It seemed pretty clear that they could not escape, at least for the present. That being so, why not take the opportunity of doing a little research work at state expense—an opportunity which he and his like were always clamoring for at home? His thoughts began to run away with him. He would find out all he could of the rites and superstitions of the tribe. He would, by the aid of his knowledge and his scientific skill, exalt the details of these rites, the expression of those superstitions, the whole physical side of their religiosity, on to a new level which should to them appear truly miraculous.

It would not be worth my troubling to tell all the negotiations, the false starts, the misunderstandings. In the end he secured what he wanted—a building which could be used as a laboratory; an unlimited supply of slaves for the lower and priests for the higher duties of laboratory assistants; and the promise that when his scientific stores were exhausted they would do their best to secure others from the coast—a promise which was scrupulously kept, so that he never went short for lack of what money could buy.

He next applied himself diligently to a study of their religion and found that it was built round various main motifs. Of these, the central one was the belief in the divinity and tremendous importance of the Priest-King. The second was a form of ancestor-worship. The third was an animal cult, in particular of the more grotesque species of the African fauna. The fourth was sex, *con variazioni*. Hascombe reflected on these facts. Tissue culture; experimental embryology; endocrine treatment; artificial parthenogenesis. He laughed and said to himself: "Well, at least I can try, and it ought to be amusing."

That was how it all started. Perhaps the best way of giving some idea of how it had developed will be for me to tell my own impressions when Hascombe took me round his laboratories. One whole quarter of the town was devoted entirely to religion—it struck me as excessive, but Hascombe reminded me that Tibet spends one-fifth of its revenues on melted butter to burn before its shrines. Facing the main square was the chief temple, built impressively enough of solid mud. On either side were the apartments, where dwelt the servants of the gods and administrators of the sacred rites. Behind were Hascombe's laboratories, some built of mud, others, under his later guidance, of wood. They were guarded night and day by patrols of giants,

and were arranged in a series of quadrangles. Within one quad-
rangle was a pool which served as an aquarium; in another,
aviaries and great henhouses; in yet another, cages with various
animals; in the fourth a little botanic garden. Behind were
stables with dozens of cattle and sheep, and a sort of experimental ward for human beings.

He took me into the nearest of the buildings. "This," he
said, "is known to the people as the Factory (it is difficult to
give the exact sense of the word, but it literally means produc-
ing-place), the Factory of Kingship or Majesty, and the Wellspring of Ancestral Immortality." I looked round, and saw
platoons of buxom and shining African women, becomingly but
unusually dressed in tight-fitting white dresses and caps, and
wearing rubber gloves. Microscopes were much in evidence, also
various receptacles from which steam was emerging. The back
of the room was screened off by a wooden screen in which were
a series of glass doors; and these doors opened into partitions,
each labeled with a name in that unknown tongue, and each
containing a number of objects like the one I had seen taken
out of the basket by the giant before we were captured. Pipes
surrounded this chamber, and appeared to be distributing heat
from a fire in one corner.

"Factory of Majesty!" I exclaimed. "Wellspring of Immortality! What the dickens do you mean?"

"If you prefer a more prosaic name," said Hascombe, "I
should call this the Institute of Religious Tissue Culture." My
mind went back to a day in 1918 when I had been taken by a
biological friend in New York to see the famous Rockefeller
Institute; and at the words "tissue culture" I saw again before
me Dr. Alexis Carrel and troops of white-garbed American girls
making cultures, sterilizing, microscopizing, incubating and the
rest of it. The Hascombe Institute was, it is true, not so well
equipped, but it had an even larger, if differently colored,
personnel.

Hascombe began his explanations. "As you probably know,
Frazer's *Golden Bough* introduced us to the idea of a sacred
Priest-King, and showed how fundamental it was in primitive
societies. The welfare of the tribe is regarded as inextricably

bound up with that of the King, and extraordinary precautions are taken to preserve him from harm. In this kingdom, in the old days, the King was hardly allowed to set his foot to the ground in case he should lose divinity; his cut hair and nail-parings were entrusted to one of the most important officials of state, whose duty it was to bury them secretly, in case some enemy should compass the King's illness or death by using them in black-magic rites. If anyone of base blood trod on the King's shadow, he paid the penalty with his life. Each year a slave was made mock-king for a week, allowed to enjoy all the King's privileges, and was decapitated at the close of his brief glory; and by this means it was supposed that the illnesses and misfortunes that might befall the King were vicariously got rid of.

"I first of all rigged up my apparatus, and with the aid of Aggers, succeeded in getting good cultures, first of chick tissues and later, by the aid of embryo-extract, of various and adult mammalian tissues. I then went to Bugala, and told him that I could increase the safety, if not of the King as an individual, at least of the life which was in him, and that I presumed that this would be equally satisfactory from a theological point of view. I pointed out that if he chose to be made guardian of the King's subsidiary lives, he would be in a much more important position then the chamberlain or the burier of the sacred nail-parings, and might make the post the most influential in the realm.

"Eventually I was allowed (under threats of death if anything untoward occurred) to remove small portions of His Majesty's subcutaneous conective tissue under a local anesthetic. In the presence of the assembled nobility I put fragments of this into a culture medium, and showed it to them under the microscope. The cultures were then put away in the incubator under a guard—relieved every eight hours—of half a dozen warriors. After three days, to my joy they had all taken and showed abundant growth. I could see that the Council was impressed, and reeled off a magnificent speech, pointing out that this growth constituted an actual increase in the quantity of the divine principle inherent in royalty; and what was more, that

I could increase it indefinitely. With that I cut each of my cultures into eight, and subcultured all the pieces. They were again put under guard, and again examined after three days. Not all of them had taken this time, and there were some murmurings and angry looks, on the ground that I had killed some of the King; but I pointed out that the King was still the King, that his little wound had completely healed, and that any successful cultures represented so much extra sacredness and protection to the state. I must say that they were very reasonable, and had good theological acumen, for they at once took the hint.

"I pointed out to Bugala, and he persuaded the rest without much difficulty, that they could now disregard some of the older implications of the doctrines of kingship. The most important new idea which I was able to introduce was *mass-production*. Our aim was to multiply the King's tissues indefinitely, to ensure that some of their protecting power should reside everywhere in the country. Thus by concentrating upon quantity, we could afford to remove some of the restrictions upon the King's mode of life. This was of course agreeable to the King; and also to Bugala, who saw himself wielding undreamt-of power. One might have supposed that such an innovation would have met with great resistance simply on account of its being an innovation; but I must admit that these people compared very favorably with the average businessman in their lack of prejudice.

"Having thus settled the principle, I had many debates with Bugala as to the best methods for enlisting the mass of the population in our scheme. What an opportunity for scientific advertising! But, unfortunately, the population could not read. However, war propaganda worked very well in more or less illiterate countries—why not here?"

Hascombe organized a series of public lectures in the capital, at which he demonstrated his regal tissues to the multitude, who were bidden to the place by royal heralds. An impressive platform group was always supplied from the ranks of the nobles. The lecturer explained how important it was for the community to become possessed of greater and greater stores of the sacred tissues. Unfortunately, the preparation was laborious, and expensive, and it behooved them all to lend a hand. It had accordingly been arranged that to everyone subscribing a cow or buffalo, or its equivalent—three goats, pigs, or sheep—a portion of the royal anatomy should be given, handsomely mounted in an ebony holder. Subculturing would be done at certain hours and days, and it would be obligatory to send the cultures for renewal. If through any negligence the tissue died, no renewal would be made. The subscription entitled the receiver to subculturing rights for a year, but was of course renewable. By this means not only would the totality of the King be much increased, to the benefit of all, but each cultureholder would possess an actual part of His Majesty, and would have the infinite joy and privilege of aiding by his own efforts the multiplication of divinity.

Then they could also serve their country by dedicating a daughter to the state. These young women would be housed and fed by the state, and taught the technique of the sacred culture. Candidates would be selected according to general fitness, but would of course, in addition, be required to attain distinction in an examination on the principles of religion. They would be appointed for a probationary period of six months. After this they would receive a permanent status, with the title of Sisters of the Sacred Tissue. From this, with age, experience, and merit, they could expect promotion to the rank of mothers, grandmothers, great-grandmothers, and grand ancestresses of the same. The merit and benefit they would receive from their close contact with the source of all benefits would overflow onto their families.

The scheme worked like wildfire. Pigs, goats, cattle, buffaloes, and Negro maidens poured in. Next year the scheme was extended to the whole country, a peripatetic laboratory making the rounds weekly.

By the close of the third year there was hardly a family in the country which did not possess at least one sacred culture. To be without one would have been like being without one's trousers—or at least without one's hat—on Fifth Avenue. Thus did Bugala effect a reformation in the national religion, enthrone himself as the most important personage in the country, and entrench applied science and Hascombe firmly in the organization of the state.

Encouraged by his success, Hascombe soon set out to capture the ancestry-worship branch of the religion as well. A public proclamation was made pointing out how much more satisfactory it would be if worship could be made not merely to the charred bones of one's forebears, but to bits of them still actually living and growing. All who were desirous of profiting by the enterprise of Bugala's Department of State should therefore bring their older relatives to the laboratory at certain specified hours, and fragments would be painlessly extracted for culture.

This, too, proved very attractive to the average citizen. Occasionally, it is true, grandfathers or aged mothers arrived in a state of indignation and protest. However, this did not matter, since, according to the law, once children were twenty-five years of age, they were not only assigned the duty of worshiping their ancestors, alive or dead, but were also given complete control over them, in order that all rites might be duly performed to the greater safety of the commonweal. Further, the ancestors soon found that the operation itself was trifling, and, what was more, that once accomplished, it had the most desirable results. For their descendants preferred to concentrate at once upon the culture which they would continue to worship after the old folks were gone, and so left their parents and grandparents much freer than before from the irksome restrictions which in all ages have beset the officially holy.

Thus, by almost every hearth in the kingdom, instead of the old-fashioned rows of red jars containing the incinerated remains of one or other of the family forebears, the new generation saw growing up a collection of family slides. Each would be taken out and reverently examined at the hour of prayer. "Grandpapa is not growing well this week," you would perhaps hear the young black devotee say; the father of the family would pray over the speck of tissue; and if that failed, it would be taken back to the factory for rejuvenation. On the other hand, what rejoicing when a rhythm of activity stirred in the cultures! A spurt on the part of great-grandmother's tissues would bring her wrinkled old smile to mind again; and sometimes it seemed as if one particular generation were all stirred simultaneously by a pulse of growth, as if combining to bless their devout descendants.

To deal with the possibility of cultures dying out, Hascombe started a central storehouse, where duplicates of every strain were kept, and it was this repository of the national tissues which had attracted my attention at the back of the laboratory. No such collection had ever existed before, he assured me. Not a necropolis, but a histopolis, if I may coin a word: not a cemetery, but a place of eternal growth.

The second building was devoted to endocrine products—an African Armour's—and was called by the people the "Factory of Ministers to the Shrines."

"Here," he said, "you will not find much new. You know the craze for 'glands' that was going on at home years ago, and its results, in the shape of pluriglandular preparations, a new genre of patent medicines, and a popular literature that threatened to outdo the Freudians, and explain human beings entirely on the basis of glandular makeup, without reference to the mind at all.

"I had only to apply my knowledge in a comparatively simple manner. The first thing was to show Bugala how, by repeated injections of prepituitary, I could make an ordinary baby grow up into a giant. This pleased him, and he introduced the idea of a sacred bodyguard, all of really gigantic stature, quite overshadowing Frederick's Grenadiers.

"I did, however, extend knowledge in several directions. I took advantage of the fact that their religion holds in reverence monstrous and imbecile forms of human beings. That is, of course, a common phenomenon in many countries, where halfwits are supposed to be inspired, and dwarfs the object of superstitious awe. So I went to work to create various new types. By employing a particular extract of adrenal cortex, I produced children who would have been a match for the infant Hercules, and, indeed, looked rather like a cross between him and a brewer's drayman. By injecting the same extract into adolescent girls I was able to provide them with the most copious mustaches, after which they found ready employment as prophetesses.

"Tampering with the postpituitary gave remarkable cases of obesity. This, together with the passion of the men for fatness in their women, Bugala took advantage of, and I believe made quite a fortune by selling as concubines female slaves treated in this way. Finally, by another pituitary treatment, I at last mastered the secret of true dwarfism, in which perfect proportions are retained.

"Of these productions, the dwarfs are retained as acolytes in the temple; a band of the obese young ladies form a sort of Society of Vestal Virgins, with special religious duties which, as the embodiment of the national ideal of beauty, they are supposed to discharge with peculiarly propitious effect; and the giants form our Regular Army.

"The Obese Virgins have set me a problem which I confess I have not yet solved. Like all races who set great store by sexual enjoyment, these people have a correspondingly exaggerated reverence for virginity. It therefore occurred to me that if I could apply Jacques Loeb's great discovery of artificial parthenogenesis to man, or, to be precise, to these young ladies, I should be able to grow a race of vestals, self-reproducing yet ever virgin, to whom in concentrated form should attach that reverence of which I have just spoken. You see, I must always remember that it is no good proposing any line of work that will not benefit the national religion. I suppose state-aided research would have much the same kinds of difficulties in a really democratic state. Well, this, as I say, has so far beaten me. I have taken the matter a step further than Bataillon with his fatherless frogs, and I have induced parthenogenesis in the eggs of reptiles and birds; but so far I have failed with mammals. However, I've not given up yet!"

Then we passed to the next laboratory, which was full of the most incredible animal monstrosities. "This laboratory is the most amusing," said Hascombe. "Its official title is 'Home of the Living Fetishes.' Here again I have simply taken a prevalent trait of the populace, and used it as a peg on which to hang research. I told you that they always had a fancy for the grotesque in animals, and used the most bizarre forms, in the shape of little clay or ivory statuettes, for fetishes.

"I thought I would see whether art could not improve upon nature, and set myself to recall my experimental embryology. I use only the simplest methods. I utilize the plasticity of the earliest stages to give double-headed and cyclopean monsters. That was, of course, done years ago in newts by Spemann and fish by Stockard; and I have merely applied the mass-production methods of Mr. Ford to their results. But my specialties are three-headed snakes, and toads with an extra heaven-pointing head. The former are a little difficult, but there is a great demand for them, and they fetch a good price. The frogs are easier: I simply apply Harrison's methods to embryo tadpoles."

He then showed me into the last building. Unlike the others, this contained no signs of research in progress, but was empty. It was draped with black hangings, and lit only from the top. In the center were rows of ebony benches, and in front of them a glittering golden ball on a stand.

"Here I am beginning my work on reinforced telepathy," he told me. "Some day you must come and see what it's all about, for it really is interesting."

You may imagine that I was pretty well flabbergasted by this catalogue of miracles. Every day I got a talk with Hascombe, and gradually the talks became recognized events of our daily routine. One day I asked if he had given up hope of escaping. He showed a queer hesitation in replying. Eventually he said, "To tell you the truth, my dear Jones, I have really hardly thought of it these last few years. It seemed so impossible at first that I deliberately put it out of my head and turned with more and more energy, I might almost say fury, to my work. And now, upon my soul, I am not quite sure whether I want to escape or not."

"Not *want* to!" I exclaimed. "Surely you can't mean that!"

"I am not so sure," he rejoined. "What I most want is to get ahead with this work of mine. Why, man, you don't realize what a chance I've got! And it is all growing so fast—I can see every kind of possibility ahead." And he broke off into silence.

However, although I was interested enough in his past

achievements, I did not feel willing to sacrifice my future to his perverted intellectual ambitions But he would not leave his work.

The experiments which most excited his imagination were those he was conducting into mass telepathy. He had received his medical training at a time when abnormal psychology was still very unfashionable in England, but had luckily been thrown in contact with a young doctor who was a keen student of hypnotism, through whom he had been introduced to some of the great pioneers, like Bramwell and Wingfield. As a result, he had become a passable hypnotist himself, with a fair knowledge of the literature.

In the early days of his captivity he became interested in the sacred dances which took place every night of full moon, and were regarded as propitiations of the celestial powers. The dancers all belong to a special sect. After a series of exciting figures, symbolizing various activities of the chase, war, and love, the leader conducts his band to a ceremonial bench. He then begins to make passes at them; and what impressed Hascombe was this, that a few seconds sufficed for them to fall back in deep hypnosis against the ebony rail. It recalled, he said, the most startling cases of collective hypnosis recorded by the French scientists. The leader next passed from one end of the bench to the other, whispering a brief sentence into each ear. He then, according to immemorial rite, approached the Priest-King, and, after having exclaimed aloud, "Lord of Majesty, command what thou wilt for thy dancers to perform," the King would thereupon command some action which had previously been kept secret.The command was often to fetch some object and deposit it at the moon-shrine; or to fight the enemies of the state; or (and this was what the company most liked) to be some animal, or bird. Whatever the command, the hypnotized men would obey it, for the leader's whispered words had been an order to hear and carry out only what the King said; and the strangest scenes would be witnessed as they ran, completely oblivious of all in their path, in search of the gourds or sheep they had been called on to procure, or lunged in a symbolic way at invisible enemies, or threw themselves on all fours and roared as lions, or galloped as zebras, or danced as cranes. The command executed, they stood like stocks or stones, until their leader, running from one to the other, touched each with a finger and shouted, "Wake." They woke, and limp, but conscious of having been the vessels of the unknown spirit, danced back to their special hut or clubhouse.

This susceptibility to hypnotic suggestion struck Hascombe, and he obtained permission to test the performers more closely. He soon established that the people were, as a race, extremely prone to dissociation, and could be made to lapse into deep hypnosis with great ease, but a hypnosis in which the subconscious, though completely cut off from the waking self, comprised portions of the personality not retained in the hypnotic selves of Europeans. Like most who have fluttered round the psychological candle, he had been interested in the notion of telepathy; and now, with this supply of hypnotic subjects under his hands, began some real investigation of the problem.

By picking his subjects, he was soon able to demonstrate the existence of telepathy, by making suggestions to one hypnotized man who transferred them without physical intermediation to another at a distance. Later—and this was the culmination of his work—he found that when he made a suggestion to several subjects at once, the telepathic effect was much stronger than if he had done it to one at a time—the hypnotized minds were reinforcing each other. "I'm after the super-consciousness," Hascombe said, "and I've already got the rudiments of it."

I must confess that I got almost as excited as Hascombe over the possibilities thus opened up. It certainly seemed as if he were right in principle. If all the subjects were in practically the same psychological state, extraordinary reinforcing effects were observed. At first the attainment of this similarity of condition was very difficult; gradually, however, we discovered that it was possible to tune hypnotic subjects to the same pitch, if I may use the metaphor, and then the fun really began.

First of all we found that with increasing reinforcement, we could get telepathy conducted to greater and greater distances, until finally we could transmit commands from the capital to the national boundary, nearly a hundred miles. We next found that it was not necessary for the subject to be in hypnosis to receive the telepathic command. Almost everybody, but especially those of equable temperament, could thus be influenced. Most extraordinary of all, however, were what we at first christened "near effects," since their transmission to a distance was not found possible until later. If, after Hascombe had suggested some simple command to a largish group of hypnotized subjects, he or I went right up among them, we would experience the most extraordinary sensation, as of some superhuman personality repeating the command in a menacing and overwhelming way and, whereas with one part of ourselves we felt, if I may say so, as if we were only a part of the command, or of something much bigger than ourselves which was commanding. And this, Hascombe claimed, was the first real beginning of the super-consciousness.

Bugala, of course, had to be considered. Hascombe, with the old Tibetan prayer-wheel at the back of his mind, suggested that eventually he would be able to induce hypnosis in the whole population, and then transmit a prayer. This would ensure that the daily prayer, for instance, was really said by the whole population, and, what is more, simultaneously, which would undoubtedly much enhance its efficacy. And it would make it possible in times of calamity or battle to keep the whole praying force of the nation at work for long spells together.

Bugala was deeply interested. He saw himself, through this mental machinery, planting such ideas as he wished in the brain-cases of his people. He saw himself willing an order; and the whole population rousing itself out of trance to execute it. He dreamt dreams before which those of the proprietor of a newspaper syndicate, even those of a director of propaganda in wartime, would be pale and timid. Naturally, he wished to receive personal instruction in the methods himself; and, equally naturally, we could not refuse him, though I must say that I often felt a little uneasy as to what he might choose to do if he ever decided to override Hascombe and to start experimenting on his own. This, combined with my constant longing to get away from the place, led me to cast about again for means of escape. Then it occurred to me that this very method about which I had such gloomy presentiments might itself be made the key to our prison.

So one day, after getting Hascombe worked up about the loss to humanity it would be to let this great discovery die with him in Africa, I set to in earnest. "My dear Hascombe," I said, "you must get home out of this. What is there to prevent your saying to Bugala that your experiments are nearly crowned with success, but that for certain tests you must have a much greater number of subjects at your disposal? You can then get a battery of two hundred men, and after you have tuned them, the reinforcement will be so great that you will have at your disposal a mental force big enough to affect the whole population. Then, of course, one fine day we should raise the potential of our mind-battery to the highest possible level, and send out through it a general hypnotic influence. The whole country, men, women, and children, would sink into stupor. Next we should give our experimental squad the suggestion to broadcast 'sleep for a week.' The telepathic message would be relayed to each of the thousands of minds waiting receptively for it, and would take root in them, until the whole nation became a single super-consciousness, conscious only of the one thought 'sleep' which we had thrown into it."

The reader will perhaps ask how we ourselves expected to escape from the clutches of the super-consciousness we had created. Well, we had discovered that metal was relatively impervious to the telepathic effect, and had prepared for ourselves a sort of tin pulpit, behind which we could stand while conducting experiments. This, combined with caps of metal foil, enormously reduced the effects on ourselves. We had not informed Bugala of this property of metal.

Hascombe was silent. At length he spoke. "I like the idea," he said; "I like to think that if I ever do get back to England and to scientific recognition, my discovery will have given me the means of escape."

From that moment we worked assiduously to perfect our method and our plans. After about five months everything seemed propitious. We had provisions packed away, and compasses. I had been allowed to keep my rifle, on promise that I would never discharge it. We had made friends with some of the men who went trading to the coast, and had got from them all the information we could about the route, without arousing their suspicions.

At last, the night arrived. We assembled our men as if for an ordinary practice, and after hypnosis had been induced, started to tune them. At this moment Bugala came in, unannounced. This was what we had been afraid of; but there had been no means of preventing it. "What shall we do?" I whispered to Hascombe, in English. "Go right ahead and be damned to it," was his answer; "we can put him to sleep with the rest."

So we welcomed him, and gave him a seat as near as possible to the tightly packed ranks of the performers. At length the preparations were finished. Hascombe went into the pulpit and said, "Attention to the words which are to be suggested." There was a slight stiffening of the bodies. "Sleep," said Hascombe. "*Sleep* is the command: command all in this land to sleep unbrokenly." Bugala leapt up with an exclamation; but the induction had already begun.

We with our metal coverings were immune. But Bugala was struck by the full force of the mental current. He sank back on his chair, helpless. For a few minutes his extraordinary will resisted the suggestion. Although he could not move, his angry eyes were open. But at length he succumbed, and he too slept.

We lost no time in starting, and made good progress through the silent country. The people were sitting about like wax figures. Women sat asleep by their milk-pails, the cow by this time far away. Fat-bellied naked children slept at their games. The houses were full of sleepers sleeping upright round their food, recalling Wordsworth's famous "party in a parlor."

So we went on, feeling pretty queer and scarcely believing in this morphic state into which we had plunged a nation. Finally the frontier was reached, where with extreme elation, we passed an immobile and gigantic frontier guard. A few miles further we had a good solid meal, and a doze. Our kit was rather heavy, and we decided to jettison some superfluous weight, in the shape of some food, specimens, and our metal headgear, or mind-protectors, which at this distance, and with the hypnosis wearing a little thin, were, we thought, no longer necessary.

About nightfall on the third day, Hascombe suddenly stopped and turned his head.

"What's the matter?" I said. "Have you seen a lion?" His reply was completely unexpected. "No. I was just wondering whether really I ought not to go back again."

"Go back again," I cried. "What in the name of God Almighty do you want to do that for?"

"It suddenly struck me that I ought to," he said, "about five minutes ago. And really, when one comes to think of it, I don't suppose I shall ever journey to the coast, and I don't expect we shall get through alive."

I was thoroughly upset and put out, and told him so. And suddenly, for a few moments, I felt I must go back too. It was like that old friend of our boyhood, the voice of conscience.

"Yes, to be sure, we ought to go back," I thought with fervor. But suddenly checking myself as the thought came under the play of reason—"*Why* should we go back?" All sorts of reasons were proffered, as it were, by unseen hands reaching up out of the hidden parts of me.

And then I realized what had happened. Bugala had waked up; he had wiped out the suggestion we had given to the super-consciousness, and in its place put in another. I could see him thinking it out, the cunning devil (one must give him credit for brains!), and hear him, after making his passes, whisper to the nation in prescribed form his new suggestion: "Will to return!" "Return!" For most of the inhabitants the command would have no meaning, for they would have been already at home. Doubtless some young men out on the hills, or truant children, or girls run off in secret to meet their lovers, were even now returning, stiffly and in somnambulistic trance, to their homes. It was only for them that the new command of the super-consciousness had any meaning—and for us.

I am putting it in a long and discursive way; at the moment I simply *saw* what had happened in a flash. I told Hascombe, I showed him it *must* be so, that nothing else would account for the sudden change. I begged and implored him to use his reason, to stick to his decision and to come on. How I regretted that, in our desire to discard all useless weight, we had left behind our metal telepathy-proof head coverings!

But Hascombe would not, or could not, see my point. I suppose he was much more imbued with all the feelings and spirit of the country, and so more susceptible. However that may be, he was immovable. He must go back; he knew it; he saw it clearly; it was his sacred duty; and much other similar rubbish. All this time the suggestion was attacking me too; and finally I felt that if I did not put more distance between me and that unisonic battery of will, I should succumb as well as he.

"Hascombe," I said, "I am going on. For God's sake, come with me." And I shouldered my pack, and set off. He was shaken, I saw, and came a few steps after me. But finally he turned, and, in spite of my frequent pauses and shouts to him to follow, made off in the direction we had come. I can assure you that it was with a gloomy soul that I continued my solitary way. I shall not bore you with my adventures. Suffice it to say that at last I got to a white outpost, weak with fatigue and poor food and fever.

I kept very quiet about my adventures, only giving out that our expedition had lost its way and that my men had run away or been killed by the local tribes. At last I reached England. But I was a broken man, and a profound gloom had invaded my mind at the thought of Hascombe and the way he had been caught in his own net. I never found out what happened to him, and I do not suppose that I am likely to find out now. You may ask why I did not try to organize a rescue expedition; or why, at least, I did not bring Hascombe's discoveries before the Royal Society or the Metaphysical Institute. I can only repeat that I was a broken man. I did not expect to be believed; I was not at all sure that I could repeat our results, even on the same human material, much less with men of another race; I dreaded ridicule; and finally I was tormented by doubts as to whether the knowledge of mass-telepathy would not be a curse rather than a blessing to mankind.

However, I am an oldish man now and, what is more, old for my years. I want to get the story off my chest. Besides, old men like sermonizing and you must forgive, gentle reader, the sermonical turn which I now feel I must take. The question I want to raise is this: Dr. Hascombe attained to an unsurpassed power in a number of applications of science—but *to what end did all this power serve?* It is the merest cant and twaddle to go on asserting, as most of our press and people continue to do, that increase of scientific knowledge and power must in itself be good. I commend to the great public the obvious moral of my story and ask them to think what they propose to do with the power which is gradually being accumulated for them by the labors of those who labor because they like power, or because they want to find the truth about how things work.